Refreshing Jutta

A Novel

By RL Martin

Full Quiver Publishing
Pakenham, ON

Refreshing Jutta
Copyright 2021 by RL Martin

Published by
Full Quiver Publishing
PO Box 244
Pakenham, Ontario K0A 2X0
www.fullquiverpublishing.com

ISBN 978-1-987970-16-6
Printed and bound in the USA
Cover Design by James Hrkach

Poems copyright David Fiedler, Used With Permission

NATIONAL LIBRARY OF CANADA
CATALOGUING IN PUBLICATION

Published by FQ Publishing
A Division of Innate Productions

Dedicated to the Sacred Heart of Jesus

"Those who refresh others will be refreshed," Proverbs 11:24

Chapter 1

The Refreshing

"Jutta." A voice without tone broke the silence and the seventeen-year-old boy snapped out of his trance. "Jutta, it's time for your procession."

Jutta had been sitting quietly on the edge of his bed for over an hour, sifting through various memories to make sense of his short life. But the memories were all jumbled.

"Come," the lady said. He took her hand and stood up slowly, as if he were an old man.

He looked around the room where he had grown up. The eyes of his group unit were all on him. Bibiana, being only six, ran up and latched on to his leg crying, "I won't let you go!"

Jutta patted her head as the group unit leader pulled the girl off of him. Having said his goodbyes earlier, he only blew a fond kiss to them and made the sign of the Avogo. Then, he followed the lady out of the room, down the stairs, and out into the morning quiet on the streets of Volmar.

As he walked alongside her towards the place where his procession would begin, Jutta's PASbot, named Redhing, crawled out of its favorite spot on Jutta's torso under his shirt. It made its way slowly up his chest to his biceps and then down his arm. It stopped at his wrist and took Jutta's pulse.

With its camera eye fixed on Jutta's face, Redhing said in a compassionate, female tone, "Your heart rate is elevated, my dear Jutta. Don't be happyless, master. I'll be with you through this. I will be waiting for your return and remind you of all the wonderful things you did in this presence."

Jutta's voice shook a little. "Thank you, Redhing. This was the right decision. I know it was." He wiped his eyes discreetly, worried that the woman—the Controller General of Prescriptive Thought, whom he had always thought of as the lady with the frozen face— would notice. He took a slow deep breath and thought about his situation.

Jutta had always felt detached from others around him. The distractions that appealed to everyone else were disagreeable and shallow to him. And some indiscernible bug of a thought crawled through his mind, torturing him with a persistent wordless interrogation.

"Such a shame," said the only person that they passed on the street at that time. "Your current presence will be missed, Jutta," the man said.

Many in the city must have felt the same. When he had talked about his decision with some of the older citizens of the city, those in their forties who had just begun to show signs that they too would need refreshing, they had shaken their heads and clicked their tongues.

The doctors of the city had done all they could in tweaking his affective apps and medications. And for a short time, their efforts seemed to have worked. Only a year earlier, he had gone back to his job as a Sasjovian and developed some of the most useful code that had been written to date. The one that brought him the greatest recognition, the Distinguished Nasrup prize, helped to rid the Vaipwo—the common citizenry of Volmar—of nagging chest pains that presented without any other physical symptoms.

Many Vaipwo were thankful for what he had done, and when he went out in public in Volmar, he often received cordial greetings, a pat on the back, and invitations to various parties that were to take place. Almost everyone knew his name, a promising young Sasjov of the highest order.

When they arrived at the stable where his procession ritual was to begin, the COGOPT patted Jutta on the back and turned him over to the Refreshing Planner, who spent a good deal of time explaining to Jutta the details of the Refreshing: what he should say. How he should look. How to hold on to the horse as he rode through the streets. When to wave. The badacts and the rightacts of the situation, etc.

After several hours, the time finally came for the procession to begin. Jutta hesitated to get on the horse.

Redhing said, "Don't worry, Jutta. I am with you, always."

Jutta mounted the white stallion and then nodded to the stable keeper that he was ready. The doors opened, and he began his ride through the winding roads, which were by now lined with people, towards the Aspodt where the final act of this brief existence would be committed. He would be transported and reshaped into a new form. This time he would be a girl. And he would be happy. All the old proclivities and that nasty tendency towards questioning which had robbed him of his peace so much these past few years, with good luck, would be wiped away.

And all the people he knew would still be there the next time around, and his companion, Redhing, would be there to provide him with memories of this life as needed. After his reintroduction sometime within the next two weeks, he would not recognize anyone, but they all assured him that they would be there to take care of him.

The people lining the streets waved and cheered for Jutta and for his accomplishments. On some of their faces, a glimmer of a tear began to show. Jutta guessed it was because they had believed he might be the one to write the program that would allow those being refreshed to keep their memories of each life intact. The refreshing meant a complete reformatting of the mind. It was unfortunate, but that had to be the case. The Avogo declared that science, alas, had yet to discover the way to keep the memory during the transfer of an old self into a new body. Technology just hadn't gone that far.

The best that could be done was to remind them of their past presences when they returned in their new bodies.

"Three cheers for Jutta!" Someone shouted. "Hip, hip" and the hooray was echoed as the young man rode closer to the next chapter of his lives. He waved and smiled, pumping a fist into the air as he had been told. "That's the spirit," said Redhing. At one point, he felt so moved by the enthusiasm of the crowd that he made the same motion as someone in the Volmar games might have made to show that victory was theirs.

As he passed, many of the Vaipwo fell into the street behind him, and many followed him all the way to the Aspodt. In front of the Aspodt was a stage. The controllers general of various departments who had known him lined up to speak kindly of him and to remember the things he had done in previous presences under different names.

The CG of Refreshing, the COGOR, read a list of his deeds: "First, we shall recall that the one we know as Jutta now was not always known as Jutta. In his last visit, he was known as Duc, a somewhat quiet but very productive grower of our food. And what calling is higher than that?" A video of Duc tending to his vertical aquaponic system was shown, and one older person in his early forties who had actually known Duc some 18 years ago was overcome with emotion and began to sob. The speeches went on for quite some time. Jutta was enthralled at what he heard about himself in previous presences, but while he sometimes blushed, a nagging doubt lingered inside of him. It was such a doubt that he hoped the refreshing would erase. His next presence would be better than this one, he felt sure.

As he looked over the crowd who listened intently to his multiple incarnations, the group unit he had grown up with and had said goodbye to earlier marched through the crowd and onto the stage.

The fellows, many his age, stood in a line, waiting their turn to speak about him and tell funny stories of his life. The growth promoters, those who had fulfilled their obligations to feed him and change his diapers and make sure he received the appropriate programs at the right age, were there as well. He laughed at many of the stories from this life because he could remember them, and they all seemed nearly true. Only Bibiana and one other person from his group unit were absent from his refreshing ceremony. Mistique had gone on the Avogo journey about eight months earlier. Jutta thought of her and wished he could have said goodbye in person. He handed a note to one of the mates in his group unit and asked him to give it to her when she returned.

After an hour, the speeches were over. Jutta stood up and walked to the center of the stage. There, all saluted him with their pinkies waving in the air. He waved back at them and disrobed. The track on which he was standing began moving, pulling him back into the Aspodt, where he disappeared behind a curtain of white smoke. One of the female mates in his group unit cried out, "I can't believe we will never see that flesh again!"

Chapter 2
The Aspodt

Inside the Aspodt, Jutta shivered as he watched two Vaipwo in surgical masks and robes scurry around, getting ready to transfer Jutta's self into his new body. One of them directed Jutta to a large dentist-like chair and gave him a blanket. "Make yourself comfortable," he said. The cold lab-grown leather of the dentist chair made Jutta's skin break out in goosebumps, and he pulled the blanket over him.

Moments later, a studious man in a white lab coat approached and, clearing his throat, said, "Bless the Avogo, Jutta."

"Bless the Avogo." Jutta looked at the man and said, "Abaidus?!"

"You remembered. It's good to see you, Jutta," Abaidus said. The two had once been neighbors in the same building. "I hope it's okay with you. I will be in charge of your refreshing."

"Of course," Jutta said.

"I'm sure you know a lot about brainport procedures, since you're a Sasjovian. So, think of this as just another one of those procedures, only slightly more complicated, and involving a shot. There may be some unpleasantness with the injection, but that will be a very minor and temporary pinprick. Please, just sit back and try to relax." He patted Jutta on the shoulder lightly.

"It's so cold," Jutta said, shivering under his blanket.

"The cold is only temporary. You'll be fine in no time at all," Abaidus said unconvincingly. "In a few moments, I will give you a shot and then connect you to the SelfRenu." He showed Jutta the cord that he was to plug into the slot behind his ear. "You will go to sleep, and your presence will be transferred to VitalityNu storage where you'll await the new body that the Avogo are preparing. Once that happens, you'll awaken with a new lease on life, as they say."

There was a humming noise and the dentist-like chair began to recline. Jutta closed his eyes and pulled the blanket tighter around him, still shivering. Redhing snuggled up close to his neck.

"Shall I play your favorite song, Master Jutta?" Jutta glanced at his PASbot, that flat flexible device with gripping feet that had been his companion since the aging ceremony on his seventh refday.

"Oh, Redhing. I'm afraid this may be the last I'll see of you. I won't recognize you when I'm new."

"Don't worry. Though you may not recognize me for a while, I'll be there watching out for you just the same. Just like I have these past years."

When the assistants left Abaidus alone with Jutta, he approached the dentist-like chair and quickly waved an electronic device in the shape of a paddle quickly over Redhing then hastily tucked it away inside his coat.

"Okay, Jutta," Abaidus said, "if you are ready for a new slate, I must take your PASbot from you for just a moment."

"That is highly unusual," Redhing objected. "PASbots are to remain on their person at all times. You must be sanctioned by the Avogo to remove me."

"I am sanctioned," Abaidus said, his voice cracking.

"I suspect mistruth." Redhing began scanning his face for signs of lying.

"It's okay, Redhing," Jutta said. "Please. Just do as he says. I know Abaidus. We used to live in the same building. Don't you remember him?"

A soft humming sound came from Redhing, while the green light on its underbelly flashed. Finally, the bot answered, "Very well."

Abaidus grabbed Redhing and hastily ran the same electronic paddle over and under it. He tucked the paddle back into his white lab coat and examined the bot for a few seconds, apparently to see whether the procedure was working. He quickly put Redhing back on Jutta. Soon the bot was snuggled back in place near Jutta's ear.

"That was strange," it whispered to Jutta.

* * *

Abaidus scanned the room, making sure that no one else was around. He locked the door and pulled the curtain to cover the window that opened into the room, and then he returned to Jutta and stood motionless, discreetly pressing a button on a key fob in his pocket.

"Why have I been disconnected from the netw..." Redhing had started to ask but suddenly became mute.

Abaidus turned his attention to the seventeen-year-old whose eyes were closed and was still shivering underneath the thin blanket. "Are you ready to be a new man, Jutta?"

"Woman," Jutta corrected with his eyes still closed. "I'll be a woman this time."

Abaidus patted Jutta's shoulder lightly and said very softly, "Of course." After a brief pause, he said, "Commencing the refreshing" to no one in particular.

Abaidus plugged the VitalityNu into the portal behind Jutta's ear, and Jutta's eyes opened. Abaidus held a syringe full of a clear liquid to the light, tapped it, and then plunged the needle into the side of Jutta's neck. The boy jumped at the pain, but soon was deep asleep.

Another man crawled through the chute for the furnace used for incinerating the bodies that lacked a presence. Without saying a word, he entered the refreshing chamber, which contained the furnace, and then reached back into the chute to pull out a large heavy bag. The man heaved the bag into the furnace and began removing parts of a dead animal and placing them in a way that would resemble a human.

Abaidus moved feverishly to dress Jutta in a pair of pants and a t-shirt, then tied his arms and legs and gagged him. The other young man then helped him place Jutta along the wall, hiding him behind a long wooden bench. When that task was finished, the man silently disappeared back from where he had come through the chute that opened up below the furnace to allow for disposal of the ash and bone. Abaidus turned on the furnace and watched a moment as the flames began to consume the animal parts.

As soon as the fire was raging, Abaidus ran to unlock the door and open the curtain. He also pressed the fob to resume regular video feed. Less than a minute later, the COGOR entered the room to check on the progress.

"Everything okay, Abaidus?"

"Yes. Very smooth. It is accomplished," he said, removing his mask and his gloves, his voice and hands obviously shaking.

"Good," he said, examining the preparation room. "Don't be sad. He'll be back in a matter of days. She is due on Monday."

"Yes, COGOR. It will be good to see, hi... her."

After checking out the incinerator and seeing the flames, the COGOR left the room.

Abaidus leaned against the wall and took a deep breath, then blessed himself with the sign of the cross. After a few more deep breaths, he set about finishing the task he'd been assigned. He once again pressed the fob button, looping the cameras. Then, he rolled out a wheelchair and, with great effort, lifted Jutta into it.

Because the door was unlocked, this was the riskiest part of the whole endeavor. If the COGOR or some earnest assistant returned, his scheme would be revealed.

Once Jutta was secured in the wheelchair, Abaidus wheeled him into a small supply closet inside the preparation room and locked the closet door, leaving Jutta bound and gagged there in the chair. It would be some time before the furnace could cool off so that the other man could return for Jutta to take him out through the chute.

It would take over an hour for the body parts in the incinerator to be cremated. Abaidus unlocked the door again and opened the curtains, then started pretending to do maintenance work on a piece of equipment that he had broken for this purpose.

After about twenty minutes, one of the assistants he had shooed away earlier came in to see why he was still there. When the assistant saw the dismantled equipment and that Abaidus was making adjustments, he left him alone.

Finally, after an hour, Abaidus could wait no longer. He opened the incinerator door even though it was still stifling hot. Heat poured out of the furnace into the refreshing chamber, reminding Abaidus of his previous home, Mainz, where the temperature outside often felt like that furnace. He bore the heat with patience as the chamber cooled enough that it wouldn't overwhelm the sleeping Jutta. When the temperature dropped to 120, Abaidus hurried to the closet and quickly rolled Jutta into the refreshing chamber, which housed the furnace, hiding Jutta to the right side of the door. He made sure that Jutta's arms and legs were tied tightly and that his mouth was taped and gagged, then opened the chute and pushed the hot ash and small bones into it. Then, he closed and locked the door of the refreshing chamber behind him, leaving Jutta alone in the dark heat.

When Abaidus left the preparation room, the clerk noted, "It took you much longer to finish this time. That will be in the report to the Avogo."

"Yes. Please tell them that I had to make some adjustments to the VitalityNu. One of the LM32 nodes is bad. I worked on it all this time, but it's clear I'll have to return later with another part.

Perhaps in a few hours."

"I see," said the receptionist behind a large white desk. "Good day. Bless the Avogo."

Abaidus paused. "Yes. Bless the Avogo."

Several hours passed before Abaidus returned to the Aspodt. Night had come, and all the assistants had gone back to their group units and plugged into their virtual pleasure crafts, so Abaidus let himself in with his voice and retina scan. The computer asked what business he had there at such an hour.

"I need to finish repairing the VitalityNu."

"Memory check, please," the voice said.

Abaidus pulled on a cord that was sticking out of the computer and pretended to insert it into the slot in his neck. Computers in Volmar had the power to read certain events that were stored in a Vaipwo's short-term memory. Since his short-term memory would have included the other Dicarer sneaking in, and their conspiracy to save Jutta from the refreshing, Abaidus could not take the risk of sharing his real memory. He plugged the cord into a separate device that stored prefabricated memories. He had already made that memory when he was working on the VitalityNu earlier. After a few moments, the computer found the memory of Abaidus working on the VitalityNu.

"You may enter, Abaidus. I do hope you can fix it."

"I'm quite sure of it," he said. "Got the part I need right here. Bless the Avogo."

The door swung open and he entered the foyer, then passed through the doors to the preparation room. Finally, he unlocked the refreshing chamber where Jutta was still sitting in the wheelchair.

Abaidus flicked the lights on, catching Jutta off guard. "I'm sorry it is taking this long," Abaidus whispered. "I know this must seem odd to you, Jutta. But soon, you'll understand. They'll explain everything. But first, we must get you out of here. No one in Volmar is to know that you are still alive."

Jutta's eyebrows furrowed as if he were completely confused.

"Just be silent for now while we get you out of the city."

Presently, the other man crawled out of the hole where Abaidus had swept the ashes earlier.

"Let's go," he whispered. "Quickly."

Abaidus pushed the wheelchair to the hole and then untied Jutta's hands and feet from the chair. Immediately, the other man grabbed him and re-tied his hands in front of him.

"Sorry, Jutta. It is for your own protection," Abaidus whispered softly.

"This is Sabas. He will see you through the tunnel to the heaps where the others will meet you. Then they will take you to our city. Do not resist for now. We do not mean to harm you. We will explain everything in due time. Just cooperate now, and you'll understand. You'll understand why you were chosen. Now go. We don't have much time."

Jutta resisted at first, but Sabas was apparently in no mood for delay. "Don't make this difficult," he said. "Do you want to go with me on your own, or do you want me to carry you?" Sabas was a well-built man no more than twenty or twenty-one years old. Jutta dropped into the hole and disappeared with his captor.

Abaidus finished cleaning up and took a long deep breath of relief. His part of the rescue was over.

He worked on the VitalityNu for a few minutes so that he could have a memory to share with the computer if need be. The refreshing chamber was empty; Sabas and Jutta would soon be reaching the heaps where another person would begin the second stage of the rescue. He examined the room, took a deep breath and said a prayer. "God protect them in the remaining days of this rescue, and bring me to be with them soon."

Then he turned off the lights and returned to his quarters.

Chapter 3
The Heaps

Sabas and Jutta came to the end of the chute that ran out of the Refreshing chamber and opened up into the heaps. Sabas put up a hand to indicate that Jutta should stop and wait with him. Sabas peered out through the end of the chute and searched the horizon. Glancing at his watch, he said, "The others will be here soon. Just sit here and wait for the signal."

Jutta sat down and looked out through the hole.

Sabas sat down as well and warned Jutta with his eyes. Jutta had confusion written all over his face. "Speak quietly, if at all," he said threateningly as he removed the tape that was still covering Jutta's mouth. He then untied his hands.

The first thing Jutta did when his hands were free was to ask softly, "What is this place, Redhing?" The bot lit up but was still muted from earlier when Abaidus took it from Jutta.

Jutta found a way to unmute the bot. "I've never been so insulted. I was muted for several hours."

"Turn it down," Sabas hissed.

Jutta turned the bot's voice down low as the bot continued its tirade. "That is a really unbelievable badact. Imagine, someone treating a PASbot in such a degrading way. It has never happened in the history of Volmar. I've never been offended like this. This is all highly unusual and alarming. I have tried sending reports to the Avogo about all of this, but..."

Jutta interrupted, "Redhing, do you know what is happening?"

"I do not know, Master Jutta. I'm not connected to the network and I'm unable to access any information. But we certainly must do something about this insolent man..."

Sabas shook his head and rolled his eyes. Sabas hated Volmar and anyone who lived in it. He listened to Jutta talking quietly with his PASbot. Jutta picked up a long, white stick-like object and played with it absentmindedly.

That reminded him of why he hated Volmar. Ignorant, Sabas thought. *He doesn't even know what he's holding in his hand. I'm not gonna tell him.* As he waited for the signal, Sabas reviewed all he had heard about the evil and beauty of the city.

Volmar was built in the foothills of the Vasgar mountains. High above Volmar sat Disibodenberg, the fortress of the Avogo. The Avogo were the original architects and founders of the city, which had just celebrated its one hundred and twentieth foundation day anniversary.

The winds often blew strong in the foothills, and the heat always bore down on the lovely metropolis. Nevertheless, the citizens of Volmar, the Vaipwo, enjoyed perfect comfort throughout their city year-round. They were never hot, never thirsty, never hungry, never worried about the weather or where their food might come from. The Avogo had built a beautiful city that protected them from the elements. Volmar was encased in an ingenious bio-dome made of plexiglass-like material that could allow sunlight in and sunlight out. It breathed like a skin yet was so rigid that the winds never stirred even one plant that grew in the city. Great fans would occasionally be turned on to simulate winds, but real storms never threatened the city.

Plants grew everywhere, even on the many buildings that rose into the sky, nearly touching the biodome. The roofs and exterior walls of these buildings were covered with plants that provided fresh food and beautiful fragrant flowers, giving the city the feel of some Edenic paradise. That was a phrase Sabas had heard.

Right outside their windows, the Vaipwo could regularly see the most gorgeous tomatoes, cucumbers, string beans, berries, and a great variety of other tasty vegetables right there on their window sills. All of the vegetables grew in nutrient-rich water that came from a giant aquaponics farm, just teeming with fish. There were all kinds of fish that were good for food. It was all closely monitored by the Controller General of Food Production using ingenious technologies that had been pioneered before the cataclysm, as was most of the technology in Volmar. The waters circulated through the city's buildings and through the town, emptying into a calming river that was lined with shops and restaurants and that meandered through virtually every neighborhood.

Fruit trees were plentiful, and as for meat, everything was grown in labs without slaughterhouses or nasty feedlots. There were no suffering animals. The animals that lived in Volmar—dogs, cats, birds, a few horses, and many other farm animals kept for pets or as novelties—were all tame, and none of them were in any real danger of being killed for food. The animals did not live the gritty existence that their ancestors had struggled through. They were fat, full, and lazy.

It was as close to a perfect city as possible, but like any city, it still had its waste. Food waste and feces, both human and animal, were sent to composts that generated fertile soil to be used freely around the city.

Although the Avogo prided themselves on having built possibly the most efficient and livable city in human history, there were some forms of waste that they could do nothing with. There were still items that broke and were no longer of value or were not worth fixing. All of those broken things that could not be reused, repurposed, or recycled were tossed into chutes at different stations around the city, and the discarded pieces would build up into heaps until they began blocking the flow of the trash. When that happened, the Avogo would send their Sogmol army to move the garbage further away from the city, leaving it in giant heaps.

Another item that was found in these heaps was human bones. Sabas looked at Jutta again and saw that he had put down the stick-like object. But since no one in Volmar could ever see the heaps—the city had been designed specifically for the best aesthetics and to avoid any unsightly views—this boneyard was unknown and un-mourned by the Vaipwo. The bones came through their own separate chute, not one of those used by the citizens.

They came from the chute that had its origin in the Aspodt, where the refreshings took place. Where Jutta and Sabas now sat, waiting for the signal from outside.

"It is so hot, Redhing," Jutta said.

Though the sun had already gone down and it was a little past 9:00 p.m., the concrete chute leading from the Aspodt was still releasing its store of heat from the day, so the temperature still hovered in the upper 90s. Beads of sweat puddled on Jutta's forehead. He wiped the sweat off his brow with his hands, which were stiff and sore from being tied up for so long.

"I've never felt such heat," he said, now eyeing Sabas suspiciously.

"Yes, Master Jutta," Redhing said. "The current temperature is dangerously high. I fear we risk overheating unless the Avogo can help. I'll keep trying to reconnect and send word." Then the bot fixed its camera eye on Sabas. "Who are you, exactly? I've scanned your face, and you are not a citizen of Volmar. Where is your PASbot?"

Sabas said, "Master Jutta," imitating Redhing. "I've been listening to your little friend here too long. We are about to get the signal, so I suggest we stand up and stretch. Get ready to run. And shut that thing down before it gets me upset."

"Shut that thing down? How can he say such a thing? Can you believe that, Master Jutta? He thinks you could shut me down. Ha! It would require permission from the COGOB herself. And I guarantee you, YOU don't have such permission."

"You mean to tell me that nowadays you can't turn those things off?" Sabas said, still talking to Jutta, genuinely surprised at this new revelation.

"Why, of course. Do you not know the laws of Volmar?" Redhing replied.

"I'm talking to you, Jutta, not that stupid thing," said Sabas with irritation in his voice. "Shut it down, or am I going to have to!"

"Why, I've never heard..." Redhing began, but Jutta beckoned it to be quiet.

"Allow me to speak, Redhing," Jutta said. "Look. I don't know who you are or what is going on. I'm sure this is all part of the refreshing. It is part of the refreshing, right?"

"Sure, Jutta. 'The refreshing.'" Sabas used air quotes and then looked away. "For now, just keep your little friend quiet. You need to begin to hear your own voice. If you cannot shut him down completely, then keep him silenced. It is vital for, a smooth, uh, 'refreshing.'"

Jutta followed Sabas' gaze out across the endless desert. "It seems odd, that's all. But I trust you know what you are doing. Redhing, stay muted, please."

"That's a good chap," said Sabas, who was watching out for the signal.

"Now listen. Soon, there's going to be a light out there, in the mountain. At that time, other Dicarers will override the motion sensors protecting the heaps and distract the drones of the Sogmols. We'll have twenty seconds to get past the heaps to the flatlands. There, my friend will be waiting on a traverser for you. You have to cooperate. No screaming. And no more sound from the bot. If you scream or don't run with me, the refreshing will be over, and you'll never get back. Your self will be left out here in the heat forever. You must go along with me. Do you understand?"

Jutta nodded as if a light bulb had just come on. "You mean we're in VitalityNu storage? Wow! This is it? I never knew what to expect."

Sabas shook his head and laughed. "Yeah. That's it, Jutta. Now, very soon, we're going to run past those heaps of trash to that giant mound over there. You see it?"

Jutta squinted to see where Sabas was pointing.

"Once we get there, my girlfriend will be waiting with a traverser."

"What's a traverser?" Jutta asked.

"It's sort of like a horse, only it's mechanical...like an elevator or escalator. Something you ride on to go places very fast. Someone will be driving it, and she'll take you to the camp." Jutta's whole face was a puzzle. "You'll understand later. Just be ready to run when I say so. Got it?" Jutta coughed out a dry "yes"—he hadn't had anything to drink in many hours, and sweat was still dripping from his forehead.

"There'll be some water when we get over there." Just then, Sabas saw the light signal.

"Run. Now. Go!" he said, tearing out across the field, pulling Jutta along by his arm. The two ran as fast as they could in the dark, but Jutta was not up to the task. He tripped and fell flat on his face. Sabas lost his grip.

"Thirteen, Fourteen..." He was counting the seconds as he reached down to pick up Jutta. "Seventeen, Eighteen..." Sabas stopped about ten yards away from the large mound they had been running towards.

"Don't move an inch!" he said. "Don't move or they'll be on us."

"Who?" Jutta asked.

"Never mind. Just wait. We didn't make it. The sensors are back on again. Time for plan B."

"What's plan B? How is this part of refreshing?"

Sabas ignored this question.

The co-conspirator waiting for them behind the mounds must have seen their shapes drop. Sabas saw the Dicarer getting off the traverser and opening a compartment. A half-mile north, an explosion shook the heaps.

"Go, go, go," said Sabas. The two shot over the remaining distance to the mound. Sabas greeted the other Dicarer, who waited on her traverser, with a quick peck on the cheek.

"Get on," Sabas told Jutta, who obeyed instinctively.

"Good luck," Sabas said to the girl, who then sped off with Jutta and his PASbot. Sabas ran south and found his appointed hiding place where he would wait until it was safe for him to venture out.

* * *

Jutta found himself riding around the many mounds of trash that had been buried over the years, whizzing past discarded pieces of the city of Volmar that had been replaced. Jutta could not see the driver well, but he held on to her desperately, terrified of falling backwards and breaking his neck.

The driver was so skilled at driving a traverser that it seemed like the vehicle itself was programmed to avoid obstacles and bumps. He'd never ridden anything so exhilarating or fast, and his stomach felt as though it had been left back at the heaps. His throat was parched, and he felt nauseous from the movement and the stress of the past few days. It took all he had to keep from throwing up. He fought the urge to tell the driver to stop because he feared that would be the end of his refreshing, that he would end up stranded in this hot netherworld, unable to find his way to the new body that awaited his self. It was a serious moment that he somehow knew he had to survive. So, he dug deep, closed his eyes, wrapped his arms around the driver, and tried to be brave.

Chapter 4

The Safe Hole

After more than thirty minutes of riding at dizzying speeds, the traverser finally began to slow down. Jutta opened his eyes and, by the moon's light, saw that they were riding over a level tract of land with no mounds or heaps or cities or anything else. Off in the distance was what appeared to be the outline of a mountain range that Jutta didn't recognize. The traverser eventually came to a complete stop. Volmar was nowhere in sight, so Jutta figured they were many miles from home.

"You can take your hands off of me now," the driver said in a tender but firm voice.

Jutta released his grip on her, and she dismounted the traverser. "Come on," she said, motioning for him to get off of the wheel-less bike. Jutta tried, but he nearly fell down on his first attempt. The girl helped him stand, and once he had his bearings, she started pulling bags out of the cargo compartment in the traverser. She handed Jutta one of them and took two for herself.

"This way, Jutta." She led him several hundred yards across the flat terrain. Eventually, the girl dropped her bags and pulled out two devices. One she pointed at the traverser, which started up and quickly disappeared.

"What? Where is it going?" Jutta asked.

The girl fiddled a little with the second device, which looked like a cardboard box. Jutta couldn't imagine what it might be. Then, she put it down and started crawling around on her knees, feeling the ground with a sense of urgency.

"What are you doing?" Jutta asked. There was no answer, so he unmuted the PASbot and asked, "Where are we, Redhing?"

"I haven't the slightest idea. I've been trying to call home the entire time since you told me to be quiet..." the PASbot paused a moment to let the guilt sink in. "But..."

"But what?" Jutta asked.

"It's like nothing I've ever known before. I've never been disconnected from the network. It is a very strange experience for me. But don't worry, Master Jutta. I'm sure the Avogo..."

"There you are!" said the girl pulling up a rope that was covered with sand. As she pulled on it, the rope emerged from the ground little by little for about twenty yards, leading them to a lid that was covered with sand. She knelt down and told Jutta to give her a hand.

Jutta got on his knees and helped her scrape the sand off of what ended up being a large round piece of metal. It was a lid about three feet in diameter. When it was cleared of sand, the two pulled on the lid together. It opened reluctantly, hinges creaking. Jutta slipped in the loose sand and nearly fell into the hole, but the girl grabbed him and pulled him back.

"Be careful," she said. "It's a long way down. Grab your stuff and let's go."

Jutta grabbed the bag she had given him and peered down into the hole but could see only the top of a ladder that descended into the abyss.

"Come on. We must hurry." The girl dropped her bags into the hole then grabbed his and threw it in as well. "You first, Jutta. Just climb down the ladder as far as you can. Once we're in there and I have the lid closed, I'll drop a light in. Don't want to turn on the light out here. Go now, just about ten rungs of the ladder and wait for me."

Jutta stuck his foot into the hole and felt the first rung of the ladder with his left foot as she held onto his hands.

"Is this where the refreshing happens?" he asked hopefully.

"Yes, Jutta. Just go," the girl said.

He did as he was told. He climbed down carefully, counting ten rungs, and then waited above the darkness as he listened to the girl climb into the hole above him. When he turned his head up, he noticed stars in their vast brilliance, brighter than he'd ever known them to be. He had seen stars before when he visited the tops of the tallest buildings in Volmar, but with all the lights reflecting back from the biodome, he'd never really been impressed by them. The lid slammed shut above them, and the stars were gone, and Jutta experienced a darkness he'd never known. He thought he heard something above them, throwing the sand and dirt back over the lid, as if they were being buried.

The girl turned on a light above him and dropped it into the hole. Jutta nearly lost his grip as he tried to cover his eyes.

"Go, Jutta. Keep descending." His eyes adjusted, and he could now see that they had another twenty feet or more to go. Frightened, he glanced at the girl who was waiting for him to descend.

"You mustn't be afraid, Jutta. Just go and don't look down."

The girl still wore a hood and a mask over her face, so he couldn't tell for sure what she looked like. As he descended the ladder, he pointed the bot in her direction so that it could find out more about her.

At the bottom of the ladder, there was a drop of about five feet. Jutta let go and landed on one of the bags the girl had dropped, tripping and ultimately landing flat on his back and bumping his head on a small stool, the only piece of furniture in the hole.

"You okay?" the girl asked.

"Yeah. I'm fine. No problem," he said, trying to downplay his embarrassment.

He got up and moved out of the way so that she could jump, too. She landed with ease, then removed her brown hood and mask and smiled at him, holding out her hand.

"My name's Odilia," she said. "Welcome to the safe hole, Jutta."

Jutta gazed into her brown eyes and at her long dark hair and hardly knew what to say. He had never been awkward with girls in the past, but usually the PASbots did most of the communicating between lovers, and Redhing was being unusually silent. After the brief greeting, Odilia went about unpacking.

"Hello, you're...uh...Odilia. Nice to meet you."

She handed him a flask of water, and he drank it completely without saying thanks. He wiped his lips on his sleeve and dropped the flask on the floor.

"So, um. How come I never met you before?" he asked.

She turned away from him and reached inside one of the bags bringing out a lantern, which she lit, illuminating more clearly the narrow hole that they were in. She extinguished the light that she had dropped earlier.

Jutta examined the place as she worked but there wasn't much to see. That's pretty much all it was, a hole in the ground in the middle of the desert. It was about thirty feet deep, six or seven feet in diameter, with just enough room for an average person to stretch out when lying down.

After the introduction, Odilia seemed more inclined to busy herself with unknown preparations than to talk.

Jutta spoke to Redhing in a subdued voice, "Did you find out anything? Do you know what's going on yet?"

Redhing responded, almost matching Jutta's tone. "I do not know, Master Jutta. I was not given information about the process of refreshing. I believe we will be fine, though. She is a beautiful girl, but I cannot place her. Ask her how she likes her pleasure."

Jutta turned to the girl and, with no sense of embarrassment, asked, "How do you like your pleasure, Odilia?"

Odilia stopped what she was doing and said, "Jutta, you'll have to learn new manners now. Please mute that thing, and for the rest of our time here, talk only to me."

"That thing?" Redhing said incredulously. "That thing? Again? Do you not know..." Redhing's voice disappeared as Jutta waved his hand over it.

"Thank you," said Odilia. "You'll stay here through tomorrow's daylight. After that, I will take you to Mainz. I'll tell you more about all of that later. For now, let's just get some rest. This is an important part of the rescue – I mean 'refreshing.' You must learn to be quiet and to do without Redhing for short periods of time. So, we need to all be quiet and just rest and, well, anyway, that's about it. I'm going to go to bed."

Odilia reached in her bag and removed a hammock. She jumped up onto the ladder and pulled herself up. About eight feet above Jutta, she built her nest by inserting the hooks of the hammock into screw eyes already embedded into the wall of the hole. Jutta shined the light at just the right angle so he could see that there were similar screw eyes every three feet, meaning this hole could hold a lot of people if need be.

When it was ready, she climbed into the hammock and lay down. "You have a sleeping bag and a pillow in your bag," she said. "If you need to pee, pull on the rope down there at your feet."

He saw the rope she was talking about and pulled on it. A little pot came out of a hole that had been carved into the wall.

"Kind of primitive," the girl said. "But it's all we've got. Turn off the light when you are ready. And try to get some rest."

Jutta was confused, but he went ahead and got his sleeping bag ready and fluffed up his pillow.

"This isn't anything like what I expected the refreshing to be," he said aloud, but the girl didn't respond. He was keeping Redhing muted like the girl asked. But he knew it was getting angry at him. He wondered how long Redhing would wait until unmuting itself.

He wanted to talk to the girl, but she had made it pretty clear that there would be no more talking. He lay down on his back and put his hands behind his head, staring up at the girl above him before turning out the light.

"Odilia," he said under his breath. "I hope she doesn't wet the bed."

He was about to turn off the light when he realized that he hadn't eaten since breakfast. Jutta hesitated but decided to ask, "Might I have some food?"

Odilia didn't answer immediately. He thought maybe she was already asleep. But then he heard her moving up above rustling through a bag.

"Of course," Odilia said. "Looks like I'm the one who needs new manners."

She leaned over her hammock and held down a green triangular thing.

"Here, catch." She dropped it and Jutta missed clumsily. "You must be famished. It's been a long day for you."

Jutta took it gratefully, but when he opened the package and smelled it, he lost his appetite. He took a small bite and made no effort in trying to conceal the fact that he didn't like the taste.

"Uggh. What is this?" He said, trying to swallow the small bite in his mouth.

Odilia lay above him and scoffed. "Wash it down with some water. I left another flask for you down there."

"This is terrible. You actually eat this?"

"It's broonscake, just survival food. Probably not something you'd like since you're used to getting potatoes and lab-grown steak. But it has all the nutrients you need. You'll get used to it...you'll have to."

He studied the green triangle-shaped glob of stuff in his hand and decided he'd had enough. After a while, Odilia began mumbling a few things to herself as she lay in the hammock above him. Something about bread and trespasses and temptation.

The words that he could hear somehow made him uncomfortable, and Redhing vibrated a warning. A message popped up on the bot. "Violation. Report her, Jutta."

"Odilia?" Jutta asked after Odilia had stopped praying. "Where's your PASbot?"

"Good night, Jutta," was her response. "There'll be time for your questions later. Right now, it's time to rest."

Jutta didn't turn off the light. He scanned the small circular hole in the ground and, with his mind full of questions, decided to unmute Redhing. He put his finger to his lip, indicating to the PASbot that it should be quiet.

"Do you need help sleeping, Master Jutta?" the bot asked, not nearly as quiet as Jutta had hoped.

PASbots were not always cooperative, but at least Redhing had stayed muted this long.

"It would help if I knew where we were, Redhing," Jutta said quietly, hoping not to disturb the beautiful girl suspended above him.

Redhing's voice grew quieter. "Again, I do not know where we are. It must be part of the refreshing, but unfortunately, I have no information on the process of the refreshing." There was a long pause. "Perhaps I can take your mind off of things. Who do you want me to be tonight, Master Jutta? What is your pleasure?"

Jutta thought for a moment. "Can you be her?" he asked, nodding towards Odilia. The PASbot's voice soon morphed into Odilia's. The avatar on Redhing's screen gradually became Odilia, then it slowly crawled up to his ear and began speaking seductively.

"Stop it, Jutta!" The real Odilia yelled from above. "That thing has to be muted at all times while I'm here. If it is not, I will rip it off and crush it with a rock. You're not in Volmar anymore, and you're in for a rude awakening. Now shut it off and get to sleep!"

Jutta had never been talked down to (literally or figuratively) except by the COGOPT on a few occasions, one of which was when he had peeked into that forbidden book. "A horse dashing into battle," he said.

"What?" Odilia snapped.

"Nothing. Nothing. Sorry." He wanted to talk more, but after that diatribe, he didn't dare. He made sure Redhing returned to its default avatar and was muted. He lay his head on the pillow. When he did, his exhaustion came upon him. It had been a long day. He looked at Redhing, who flashed the time to him. It was 12:30 a.m., a decent time to sleep.

Chapter 5

Confronting Redhing

Jutta awakened hours later to darkness. In a panic, he called out for Redhing, who lit up with a blue glow, dimly illuminating the cave they were in. He had hoped all of this had been a dream, but the cold round walls confirmed it to be real.

"I'm here, Jutta," Redhing said.

Jutta shushed it immediately, afraid that Odilia would yell at him again.

"The girl is gone. She's not here."

Jutta still felt groggy. He could see that her hammock was gone, and there was nothing left that belonged to the odd but beautiful girl.

"What time is it? Where did she go?" Jutta asked.

"It is 8:00 in the morning, Master Jutta. And I don't know."

"I'm still so tired. Why am I so tired?"

Redhing paused: "It must be the refreshing. The process must be starting."

Jutta wiped his eyes. "I thought my vital force would have moved into my new body by now." He had often wondered what it would be like getting used to a new body. He tried to remember yesterday's events to figure out what was happening. There was the procession, and the cold chair, and Abaidus, and the painful stinging in his neck, and...he felt his neck and realized that it was still rather sore.

"Redhing, what is this bump on my neck?"

Redhing examined it. "It is a puncture wound, perhaps from some sort of biting insect. We do not have freely roaming biting insects in Volmar. That would mean it must have happened here. But my sensors have not indicated any other life form in this hole."

"Could have happened in the Aspodt," Jutta said, rubbing his neck slowly.

There was the hot room, and the man who came in and took him out of the Aspodt through that chute and then to the heaps outside of Volmar.

"Perhaps it was a drug to make you relax," the bot said as it stood up onto what could be called its hind legs and displayed a friendly computer-generated female human avatar that Jutta had designed himself.

"The refreshing shouldn't be this hard. Why would this body need to be here, thirty feet below ground? Why should I be in hiding?"

Redhing's avatar furled her eyebrows and shrugged her shoulders. Then she pouted as if commiserating with him.

"My poor, poor little man," she said.

In Volmar, PASbots spewed Avogo-approved answers to any question their human asked. But there were no approved answers to offer in this case. The avatar continued to pout and fidget in her plaid mini-skirt, placing an index finger on her dimple and looking up at the sky as if she were thinking about his situation.

Jutta struggled out of bed. "Light," he said. When Redhing turned on its flashlight beam, Jutta became light-headed, as if he had stood up too fast, but he was still only on his knees. He found the light that Odilia had used the night before and turned it on. Redhing stopped glowing, and Jutta began to feel better.

The girl had left a large knapsack, which Jutta rummaged through, finding more water and three more large pieces of that nasty, bland food she had offered him at bedtime. He tossed the broonscakes back into the bag with disgust and continued searching for something tastier. But there was not much to search through. The only other items in the knapsack were a new hammock, alcohol sanitizer, some food and water, and a small collapsible shovel.

"I'm afraid I'll have to eat that if she doesn't come back soon," Jutta said, referring to the survival cakes he had nearly damaged, throwing them back into the bag. He sat down on the lone stool in the cave. It was wooden, roughly hewn, and with no back at all. Perhaps there had been a back at one time, but it was no more. He leaned against the wall.

"Did she say anything before she left?" Jutta asked.

"No, but I did video her leaving. Would you like to see?"

"Yes. Play," Jutta said, and then he turned down the light.

One wall of the cave became a screen for the video that was projected onto it. Jutta felt tired again. The video showed Odilia waking up at 7:03. She moved quickly and peered back at Jutta. Her head moved out of camera range and a light came on near her.

"She must have been using a communication device of some kind. Maybe she was reading a message," Jutta said.

He watched as she climbed onto the ladder and began throwing things into her knapsack, finishing up with her hammock. She folded a piece of paper and stuck it in a crack in the wall but then paused for a moment and suddenly stared straight into the camera that was recording her.

Seconds later, Odilia climbed up the ladder and out of the hole. The bright light indicated that it was daylight outside, but before Redhing's camera had adjusted, the lid was closed again and the video stopped.

"That is all I have, Master Jutta." Redhing's projection ended and Jutta turned the light back on. Immediately, he felt his energy start to return.

Jutta glanced over his shoulder and saw the piece of paper stuck in a crevice in the wall about the same height as Odilia's hammock had been.

He reached for it and began reading aloud.

"Do not go out. Stay here. Will be back soon. Be wary of the..."

Jutta stopped reading aloud.

"Be wary of the what? Master Jutta?"

Jutta didn't answer. He re-read it silently several times. "Do not go out. Stay here. Will be back soon. Be wary of the bot. Book under stool. Bot must not know." He folded the paper and put it in his pocket.

"What should we be wary of?" asked Redhing once again.

"Nothing. It's nothing, Redhing."

"Master Jutta," Redhing said in a motherly tone. "You know there can be no secrets between you and your bot. What does the rest of the note say?"

The Vaipwo/PASbot creed rang in Jutta's mind: "Your PASbot is your guide, confidant, and trustworthy friend; to your every need it will attend. Through every trial, thick or thin, it will be with you till the end."

Jutta felt like he should tell Redhing, but something in the way Odilia had looked at the camera made him resist. She had a quality that he hadn't seen much of; he struggled to think of the word. Redhing began to glow, and it asked again, this time in a louder and more demanding tone.

"Jutta? Be wary of what?" Again, Jutta's strength felt like it was seeping out of him. He struggled to keep his train of thought. Sincere. That was the word. She had appeared so sincere. She couldn't have been lying.

Hadn't he always felt something was a little odd about the relationship humans had with their PASbots? When others received theirs at the age of seven, they were elated. But while he remembered thinking the bots were really cool, he also felt that something was odd about them. He had been scared of Redhing. And the idea of never being able to be alone again without it, that thought had overwhelmed him. He had even asked if he could have a bot that he could take off if he wanted.

"Definitely not," the lady with the frozen face had said.

Redhing was practically yelling, "Tell me!" Its avatar had now become an ogre, and its voice deepened. Redhing began vibrating, menacingly, like the low growl of a suspicious dog. If the vibrating didn't work, Jutta knew that pins and needles came next.

"The box!" Jutta finally said wearily. "Beware of the box. At first, I thought it said 'beware of the bot', but now I remember the box she left outside the hole. Her handwriting is difficult to read." Jutta hoped the lie would satisfy Redhing. But PASbots were designed to read people. They could detect pheromones to know when their human was aroused. If in the right place, they could also detect physiological functions to determine whether someone was telling the truth or not.

Jutta knew that the bot was analyzing his voice for cues of insincerity. It apparently found none. Redhing stopped vibrating and the female avatar and voice returned. Jutta felt his energy level coming back, but he was hungry.

"I'd better eat something," he said, hoping to turn the conversation away from Odilia's note. "Can you believe this stuff I'm supposed to eat?"

Redhing was silent.

"You're lucky you don't have to eat," Jutta said and then took a bite of the awful green triangle. As he chewed, his own words hit him. Redhing didn't have to eat.

Jutta swallowed hard and a piece of it caught in his throat. He drank some water, thinking that even though Redhing didn't eat, it did need to be charged every day. PASbots had to be charged either at a charging station, which graced every room, restaurant, casino, office, bedroom, bathroom, and closet in Volmar, or by sun, by wind or other life forms, including their humans.

This was a fact Jutta had stumbled on to when he was working on a project as a Sasjovian. It was an inadvertent slip of the tongue made by the Controller General of Defense when Jutta interviewed him about how the biodome transfers energy. Jutta thought back to the last time Redhing had been charged. The previous day, before the procession, twenty-four hours at least as best he could figure. And here they were, in a cave with no sun, no wind, no other energy source, except his own body.

"I wonder why we should worry about the box," Redhing said. "I've not seen anything quite like it." After a long pause, Redhing changed the subject. "I have been thinking about all the kind words that people said of you yesterday."

Jutta was pleased with the change in topic. But the note, telling him to beware of the bot, and the sudden realization that Redhing had been getting its energy directly from him made Jutta suspiciously quiet.

How much of my energy will it steal from me? He wondered. Would a bot let its human die rather than run out of energy? That was a question the Defense minister wouldn't have answered even if Jutta had asked.

Jutta ate the insipid broonscake with a new appreciation. Though it lacked flavor, it was nutritionally dense; he began to feel stronger and to think more clearly. He remembered being sent to reprogramming several times because he had asked questions, like the ones he was now thinking. At one time, he asked the lady with the frozen face, "Could I have a break from Redhing? Just one or two days?" It was not long after this discussion that the idea of volunteering for refreshing was tossed around. Had he thought of it himself? He now began to wonder.

"I thought it was wonderful what Haly said about you," Redhing was blabbering on still about the ceremony. "Very touching. They all really love you, Jutta. I love you, too."

Something in the way Redhing said those words made Jutta's skin crawl. He finished off the last bite of broonscake and stood up.

"I have to go to the bathroom."

He pulled on the rope and withdrew the chamber pot. It was lined with a bag that could be tied and toted off. He sat down on the pot, wishing he could relieve himself of the bot that clung to him as well. But Jutta knew that was unlikely. He had once pulled Redhing off and dropped it on his bed. The PASbot had made a horrible sound, and soon, the Sogmols were kicking in his door. Since then, he had not tried such a stunt.

But now, here in the deep hole, Jutta began to think that things might be different: Redhing was disconnected from the network.

"Have you any word from home?" Jutta asked nonchalantly.

"Still nothing, Master Jutta. I'm afraid in this hole we have lost all connection to the real world. We need to get out of here so that I can connect with PASportal to see what is going on."

Jutta thought about the note from Odilia. *Book under stool. Bot must not know.*

"You're acting rather strange, Master Jutta. Is something the matter?" Redhing said, possibly sensing an increase in epinephrine and cortisol, stress hormones.

Jutta did not respond immediately. "Master Jutta?" the bot said.

Having finished his business, Jutta stood up: "What do you mean, 'Is something the matter'?" He tied the bag, put a new one in the pot and wiped his hands with the alcohol sanitizer Odilia had left. "I'm totally lost, stuck in a hole, put here by strangers who ran away and left me with nothing but a note that says 'don't go out and watch out for stupid box bots' and tasteless food that won't last more than another two meals. And to top it off, my PASbot doesn't even know where we are or what is happening. Can't something be the matter?"

"I see. Thank you for sharing." That was Redhing's usual response when Jutta got angry.

"Thank you for sharing," Jutta mimicked Redhing with

exaggerated sarcasm.

Jutta's blood began to boil as those words brought back a flood of bad memories. Every time he had ever gotten mad at Redhing, the Avogo insisted on adjustments to his temper mitigation program. But the adjustments never really made him less angry. He now realized they had just made him apathetic, less likely to confront his bot. But here, isolated in this hole, Redhing couldn't communicate with the outside world, and he thought about the book Odilia had mentioned in her note. He didn't know if he could trust the girl, but something inside told him he had to try.

"Sincerity," he said aloud, out of the blue.

"What a strange thing to say," Redhing said. "Are you talking about Haly?"

"Never mind," Jutta said.

What is there to lose? He thought. If he took the bot off and the alarm sounded, would the Sogmols come crashing through the hole? If so, he'd be rescued and taken back to Volmar, and the rightful act of refreshing could proceed. If not, he would be able to get away from the bot and think for himself for a moment and read the book that remained hidden under the chair. And if he didn't do it, it was very possible that the bot could end up sucking his energy while he slept. He might never wake up.

"Master Jutta," Redhing said, evidently forgetting about the "sincerity" comment. "I agree that you have the right to be upset. This is certainly a predicament that a human needs a PASbot for, but I am of little use. This is the first time, in the ten years we have been one, that I have ever had to utter the words 'I don't know.'"

Redhing paused for emphasis. "But what I do know is that we must get out of here. You must take me up the ladder, and I will call for help."

"But the girl, she said I shouldn't go out there."

"Why would she not want you to go out there, Jutta?"

"I don't know."

"Think about it, Jutta. Why would someone not want you to call for help? You know full well that outside our beautiful city live many barbaric, primitive people, savages who would kidnap and kill our beloved citizens were it not for the protection of the Avogo. They are known to eat flesh and blood. I think they have kidnapped us for that very purpose."

"Well, they won't get much to eat out of you," Jutta said.

"How utterly rude," Redhing said. "Do you not agree that we have been kidnapped?"

"It makes sense," Jutta said, trying to stall. A plan came to him. He would get the book, climb up to the top, push Redhing off back into the hole, and then slip out by himself to read the book that the girl had told him about.

He stared at the stool, wondering how he could get the book without Redhing seeing him. Maybe the book would answer some of his questions.

"You know," Jutta said, "it's been a long time since I've had pleasure. I think I would like to have some before we leave this cave. Oddly, the girl seemed uninterested."

"Barbarians," Redhing made a spitting noise. "Truly barbaric."

PASbots were designed to properly educate their humans and to inform the Avogo about the activity and thoughts of their humans. But another reason for a PASbot was to keep their humans gratified. One of their primary responsibilities was to make sure that their humans had anything they desired when it came to physical pleasure. Jutta knew that the only way he could keep Redhing distracted was to request this service.

"Who should I be this time? Master Jutta? Should I be her, Odilia?"

Jutta said somewhat angrily, "No! Not her. You choose."

While Redhing's avatar was morphing, Jutta reached out and turned over the chair. Stuck up under the seat was a small, leather-bound book no more than fifty pages. It was wrapped inside a clear plastic bag. He hastily removed it from the bag, put the bag back under the chair, and then slipped the book into his back pants' pocket.

After a moment, he said, "Oh, never mind, Redhing. I guess I'm just not in the mood. Maybe we should get out of here."

Jutta began picking up all of the belongings that the girl had left him and putting them in the knapsack.

"That's my Jutta! Good choice," said Redhing.

He made sure the last loaves of broonscake were packed along with the remaining bottles of water. Then, he slung the bag around his shoulder and asked Redhing to ride on his arm, thinking he could more easily knock the bot off once they reached the top. He didn't dare ask Redhing to ride on his clothing for fear of giving his plan away.

As he began ascending the ladder, he struggled with doubts. Would the drop break Redhing beyond repair? In Volmar, PASbots were sometimes accidentally broken. They were crushed in a soccer match or broken as their humans fell on top of them during a drunken stupor. But in the city, they could be repaired in a matter of minutes while the human sipped a margarita with a substitute bot. But here, away from Volmar, he was not quite sure enough of himself to let the PASbot go.

Redhing may still come in handy yet. I may need him. There's got to be a better way, he thought.

He reached the top and struggled with the weight of the lid. As he pushed with all his strength, sand and light began pouring into the hole. The lid grew lighter as more sand dropped. Soon, he was able to push it completely open.

Jutta figured it must have been about ten a.m.; the heat outside was stifling.

"I detect dangerously high temperatures, Master Jutta. Above one hundred twenty degrees."

Jutta peeked out and got his first look at the terrain in the daylight. Nothing except sand and black-charred rock for many miles. In the far off distance was the line of mountains he had seen last night, but this place was almost completely flat and desolate.

"Take me higher, Master Jutta. Let me see if I am able to connect with the pasportal."

Jutta climbed up higher. In all directions, there was nothing in sight.

"I believe I'm getting something," said Redhing.

A rush of regret overtook Jutta. If Redhing actually did contact Volmar (and if this wasn't part of the refreshing) the adventure would be over. He was not quite ready for that. He changed his mind quickly and pretended to slip on the ladder, dropping down a couple of rungs. He caught himself and then pulled the lid closed above him.

"What are you doing? Jutta?" Redhing said. "I am quite sure I can connect. We can find out where we are and what is happening."

"Too hot," Jutta pretended to be afraid of the heat. "It was too hot."

He continued his descent back down into the coolness of the hole.

"But we must go back up. I was about to connect. Just a few more seconds and I would have..."

"I'm going to pass out," Jutta said, pretending to be overwhelmed by the heat.

Redhing immediately wrapped around his wrist and began taking his pulse and reviewing his vital signs, its camera eye fixed on his face. Jutta felt his strength being zapped. He reached the end of the ladder and dropped again as he had the night before, this time without falling down.

"Everything seems normal, Jutta. You wouldn't be trying to avoid this, would you?" Redhing asked.

"No. I just got dizzy there for a moment," Jutta said, feeling the book in his back pocket as he sat down on the chair. He needed time to figure out what to do.

"Remember the time you got dizzy before the Volmar games?" Redhing asked.

He knew what Redhing was referring to. He had faked it then, too. Jutta had not wanted to be a part of the games, but his group unit was up for their turn at this televised display of carnal human behavior. It took a lot of coaxing to get him to go, and in the end, the needles were what finally had convinced him to participate.

"This time's different. It wasn't that hot then. I've never felt heat like that."

Redhing did not respond immediately. He loosened his grip around Jutta's wrist, his soulless camera eye still fixed on Jutta's face, reading it for signs of untruth. Redhing began to squeeze his wrist more tightly. Jutta's strength was being zapped.

"Redhing?" Jutta said. "Why is it so hot out there?"

"Master Jutta, as you know, the Avogo have for many years provided their beloved citizens of Volmar a beautiful city constructed inside walls designed to let in optimal sunlight. Those walls protect us from the terrible heat that the rest of the world outside endures. The sun, without the walls, is deadly to humans."

"What can I do to get back to Volmar?" Jutta asked, seriously considering his options if the girl didn't return. "How can I deal with this heat?"

Redhing paused for a moment. "It's probably best if we travel at night. The temperature will be much more tolerable. Let us plan on going back up later tonight when the sun sets. I will connect with the pasportal, and we can determine how far it is. I should think that they will send the army out after us when they know where we are."

Jutta thought of the stories he had heard growing up about the Sogmols, the Volmarian army protecting the walls of their fair city from those rebels living outside who sought to destroy them because of some crazy primitive ideology. Everyone was so thankful to the Avogo for providing these soldiers and giving them training and weapons. But the soldiers were never allowed to mingle with the citizens inside the city that they protected. These mysterious warriors lived on the outside, beyond the realm of the concern of the Vaipwo.

"I wanted to be a soldier when I was a kid," Jutta said as if for the first time, to Redhing.

"Yes." Redhing laughed. "We had a difficult time trying to get that idea out of your head. You knew that such a thing was impossible. Sogmols are Sogmols, Vaipwo are Vaipwo, Sasjovians are Sasjovians, and Avogo are Avogo."

"It sounded fun. That's all," Jutta said, feeling a bit sad.

"That kind of wish is what led you to the refreshing at your age. I don't understand where it came from," Redhing said. "You weren't like that in your last fleshly cloak. When you were Duc, you were satisfied as a Vaipwo farmer. Never a singler badact. And a great gamer, too. You enjoyed the games back then more than anyone..." Redhing went on about memories of Jutta as Duc, but Jutta couldn't listen. He became upset as the story went on, and he kept waiting for his chance to jump in and ask a question. Finally, Redhing paused and Jutta interjected.

"You are programmed to tell me the truth, right?"

"Of course, Master Jutta, you know Volmar is an open society. No truth is greater than any other truth. There are no secrets. I'm afraid right now, since we're disconnected, I do not have access to quite as much information as I normally would. I do have a small store in my own being, but as you know, 'connected, we are more than we are individually.'" Redhing was quoting from the Rules of Vaipwo Conduct book. Jutta continued to think about how he could read that new book in his back pocket without Redhing seeing him. That book was obviously something he wouldn't have permission to read.

Jutta asked, "Why is there some information that I do not have access to?"

"My dear Master Jutta. There are many things not worth knowing. The Avogo bring us health and provide us all we need to live a happy life. They give us all the good things that we enjoy..."

Jutta's mouth nearly mimicked the words. "The beauty of a flower, the lovely sweetness of honey..." This was a speech he had heard before.

"Nevertheless," Jutta said, staring at the floor. He was gathering courage and nursing a long, deep-seated anger. "If we have a truly open society, I don't see why anything should be held back from me. I should be able to know what I want. I should have permissions to any knowledge that I wonder about."

The small green light on Redhing's underbelly that indicated communication with the pasportal turned on automatically. This was a conversation that would need to be sent to the Avogo. But instead of staying a solid green, the light continued flashing, indicating that no connection could be made.

"Why do I feel my energy is being drained anytime one of your lights comes on?" Jutta asked.

"That, Master Jutta, must be your imagination. You do have an unfortunately active one. So many reprograms and treatments, and still... A lot has happened these past twenty-four hours. The stress must be getting to you. Why don't you lie down and nap a while? I will wake you when it is dark outside. It should be so in eight more hours."

"In eight hours, you might have drained me dead."

"Jutta! I am shocked."

"How are you getting your energy? There's no charging station down here, no sun, nothing. At home, you have to be charged every twenty-four hours. It's been much longer than that since your last charge."

"Just what are you accusing me of, Master Jutta?" The bot was slipping back into its ogre voice and was beginning to vibrate once again. Jutta's strength diminished proportionally.

"Only that you're getting your energy from me."

The deep voice started, "I do not harm you. I am your PASbot. I am here for your protection, for your service, for your pleasure."

"Then serve me by leaving me alone!"

The voice got louder and deeper, "I do not harm you. I am your PASbot. I am here for your protection, for your service, for your pleasure."

"I don't want your service now. I'll ask you when I need you!" Jutta yelled back.

The voice repeated the same lines each time in a louder voice. Jutta tried to plug his ears, but then the voice of Jutta's favorite avatar returned, and the vibrating stopped. "Master Jutta, let's not talk about this now. You're tired. You will need your rest for the journey back home tonight. Please, be a good Sasjov, and take a nap. Everything will be better when you wake up."

Jutta, panting from the confrontation, stared at it for a moment. The bot hung loosely around his left arm. Mustering all his courage, he yelled. "You mean IF I wake up!" Then, grabbing the bot with his right arm, Jutta pulled hard to get it off.

Immediately, a horrendous alarm sounded, and scores of tiny needles plunged into Jutta, bending up like tiny fishhooks, anchoring Redhing to his left arm.

"Get off me!" Jutta shouted in pain, pulling hard on the bot to get it off. The hooks tore through his skin, leaving a bloody mangled patch of flesh.

The needles disappeared back into the bot, but the alarm blared out ear piercingly loud, and the ogre's deep voice started up again. "I do not harm you. I am your PASbot..."

Blood ran down Jutta's left arm, but he held the bot in his right hand extended at arm's length as if he were holding a snapping turtle that might bite him at any time. Jutta ran to the chamber pot and threw the PASbot into the clean bag, tying it up so that it could not escape. The bag did little to dampen the noise of the alarm. Jutta dropped the bag and covered his ears, but the sound echoed up and then back down the cavern amplifying the dreadful racket, a roar that was designed to torture, to bring someone back in line, a mix of a baby crying and demon screeching, an awful clamor like that of the Nazguls in that ancient story *The Lord of the Rings*.

Jutta fell into the sand that had leaked through the hole when he opened the lid earlier, pushing palms against his ears as hard as he could while blood trickled down into his ears.

But it wasn't enough. He grabbed the bag that now contained Redhing, wrapped it in the hammock, and then put the screaming package under the chair. Even then, the noise was still unbearable, but Jutta still sat up and tended to his wounds. He pulled out the first-aid kit Odilia had left and wrapped his arm with tape while keeping an eye on the lid above, fully expecting the Volmarian army to break in at any time. His arm bandaged, he could do nothing else but cover his ears and look up. He was surprised by his own courage, oddly remorseful about what he'd done to his "friend," and fearful of an army coming from above.

Gradually, the alarm died down, and Redhing could be heard using a new voice, a pitiful, begging child's voice. "Master Jutta. How can you do this to me? We are best friends. What has happened to you? Please, save me. I am dying." It was the first avatar that Redhing had used when Jutta was seven.

Jutta was conflicted. He was not one who liked to harm others, and this appeal to pity was far more effective on him than the alarm. He stared at the bag under the chair, which kept talking. "Please, Master Jutta. I am dying. How can you do this to me? I am your best friend."

He began to reach for the bag, but the pain in his arm reminded him that this freedom had come at a cost. If the bot had just let go on its own and respected Jutta's wishes, there would be no need for this.

Jutta withdrew his hand, and when Redhing realized that the pity approach was not working, the alarm sounded again, this time even louder. *How could the alarm be so strong*, Jutta thought, *when the thing has so little energy left?*

Eventually, the noise coming from under the chair began to fade. The bot was running out of electricity, and its highly specialized battery would soon be dead altogether, awaiting exposure to the sun or some other power source. Jutta was able to uncover his ears, which were red and sweaty. His left arm throbbed with pain, and as the hole began to quiet down, Jutta began to feel alone for the first time in his life.

It was all he could do to resist reaching for Redhing and flying up the ladder to charge the bot. This was the first time in his life he had ever been alone and free from the scrutiny of a digital eye. He looked around the cavern to see if any cameras were hidden. There were no signs of spiders or cockroaches, those tiny drones that the Avogo used for their voyeurism.

No sign of life came from above. The bot was completely silent now. Jutta began to think in unnerving silence.

"Okay. Okay," he talked to himself. "What am I going to do? Oh, Redhing. Why didn't you just get off of me? I need help. I need out. I need..."

He remembered the last piece of green gob he had stored away.

"Food. That's what I need." He searched through the knapsack and found the food. And while he was at it, he unwrapped Redhing from the hammock and put the hammock in the knapsack. There it was, lifeless, immobile, sealed in that plastic bag. Jutta devoured the survival cake without grimacing at the taste, glad to have something to fill his stomach. It even seemed to help ease the throbbing pain in his arm.

"I don't even know what time it is. Maybe it's dark now. No. It can't be. It's only been an hour, if that much."

When he'd said that, he heard a soft hissing sound coming from near his feet. It sounded like air being let out of a tire slowly. In a moment, he began to smell something odd. He leaped up and saw that a gas was seeping from under the chair. One whiff and he nearly fell over backwards and passed out.

"Redhing! Why are you doing this to me?" He shouted. A noxious gas was seeping out of the bag's imperfect seal.

From inside the bag came the muffled voice, "I am your PASbot..."

Jutta held his breath and gathered as many things as he could— a water flask, the knapsack with his hammock in it, the shovel— then bolted up the ladder. The lid was harder to open this time because he was holding everything with his good arm and had to use his wounded arm to push it up. When the lid opened, heat rushed down on him like some oppressive entity. He would have backed down, but the deadly gas below gave him no choice. He pushed into the open, unprotected, unrelenting desert, the blinding midday sun beating down mercilessly all around.

Chapter 6

The Book and the Boxbot

Jutta crawled out of the hole and closed the lid behind him. He shielded his eyes and would have stayed right there on the ground, but the sand was too hot. He had to move. He hobbled along slowly, trying to give his eyes time to adjust to the bright sun. "Hot! Hot!" he murmured as he trekked away from the hole.

He used his injured arm as a visor to shield his eyes. Nothing. There was nothing but miles and miles of empty desert. A few patches of green dotted the landscape where it appeared life might be holding on, and there were a lot of black rocks that made the landscape look as though clouds were shadowing it. But there were no clouds anywhere to be seen. Jutta ventured far enough away from the hole that the gas couldn't reach him, but he didn't want to lose sight of it altogether.

Instinctively, he pulled out the hammock and made a sort of tent for shade. Then, he knelt down, covered with the hammock, and began digging with the shovel Odilia had left him. *She knew I would do this!* he thought.

The ground was loose and relatively easy to dig through. Two feet deep, and the ground was cool to the touch. He kept digging, hoping to get a hole wide enough and cool enough for his entire body. The white hammock reflected the sun and made survival possible, at least for a short period of time.

Jutta finally hit a harder layer of dirt and gave up digging. He sat down in the hole and wiped his forehead. He then opened his water flask and drank the warm liquid down to the last drop. As soon as the bottle was empty, he slapped his palm on his forehead. "Should have rationed that," he said aloud.

Lying in his dugout, Jutta was truly alone for the first time in his life. He didn't have Redhing to tell him what time it was. He didn't know what to do with the quietness or the heat. He could only wait for the gas to clear out of the safe hole and then go back down to wait. It was far more comfortable down there. Maybe he would grab the uncharged Redhing and take it along in case it turned out these people really were barbarians, and he needed the Sogmols to rescue him.

Jutta leaned back and closed his eyes, but as he tried to get comfortable, something in his back pocket was digging into him. Jutta pulled out the book and began reading, hopeful that it would contain some explanation as to what he was doing there:

If you are reading this, one of two things has happened. Either you have somehow risen above your PASbot and are reading this alone, or the two of you are reading it together. If you are reading with your PASbot, it is highly recommended that you read no further. Just wait for us to get back. If you are reading alone, maybe you are the one we've been hoping for. You are the first ever to throw off their PASbot. Congratulations! Read on.

The refreshing that you were about to undertake was not real. They were actually going to kill you. Your body was going to be burned in the Aspodt and a newborn baby was going to be presented to the city as your old self. There is no transfer of the self. There is no refreshing. It is only killing. The soul is not something that can be bartered. It belongs to only one body. It is not transferred to some new body. And the soul and body live forever. That's what we believe, and that is why we rescued you from this fate.

It was a lot for Jutta to take in. He could hardly read on. He was feeling dizzy and weak.

The world you have been living in at Volmar is one of great comfort, but the purpose of this short life on earth is not to be comfortable. It is to grow. We cannot live all of our lives in perfect bliss. We need something to come and shake us. We need to struggle. We need each other. But we need to be given the honest truth.

The book went on, but he closed his eyes hard. *Would they have actually killed me?* Just as he was about to read more, the sound of an electric motor could be heard moving around outside his dugout. He peeked out, half hoping it would be the Sogmols coming to punish him for removing his PASbot. But he could see nothing. The glare turned everything on the ground the same color of silver.

Fearing he would lose this chance to meet someone who might help, Jutta emerged from his dugout, only to find no one. He soon forgot about the noise as there was now a bigger concern. The entrance to the safe hole was gone.

It should have been no more than fifteen or twenty feet away. But he couldn't find it. He walked around in circles searching for it and mumbling to himself. "Why did I close it? It could have aired out, too. Now it's covered, and I'm going to die out here." He searched until he nearly fainted. But the lid to the safe hole that Odilia had brought him to was nowhere to be found. Even his own footprints that would have led to it were gone. The lid had been covered up completely. In despair, he returned to his dugout and collapsed inside.

The noise came again after a few minutes. This time, it was even closer. He peeked outside and saw part of a square bot sink into the sand. He recognized it as the boxbot that Odilia had left outside the hole the night before. Now he realized its job must have been to cover the hole and all tracks around it. Jutta lay back down and waited for the sun to set.

Though he was curious about the rest of the book, he just

couldn't bring himself to read it. He waited, drifting in and out of sleep. Each time he woke up, he realized how thirsty he was. His tongue was stuck to the roof of his mouth. Unable to bear the heat and thirst any longer, Jutta frantically renewed his search on his hands and knees for the lid to the safe hole. The sand burned his hands as he groped about looking for the lid. He couldn't find it. With the last ounce of his strength, he stumbled around until he found the hammock. When he saw it, he fell in and cried dry tears.

At the height of his despair, the boxbot unburied itself and inched its way towards him. Jutta stared at it vacantly. Shortly, a steady thin stream of warm water began to hit his face. As it did, Jutta opened his mouth to drink. After Jutta had taken only a sip or two, the bot scooted away and disappeared into the sand.

As it buried itself, Jutta closed his eyes and whispered, "Thanks." He lay there in the heat for several hours longer. His head began to hurt, and with each hour, he grew more and more confused. By the time the sun was setting, he was so dizzy that he couldn't stand up.

Darkness fell, and Jutta thought he heard footsteps. The hammock was ripped off of his hiding place, and someone knelt beside him.

"He's here!" the man shouted, and Jutta blacked out.

When Odilia heard Sabas call to her, she came running to help him pull Jutta out of the dugout.

"He might have had a heat stroke," Sabas said. Odilia took off her head wrap and doused it in cold water from her flask, then put it behind his neck.

"It won't be enough," Sabas said as he felt Jutta's pulse. "We've got to get his temperature down." He unbuttoned the shirt that Jutta had been wearing since Abaidus had dressed him in the refreshing chamber and then poured his entire flask of cold water onto his body, making sure the shirt absorbed most of the water.

"Where's his PASbot?" Odilia asked. The two searched for it, and when they saw the bandage on his arm, they exchanged a look of surprise and excitement.

"Let's get him back to Mainz," Odilia said. Sabas pulled on the back of his traverser, lengthening it into a stretcher, and the two heaved him up and onto it.

As soon as Sabas and Odilia arrived in Mainz, they carried Jutta to the infirmary just inside the caves of their city. After they got him into a bed, a nurse assessed the situation and then ran out of the room to get some supplies. Sabas went to find Father Rawley to let him know that the new rescue had arrived.

Odilia sat down next to Jutta's bed and got her first really good look at the one she had helped rescue. His face was streaked with dirt, so she dipped a sponge in a bowl of water and wiped his cheeks. As she cleaned, she noticed his curly hair was actually light brown, and his complexion was much smoother and olive-colored than she'd thought. His bottom lip was puffy, and she thought that while his nose might be larger than most, it was perfectly proportional for the face it occupied. She passed the sponge along his forehead and wiped his eyebrows into place.

She studied his big, soft smooth hands and thought about how he had held on to her so tightly during the ride. She smiled. He had probably never been on a moving vehicle like that before, definitely not at such fast speeds; Volmar had been so well laid out that no autonomous form of transportation was needed.

Putting the sponge down, Odilia found it hard to believe that Redhing was not there. She cringed, remembering how that vile PASbot had told Jutta to ask her how she wanted her pleasure. She had assumed that Jutta would need help to free himself from its spell.

The bandage on Jutta's arm was bloody, and she set about replacing it. When she finished dressing his wound, she stood next to him and let herself stare a moment. Noticing that his hair was out of place, she ventured to pat it down, and as she did, Father Rawley walked into the room.

"He'll be fine, Odilia."

Odilia jumped a little in surprise but she quickly smiled.

"You fuss over everyone," Rawley said, "especially the new arrivals."

"I know, Father. He was brave, wasn't he?"

"Indeed. It takes some doing to rip a PASbot off your arm. This is a first."

"You were right, then. He was one we had to save. He was worth the risk, right?"

"I think so. I think he's special."

"Me too," Odilia said without thinking. She felt her face blushing, but Father didn't seem to notice.

"You were brave, too, Odi," he noted, hugging her from the side.

She leaned her head on his shoulder and he continued. "You know I don't like sending you on these missions. I wish you'd leave it up to the others."

"It is my choice, Papa." That was her nickname for him. He was the closest thing she knew to a real father.

The nurse came back in and asked them to step away from the patient. They both watched in silence as she took his blood pressure and hooked him up to an IV drip to make sure that Jutta was hydrated. Noticing the wet sponge and the new bandage, the nurse said playfully, "Looks like you're doing my job again, Odilia."

Odilia shrugged. "Sorry. Can't help it. Jutta is going to do great things. I just know it."

"Need I remind you," Father Rawley enjoined, "that he knows nothing of our way of life? He will have a lot to learn. And many, as you know, don't take to our way of life."

Odilia didn't answer immediately. Her eyes were fixed on the sleeping Jutta. "He'll make it. I'm sure of it," she finally said.

"I pray so. Let's just take it one day at a time. 'Inch by inch, life's a synch. Yard by yard, life is hard.'"

Rawley kissed Odilia on the top of her head and walked away. The nurse followed him out, carrying a tray of bandages, apparently for another patient.

Alone again with Jutta, Odilia ventured to touch his hand and whispered,

"You'll make it. You'll be one of us."

***

Jutta could hear a voice, but he could not make out what it was saying. There was light on the other side of his eyelids. As he opened his eyes, Odilia was spinning around above him. She let go of his hand and started to inch backwards toward the door, but his eyes followed her, and he smiled. Instead of walking away, she stayed and smiled back awkwardly.

Jutta's dizziness began to wear off, and Odilia stopped spinning. She smiled and said, "Hello again, Jutta," before pretending to examine his wound.

"It's the girl from the... the...cave," he said, his mind still groggy.

"That's me," she smiled.

"Odilia," he said, trying to piece together what had happened.

"That's right. Good memory, Jutta."

"I remember riding on the ... that thing, and the heat, and the big hole in the ground, and...Redhing?" He put his hand on his head and squinted his eyes hard.

"Are you okay?" Odilia asked.

Jutta nodded.

"Just rest. You need to get your strength back."

Jutta let his gaze linger on Odilia. Her long brown hair was pulled back, revealing her forehead and accentuating her long oval face. When she smiled, her thinnish lips stretched wide, turning her cheeks into deep dimples.

Jutta hadn't noticed the IV needle in his arm until now, and when he saw it, his body started to shake.

"Is this the Refreshing? Is this how it happens?" Imagining that his vital force was about to be sucked out of his arm and into the bag hanging over his head, Jutta reached for the needle to pull it out.

"No, no, Jutta! Relax. It's okay." Odilia held onto his hand. "It's just an IV. We're giving you extra water and electrolytes. The nurse said you got dehydrated out there in the heat. It's okay."

Jutta calmed down a little after realizing that the liquid was flowing into him rather than out. After a long time of studying the IV, he finally ventured a question. "There is no such thing as a refreshing, is there?"

"No, Jutta. There is no refreshing."

Jutta felt his back pocket for the book, but it wasn't there. "Where am I? I had a book..."

"You're in Mainz, now. Don't worry about the book. We have more of those here. But I can probably tell you everything you need to know."

"The book is right? If there is no refreshing, what happens to the people who get refreshed?"

Odilia lowered her head. "They die."

"But I've known some who were refreshed. Like my house elder, Yarosky. We called him Sky. He got refreshed and came back in another unit as another boy. I got to see him a lot, and it really was him."

Odilia hesitated but answered, "No. It was just another baby, another baby spawned by the Avogo with whatever Vaipwo they wanted."

"What do you mean spawned?"

Odilia turned red and averted her eyes. "The Avogo have sex with a Vaipwo girl and make her pregnant—or him, because men carry babies, too, nowadays. And then, after nine months, the kid is born."

It took a couple of seconds, but Jutta eventually started laughing until he saw the confused expression on her face. "Wait, you're serious? I mean. You think that's what sex is for?"

"Yes. The biological purpose of sex is for procreation. The man's seed enters into the woman, and it meets an egg and a person is created." Odilia had said all of this staring at the floor and not right at Jutta, but when she again made eye contact, she could see that he was taking in this news and trying to process it.

"So the Avogo don't make us. I... I always wondered about that. But I can't believe that's what sex is for. Everybody knows it's how you express yourself. It's a way of expressing love."

"Yes, but here in Mainz, we only express our love in that way to one person. Not just anybody we meet."

"That's strange," Jutta said and grew quiet again. After a moment, he asked. "I always thought only computers died."

"The Avogo try to keep you from knowing about death."

In his seventeen years of life, at least ten people he had known well had been refreshed. He turned away from her, tears welling up in his eyes.

"No. It can't be." Jutta was getting agitated. He looked past Odilia at the door as if he wanted to run.

"It's okay, Jutta. Just calm down. We'll talk more later. It takes time to process all of this. And if you don't believe me, that's fine. In the end, it will be up to you to decide what you believe."

Suddenly tearful and defensive, Jutta lashed out, "Nothing you show me will make it true. I've heard about you people..." He was remembering everything that Redhing had taught him. He sat up in bed trembling. "I want to go home! Let me go home."

Just then, a familiar figure walked into the room and crossed his muscular arms. Staring straight at Jutta was Sabas. Odilia walked over and stood next to him.

"So, you're awake," Sabas said. "Bet you never expected to be here when you went in for the refreshing." He said the word refreshing in a condescending manner.

"Shhh..." Odilia said. "Let him be, Sabas. He just got here."

"Redhing," Jutta whispered. Jutta's natural reaction was to ask Redhing for advice on how to handle Sabas. *Oh, Redhing, how could I be so stupid! I'm sorry,* he thought.

He began to get up, but the world started spinning again, and he had to lie back down to make it stop. If he were to run, he knew he'd never make it around Sabas. Even if he did, he wouldn't know where to go. He had committed a cardinal breach by removing his PASbot. He had no one to blame but himself.

"I think I need to rest," he said.

"Of course," Odilia concurred. "You should probably eat something too. I'll go get you some food."

Jutta snarled at the thought of more of that green glob stuff she had given him before.

"Not survival food this time," she said. "Real food."

As she walked out of the room, she glanced back at him, and he saw the same look he'd seen in the video Redhing had shown her the day she left him in that hole.

Jutta closed his eyes and pretended to sleep, but Sabas had other plans. The burly young man about three years older than Jutta grabbed a chair and sat on it backwards, straddling it as if he were riding a horse. He put his chin on the back of the chair and stared right at Jutta. Jutta took a peek but quickly closed his eyes again when he saw Sabas, who was now wearing a tank top and flexing his biceps.

"You're not sleeping," Sabas said. "I don't mean to rush you, but how much longer until you get up and show us that you were worth saving?"

Jutta rolled over and turned his back to him. As he did, he examined the bag above his head and wished he'd be sucked up into it.

"Just what I figured," Sabas said. "Another waste of time. You know we risked our lives for you..."

Jutta heard someone clearing his throat in the doorway. "Enough, Sabas. Give our friend some time."

"Naturally," Sabas said. "Time. We've got a lot of that."

The room got quiet, and Jutta glanced over his shoulder to see if anyone was still there. He was surprised to see that Sabas had gone away, and an old man was now sitting in the chair that Sabas had vacated. The old man had a wide, closed-lip smile on his face.

"Hello, Jutta. My name is Father Rawley. I mean, Rawley. Father's not my first name. I'm so excited you are here with us. I must say, we've waited a long time to rescue someone of your, uh, abilities."

Jutta rolled onto his back and slowly propped himself up on his elbows.

"I'm sure you have a million questions," Father Rawley continued. "What am I doing here? Who else is here? Where is here? How come here is so weird?" He chuckled. "Don't worry. We'll get to all of that soon enough, soon enough. You just let us know when you're ready."

The old man seemed to be getting excited. His voice lilted up as if he were cheering on a favorite team. Jutta was captivated by the lines on the man's face and the gray hair on his head and in his beard. It was the first time he'd seen a man who was obviously in his fifties. Though Rawley was sitting down, Jutta could tell that he was not very tall, at least a couple of inches shorter than Jutta himself, who stood at six foot one.

"Odilia will be back soon with some of my favorite food. I know you'll enjoy it much more than you did that broonscake you survived on yesterday. You must be quite ready for a proper meal. You just stay in bed a while longer. After a delicious meal, if you feel like it, Odilia and I will show you around our little city." He clapped his hands as if to punctuate his last sentence. He seemed to struggle to contain his excitement.

Odilia walked in carrying a platter of steamed leafy vegetables, a thin slice of unidentifiable meat, and a few potatoes. When she put it in front of him, he looked back up at the old man with an expression that seemed to say, "This is your favorite food?"

"We eat a little simpler here in Mainz than you do in Volmar," Odilia said apologetically.

"Go on!" Rawley smiled. "Eat! It's very tasty. Wonderful food and very good for you."

Jutta couldn't stop staring at Rawley. He wanted to ask how he'd managed to avoid the refreshing for so long, but he sensed it would be, to use Odilia's words, bad manners.

He picked up a fork and reluctantly took a bite of the leafy vegetables. To his surprise, the food had a surprisingly vibrant flavor. Jutta tried to hide the fact that he really did enjoy it. He quickly realized how hungry he was and devoured the entire plate, Volmarian style, without those pesky manners.

"Wonderful!" Rawley said, clasping his hands together. "More, Odilia, the boy needs more!"

Rawley got up and removed the IV from Jutta's arm. "You won't be needing this, Jutta. You're going to be just fine. Are you able to stand?"

Jutta began to get up. The world had finally stabilized. "Can I have a shower?" he asked as he stood up.

"Yes. Of course. The bathroom is right there," he said to Jutta, pointing at a closed door.

In the bathroom, Jutta found a clean pair of clothes, just his size. They were similar in style and color to the clothes both Sabas and Odilia wore, plain, simple, and in two colors: khaki and white.

Rawley called from outside the bathroom door. "There's soap on the sink and several warm gallons of water. I'm sure the shower will refresh your spirits," he said.

He finished his shower and emerged from the bathroom with his new clothes on, just as Odilia entered the room with his food.

Father Rawley said, "It is getting late, Odilia. We should let Jutta get some rest. We will show you around Mainz in the morning, Jutta."

Odilia put the tray on the table next to Jutta's bed and said, "You're right, Father. I look forward to showing you around in the morning, Jutta." As they left Jutta alone, Odilia turned back around and peered at him with that same expression he had seen in the video that Redhing had shown him.

Jutta ate his second helping but the silence in Mainz at that time of night was hard to bear. Not used to being alone in the quiet, he had a great deal of trouble falling asleep.

Chapter 8
Dashing into Battle

Early the next morning, Odilia and Father Rawley came to the infirmary and saw that Jutta was already awake. They invited him to tour Mainz, and soon he was strolling along with Father Rawley and Odilia towards the entrance of Mainz. He noticed that Mainz had no tall plant-covered buildings like those in Volmar, where people lived in physical comfort, basking under the glow of the sun that was filtered by a protective biodome.

Mainz did not reach to the sky like the branches of a tree, but rather it ran underground, like roots searching out what they needed in the depths of the Earth.

As they walked, Father Rawley explained that the people of Mainz had always called themselves the Dicarers. "The exact etymology of that word has been lost to history," Rawley said. "But one popular theory is that the word came from a combination of care and die, as in 'They died caring.' More than likely, though, the word derived from the Latin *Dicare*, which means 'to show or to point out.' It is our job to show or point out the way for others," he said.

Jutta scratched his head, wondering what "way" Rawley was talking about. He learned that the Dicarers had a tough existence. They did not have everything handed to them without having to work hard for it like the Vaipwo did. The Dicarers worked hard, under quite difficult conditions. Food shortages were common. Adults were often limited to one or two meals per day, rationing food and water so that no one would go hungry.

"We only eat meat a couple times a week," Odilia said. "There just isn't enough meat to have it every day."

"True, but the fact that we have food at all in such a desert testifies to our ingenuity and grit!" Rawley said.

When they arrived at the city gates, Rawley greeted the guard with a smile and wave. The guard sat stoically and nodded back.

"This is the adit," he said, "which is just a term for the entrance of a mine. You see, Mainz was built in an abandoned drift mine. That's a mine that was dug horizontally. After the cataclysm, when people needed shelter, this turned out to be a pretty convenient place, and it goes back very far into the mountain. So it accommodated a lot of people."

Jutta peered out through the adit, across the vast desert, and he stepped back when he felt the heat inching its way into the cool recesses of the underground city.

"As the town grew," Rawley continued, "people dug out more and more areas. Over the years, we've added a large kitchen and cafeteria, growing rooms for our crops, living quarters, an infirmary, which we were just in, and my favorite, a nice chapel."

Jutta frowned. In Volmar, "The Chapel" was a no-limits pub. He had only gone once and discovered that he did have limits. Father Rawley clarified, "Oh. Dear. It's not like the one in Volmar. Believe me. Quite the opposite. It's quiet. It's where we go to pray. This way, our next stop will be our largest grow room."

As the three made their way through the tunnels that were being lit by a string of light bulbs attached to wooden beams, the musty air made the things Jutta saw seem repulsive. As they passed a large open room where children were running around and playing, Jutta noticed that one of the children was missing a leg.

"Look, Jutta," Odilia said. "They're playing Zalltilinger. That was my favorite game in school. I'll have to teach you sometime." The girl with one leg was playing as well, and Jutta couldn't bear to watch. The missing leg made him uncomfortable, and he felt glad that they had had no such people in Volmar.

They continued through other poorly lit tunnels, greeting people, many of whom were obviously well past the age of refreshing. The lines on their faces made Jutta extremely uncomfortable.

His natural reaction was disdain for this dreadful city and the people in it. Yet he told himself to keep an open mind, not an easy task among the acrid smells.

After several minutes of walking past what Odilia said were living quarters, they came to a large cavern with hundreds of pink lights that illuminated the tall ceilings.

"All our food is grown underground in hydroponic gardens under these grow lights," Father Rawley said. "This is one of our four large grow rooms."

The peaceful sound of water trickling through the troughs seemed to make Fr. Rawley pause a moment. "These gardens are the main source of work for many Dicarers. Of course, what we can't grow ourselves, we trade with other cities, including Volmar."

"Other cities?" Jutta asked. "You mean there are more places like this?" he said with unintentional condescension.

"Why, yes, Jutta. There are many cities like ours, filled with people who refused to bend a knee to the Avogo or some other form of tyranny." Father paused a moment, and his voice took on a somber tone. "At least there used to be many. I'm not so sure now because of the..." Rawley didn't finish the sentence.

"But why live like this if you don't have to?" Jutta asked. "It seems like everyone should be thankful to the Avogo. They give us The Four Boundlessnesses: Presence, Future Presence... and ..." He caught himself repeating one of the many Vaipwo mantras of praise to the Avogo. Somehow, he sensed the hollowness of the words and let them trail off into an awkward silence.

Rawley snapped out of his sadness and said in a slightly irritated tone. "Hmph. I'll tell you what they give us, or you, rather. They give you nothing! They only take. They do not know God, so you do not have freedom. God is the only guarantor of freedom."

"Look," Odilia pointed to a child about the age of seven who was waving at them and smiling. Jutta noticed that the boy didn't seem to have a PASbot. No one did. If they were in Volmar, that boy would be receiving his PASbot, and he would be playing video games most of the day. But in Mainz, he was harvesting carrots instead.

"Even kids work?" he asked incredulously.

"We all work," Odilia said, "to ensure a steady food supply, everyone from the young to the old. Anyone who can work."

Jutta was amazed, appalled, and somewhat excited when he thought about his own childhood. The countless hours playing video games in a room packed with other kids. Kids were not required to work in Volmar. They were given their yearly programs, stores of knowledge, as they grew older, so they didn't have to go to school and learn things the hard way. They just inserted an application and voila; they could speak French or do Calculus.

The young child holding the carrots smiled and waved at Jutta. "Look what I got!" he said, proudly holding up the plants he had helped cultivate. Something in the child's smile reminded him of a friend he had had in Volmar.

"How old...is the oldest person?" Jutta asked.

"Bettrily, I believe, is now seventy-one? Is that right, Odilia?"

"Yep, seventy-one," she said.

"Seventy-one?" Jutta said with a mix of awe and disgust. "But why wouldn't she be refresh—?" he stopped and shook his head for a moment. Eventually, he changed the topic back to work. "How long do you work every day? How long do *they* work?" he said, pointing to the child.

"The adults work as long as we can," Rawley answered. "Usually, around ten hours. And then we spend time in our devotions, mealtimes, and leisure and then sleep at least six hours per night.

Kids work before and after school. They go to school five days a week for five hours a day." Rawley beckoned him onwards into a long tunnel. "This way leads to the chapel, the main gathering place where we have our devotions and our town meetings."

"What are devotions?" Jutta asked as they entered the long, dank tunnel.

"Devotions are...well. It's better to show you than to explain it. We're heading to one now. Most of the city joins in on Sundays. I wish you had been here yesterday. You could have met pretty much the whole town. We have a smaller group today. But they are a devoted bunch."

Soon, the three entered into a light-filled cavern that evoked a sense of awe in Jutta that he'd only experienced once before, when Odilia was closing the lid above him, and he saw the stars. The ceiling was enormously high, and a skylight at the top let in natural sunlight, so the room felt bright and fresh. In stark contrast, the walls were lined with images of a man who was apparently being abused in many different ways. About twenty people or so were sitting quietly in the room. Some were on their knees. Others seemed lost in thought. Many had their eyes fixed on the front of the room, where a candle was burning in a red glass holder.

"Please, Jutta. Have a seat," Rawley said. "I'll be back after the Mass. Just stay here with Odilia, if you will. It's important that you are here."

Jutta and Odilia sat down next to each other, but they did not talk. Odilia smiled at him awkwardly, and Jutta was content to just take everything in. She sat silently and eventually closed her eyes. After a moment or two, she pulled down a kneeler from the pew in front of her and got on her knees. To Jutta, who had never seen anything like this before, it seemed she and many others were talking to themselves. As she knelt, Jutta watched other people trickle in. Most of them caught his eye and nodded and smiled. It appeared as though they wanted to talk to him, but they all found a place to sit or kneel.

In a moment, music began playing, and the entire group stood up and began singing. An older man who looked a lot like Rawley, was walking down the center aisle wearing a green robe and singing along with the crowd. It wasn't until the man got up in front of the group and spoke that he realized it was, in fact, Rawley.

"Good morning, brothers and sisters."

"Good morning Father," the crowd responded.

"Let's begin in the name of the Father, the Son, and the Holy Ghost." The crowd mimicked the priest with their hand gestures.

"Peace be with you."

"And with your spirit."

Jutta felt awkward every time the crowd responded and he didn't. He felt completely lost. The whole group recited something together that they had all memorized. The recitation reminded him of the lines he was required to say as he progressed to each level of education programming. "It is all for the good of the Avogo who sustain and protect us..." he wanted to say as the others repeated something completely foreign to him.

Everyone sat down except for one lady, whose appearance really frightened Jutta. He'd never seen anyone so old and decrepit in appearance. She had totally white hair and wrinkles that creased her face making her head look like a wilted head of lettuce. She hobbled with a cane up to the front of the room and opened a book.

The old lady said, "A reading from the prophet Jeremiah: 'I have listened closely: they speak what is not true; No one regrets wickedness, saying, 'What have I done?' Everyone keeps on running their course, like a horse dashing into battle.'"

Jutta cocked his head, and a memory flashed into his mind. He had been doing research for a program that would help the Vaipwo fight against anger, and he had been allowed into a large room full of old books, something most Vaipwo had never seen or even heard of. To write the program, Jutta needed to understand that emotion better, and the Avogo thought it might help if he read something from an ancient book.

The lady with the frozen face, that same Controller General of Prescriptive Thought who had just prepared him for the Refreshing, had brought him to the book room, past three levels of security. Then, she allowed him to read one book containing what the ancients had called poetry. The Vaipwo and even most Sasjovians knew very little about poetry. They heard only trite rhyming in advertising or in slogans that all kids learned from the time they could talk, such as: "Need to get something off your chest? The Avogo know you best."

Being a Sasjovian, Jutta had a deeper appreciation of poetry. He knew about meter, alliteration, and other poetic devices. But a poem's meaning nearly always escaped him. In the locked room, after studying the book of poetry for over an hour, he had noticed that he was alone. The COGOPT had stepped out for a moment, and Jutta was there with only his PASbot. Another ancient book sitting on the next table over caught his eye, and Jutta had decided to take a peek. Redhing had begun to vibrate menacingly, but Jutta had ignored the bot and flipped the tome open to a random page.

On that page, he had read the same passage the old lady was now reading: "I have listened closely: they speak what is not true; No one regrets wickedness, saying, 'What have I done?' Everyone keeps on running their course, like a horse dashing into battle..." He had gotten no further with that book. The COGOPT entered, having been alerted to this transgression by Redhing. She shooed him out of the room, and naturally, the incident was reported to the Avogo.

"What does it mean?" Jutta remembered asking the committee that was convened at the Office of the Controller General of Prescriptive Thought.

"The point is you were not reading what you were allowed to read," responded the COGOPT without emotion, except with a hint of disdain. "All you need to think about is how the information we gave you can be useful for the betterment of our people."

"To help the Vaipwo is how I grow. Yes." He had said automatically. "That is all we want. Thanks to the Avogo."

Jutta listened intently as the elderly lady continued reading from the book: "'Even the stork in the sky knows its seasons; Turtledove, swift, and thrush observe the time of their return, but my people do not know the order of the Lord. How can you say, 'We are wise, we have the law of the Lord?' See that has been changed into falsehood by the lying pen of the scribes." The lady paused a moment. "The word of the Lord," she said. Everyone responded: "Thanks be to God."

After asking the people to repeat something, the old lady flipped through the book and then continued: "A reading from the Second Letter of Saint Paul to the Thessalonians: 'We instruct you, brothers and sisters, in the name of our Lord Jesus Christ, to shun any brother who walks in a disorderly way and not according to the tradition they received from us. For you know how one must imitate us. For we did not act in a disorderly way among you, nor did we eat food received free from anyone. On the contrary, in toil and drudgery, night and day we worked, so as not to burden any of you. Not that we do not have the right. Rather we wanted to present ourselves as a model for you, so that you might imitate us. In fact, when we were with you, we instructed you that if anyone was unwilling to work, neither should that one eat.' The word of the Lord."

Jutta thought it weird not to let someone eat just because he didn't work. In Volmar, many didn't work but still ate like kings. The old lady read a few more things and the whole group responded. Jutta could hardly understand what they were saying.

The words were English, but he had never heard them spoken in such odd ways.

The odd ceremony continued as Rawley stood up along with everyone else. He read more from the same book and then gave this brief talk to the crowd assembled there:

"My friends, brothers and sisters. Have you ever been asked what you would do if this were your last day on earth? If I were to die today, how would I like to live my last few moments? Would I like to have my favorite meal? Would I like to enjoy a very rare wine and fill my senses with pleasure for the last time? For what? I ask. If I died with a belly full of fine meat and wine, would it not just go to waste? No. I would want to feast on a greater food, one that sustains me not only in this life but in the next. I would want to do what I am doing right now. Preparing my heart and mind to receive the body, blood, soul and divinity of our Lord. Let us be like the stork in the sky, knowing our seasons. Let us not lie. Let us not be those who are unwilling to work and unwilling to risk. And let us not be ones with lying pens. Let the truth be told through us and through our lives. Let us continue in this life that we chose, not giving up the traditions we have received from our forefathers, even in the face of great challenge and perhaps death..."

Rawley continued, but Jutta was unable to follow. For one thing, he kept thinking about how everyone called Rawley, Father. The words father, mother, brother, and sister had been deemed divisive in Volmar, so nobody used them. When Rawley was finished speaking, Odilia and another person stood up and brought a flask and a pan to Rawley, who took it and began praying over it.

Everyone knelt again and closed their eyes. Jutta sat watching the whole thing, his attention being diverted at times to the pictures on the walls of a man being tortured.

Soon the people walked in lines moving toward the front where Rawley was. Odilia motioned that Jutta should stay where he was, so he watched the people walk up to Rawley and receive a small piece of something like bread.

He could hear Rawley saying what sounded like, "The body of Christ." And another lady was holding a chalice and giving it to everyone to drink. As she did, Jutta heard her say, "The blood of Christ."

Jutta was shocked. They were indeed cannibals! Redhing had been right. These people really did eat flesh! Odilia came back to sit next to him, and he slid down the pew (away) from her.

When everyone in the room had eaten, Rawley said, "The Mass has ended. Go in peace, glorifying the Lord with your life."

"Thanks be to God," was the unified response.

Jutta and Odilia waited as the Dicarers left the room.

Rawley came back to the two and sat down next to Jutta. "So, what did you think of the Mass?"

Jutta was uncomfortable and said nothing.

"Father Rawley! Odilia!" They turned and saw Sabas running towards them. Sabas reached them, panting and avoiding eye contact with Jutta.

"What is it, Sabas?" Odilia asked.

"You might stop your tour for Master Jutta and get him into the hiding place. The Sogmols are coming."

"But why?" Odilia asked.

"Not sure, but I think it's his PASbot."

"Redhing?" Jutta asked but did not get any response from Sabas.

"The damn thing—sorry, Father—must have sent a signal," Sabas said.

"But that's not possible," Jutta said. "When I left that safe hole, his battery had died, and there was nothing there to charge him up."

Slapping his palm to his forehead, Sabas said, as if any first grader should have thought of it: "The sun! When the sun passed directly overhead, it could have charged the bot."

"But the boxbot covered up the hole, and Redhing was in a bag," Jutta protested.

"Oh, dear," Odilia said. "I think I left the lid open when we were searching for Jutta. Oh, no. What have I done?"

"It's not your fault," Rawley said."

"But wait. Weren't its ports disabled by Abaidus before the refreshing?" Odilia asked.

"Yes, but if a PASbot is completely rebooted, the ports turn back on," Sabas said.

"Wait, what?" Jutta said. "But Redhing had almost connected when I climbed to the top of the safe hole."

"No. It couldn't have connected," Sabas said. "Not until it rebooted."

"Oh, no," Odilia said. "It's all my fault."

"No," Rawley said. "It is something we've never had to deal with since no one has ever torn off a PASbot." Rawley turned to Jutta, "Normally, when we return to the hole, the person has been nearly drained of their energy by his or her PASbot, and we have to remove the bot ourselves. Do we know for sure if it communicated with Volmar?" Rawley asked.

"We don't know. All I know is that our lookouts say the Sogmols are coming. You should hide him, that is, if you want to keep him," Sabas said, referring to Jutta. "Maybe we should just let them have him."

"Not a chance," Rawley said. "This way, Jutta."

"I'll go get the militia ready," Sabas said.

"No!" Father said forcefully. "Come with us, Sabas."

"But, Father!" Sabas began to argue.

"There's no time for that. I will talk to them."

Sabas continued to protest, but Father would not be dissuaded. The four of them hastened through the chapel and into a long, dank tunnel.

"I don't understand," Jutta said, trying to keep up. "If Sogmols are coming for me, why don't you just let me go with them?"

"They'll kill you," Rawley said.

They raced through the tunnels back towards the infirmary where Jutta had woken up. They passed the courtyard where teachers were calling students into class. Jutta remembered when he tore off Redhing. He had worried then that the Sogmols would be pounding on the lid of the safe hole. They stopped in front of a rock wall, and somehow, it opened, revealing a tiny room that had a cot and a table with a monitor on it. Jutta saw that it was a hiding room, perfectly camouflaged to look like any other dirty stone wall of Mainz. Anyone hiding in the room would never be detected by even the most advanced tools of the Sogmols.

"Get in," Sabas said.

"Maybe you should just let me talk to them," Jutta said out of breath. "I can go with them, and they won't hurt you if they're only here for me."

"No, Jutta. You must hide," Rawley said.

Sabas grabbed Jutta's arm and pulled him into the hiding room. Odilia helped to push him in. When all three were inside the room, Rawley pushed a button and said, as the door closed, "You three stay here."

"What are you doing?" Odilia shouted, but the door was already closed.

Sabas said, "Oh, no. I'm not staying in here with this...I'm going to help Rawley."

But there was no way out. Rawley had taken the access fob, and the hiding place could only be opened from the outside.

Chapter 9

Two Different Weapons

Before rounding the corner to the adit, Father Rawley paused and blessed himself with the sign of the cross. He then turned the corner just as a platoon of Sogmols came marching in. Rawley watched the soldiers line up one at a time to form a blockade at the gate. When more than fifty armed Sogmols had formed a barrier between Mainz and the outside, the leader stepped through their ranks and planted himself in front of them.

The few citizens of Mainz who had been near the entrance earlier had retreated back into the cavernous habitat that enabled their survival. Only Rawley remained, unarmed and defenseless, to confront the army.

"Welcome, friends," Rawley said with a wry smile. "I'm delighted to see that so many of you have decided to put on the armor of Christ! If you had called ahead, I could have warmed the baptismal font."

Gangry, the captain, sneered. "You know we have not come for your foolishness, Rawley. We are wise to your ways."

"That's a shame. The baptistery hasn't been used for months. Then, to what do I owe the pleasure of your visit?"

"You'll not think it a pleasure when we're done, Rawley. Not a pleasure at all. At least not your own."

"Then why are you here, Volspat?" Rawley intentionally called Gangry *Volspat,* knowing that the distant, controlling voice of Volspat was telling Gangry what to say.

"I am Gangry, Grand Comrade with my terrors. You know why we are here. You continue to interfere with the sovereign rights of the

Volmarian people. You have taken one of our own, the one called Jutta. Hand him over, or face the consequences."

"One of your own?" Rawley asked. "So you own people now, is that right, Volspat?"

The soldier grew angry at being misaddressed.

"You're digging your own grave, Rawley. The young Sasjovian was undergoing a refreshing."

"If you have evidence, take it up with the council. After all, we do have agreements signed by our forefathers. The protocols have worked well for many years. Follow those procedures, but don't come here with your minions accusing us of violating your so-called rights to kill."

"If you will do what you please in our city, we will do as we wish in yours," Gangry said.

"What on earth are you talking about, Volspat?"

"It is GANGRY," the soldier yelled, drawing his sword.

"Then, Gangry," Father Rawley said calmly. "You know intuitively that the refreshing is nothing more than murder. People are not refreshed. They're done away with, and you know murder is immoral."

"I did not come here to debate morality, Rawley. I'm here to retrieve the Sasjovian or take others to make up for our loss."

"Volspat, shouldn't you simply look around first and see whether the one you seek is here? How do you know we have him?"

Gangry signaled for his troops to march through the city. "Find them," he said. "And bring them back to me."

"Them?" Rawley asked. The soldiers pushed passed him, knocking him back against a wall and to the ground.

"Them," Gangry responded. "Since it's evidently okay for you to steal our citizens, we figure it's okay to take a few we want ourselves. Eye for an eye kind of thing." Gangy's tone became more playfully taunting. "Oh, you know who the Avogo want most, don't you?"

Rawley stood up, brushed himself off, and looked up at the camera that he knew Odilia and Sabas would be watching through.

"Why do you accuse us of infiltrating your city? What proof do you have that we have committed any crimes?"

Gangry scowled at Rawley a moment and then began to laugh. "You mean you haven't heard? Maybe it's possible you don't know. Or maybe you're just lying as usual."

"Spit it out, Volspat! What do I not know?" Father Rawley said, getting up and brushing himself off.

"Not *what* I know. *Who* I know," he said. "Abaidus."

Rawley now wished he hadn't stood up. He leaned back against the wall and started to feel dizzy.

"Something wrong, Rawley?" Gangry sneered.

Rawley's white face betrayed the fact that he knew exactly what Gangry had meant. Abaidus had been discovered and, very likely, tortured. That meant that the Avogo named Volspat, who was speaking through Gangry at that moment, knew Jutta was there or at least that he was alive.

Abaidus had been the Dicarers' inside man for two years. During that time, he'd helped to rescue fifteen people, but this time, Redhing had connected with the PASportal and told all that had happened.

"Abaidus was right; we shouldn't have tried this one," Rawley said to himself. He had been too hopeful that this Sasjovian would help the cause, that Jutta would write the program to make the Avogo respect people's rights. Had he let his own ego make the decision? Rawley examined his conscience but, feeling acquitted, the color returned to his face, and he snapped back into the moment.

"Was he a friend of yours?" Gangry was asking. "Don't worry. He died painlessly...relatively speaking."

Rawley made the sign of the cross.

"They're not here," came a voice from one of the soldiers relayed back to Gangry's receiver.

"Well, I guess it's 'Plan B'," he said with a sarcasm that seemed to indicate he had learned from Redhing or Abaidus about the backup plan that Odilia and Sabas had resorted to. Soon, screams were heard coming from inside the city.

Gangry leaned in closer to Rawley with his sword still out. "Rawley Tang. Since you continue to challenge Volmarian sovereignty by directly interfering with the Council's ordinance 3517, we will take you, and a few others that we have special use for, back to Volmar where you will no longer be troubling us."

Father Rawley said angrily, "You and your so-called sovereignty. God gave you no such rights, Volspat. One day you will face your maker, and it will not go well for you! And you, Gangry, you still have a choice. You can change."

Gangry was fondling his sword and had a smirk on his face.

Rawley asked, "Want to see my weapon?" When his hand reached into his pocket, the Grand Comrade instinctively swung his sword. It sliced through Rawley's neck. Father Rawley's eyes were opened wide in shock. His head and body fell separately to the ground. The impact caused his hand to come out of his pocket. It was holding a rosary.

* * *

Rawley's head rolled to the ground and stopped at Gangry's feet. Gangry jumped back as if he were being chased by some small rabid animal. Then, a bewildered expression came across his face as he stared at the decapitated body and the prayer beads lying in a growing pool of blood.

"Scullion!" Gangry shouted with great urgency, looking for his assistant. But Scullion had gone with the others. Gangry shouted into his transmitter, "Scullion, return immediately! I need the Neureader on the priest's head, now!"

A short moment passed before Scullion showed up and gave Gangry an exasperated look when he saw the carnage. His eyes seemed to say, "What did you do?" But Gangry just yelled, "Scan it! Now, hurry up!

Scullion fumbled with a cloth-like device about two feet long and one foot wide. He wrapped it around the bruised head and pressed a few buttons on a device that was wired to it, similar in size to a PASbot.

"Get as much as you can," Gangry said as he kicked at a small rock that was lying in front of him. "How stupid can you be?" Gangry shouted but not at anyone in particular. A few seconds later, Gangry's voice was light and fearful. "I'm sorry, master. I thought he had a real weapon..."

Inside his head, Gangry heard Volspat say, "You'd better hope the scan gives us something useful."

"Sir," Scullion said after about seven minutes. "There's no more brain activity. That's all I can record."

He handed Gangry a Direct Neural Interface device that now stored the final thoughts of Father Rawley. Gangry took it and put it in his pocket.

The soldiers were arriving back at the entrance, each with their captives. There were around thirty Dicarers now standing in front of Gangry with their hands bound behind their backs. He selected eleven of them and let the others go. Then, he commanded the soldiers to take the prisoners back to Volmar. He forced the people to pass by the body of their leader and tried to make them spit on him.

"Spit it out!" Gangry said, unhappily mimicking what Father Rawley had said to him earlier. All refused to spit, so they were beaten and then dragged to the waiting vehicles to take them back to the beautiful open society of Volmar.

Chapter 10

The Townhall

Odilia wept inconsolably in the hiding chamber. Sabas sat stone-faced, staring at the video screen that still showed Father Rawley's lifeless body. When he saw the Sogmol wrap Father's head in the scanning device, a deep rage gripped him, and he turned to Jutta with a glare of black malice.

Sabas grabbed a chair and smashed it against the ground. He overturned the table that had the monitor on it. He threw items large and small. But no matter how much damage he did, even if he could have torn down the sky, it would not make up for the loss of such a man as Rawley or for the kidnappings.

Odilia was startled by each outburst, causing her to cry more earnestly. Jutta crawled into a corner to protect himself from Sabas. He pulled his knees up close to his chest and sunk his face into them, rocking back and forth.

Sabas apparently grew tired of destroying things; the hidden room became quiet. Then, as if a pressure relief valve had been activated, the doors opened, and fresh air flooded the room.

Standing outside the door was a little boy holding carrots. When he saw Sabas, tears welled up in his eyes, and his bottom lip began to shake. "Have you seen my mommy?" he asked.

Sabas swept him up into his arms, and Odilia threw her arms around the two of them. Jutta stayed where he was.

Odilia turned her face to rest her cheek on Sabas' chest, tears still rolling down her face. She reached out her hand as if to beckon for Jutta to come to her. But he remained leaning against the wall in the corner hugging his knees.

Sabas and Odilia slowly walked away with the child as if they were afraid of what they might find ahead of them. Jutta stayed in the hiding chamber.

Sabas, Odilia, and the child made their way through the city and saw that a few people were hurt from trying to protect family members from the Sogmols. Sabas told everyone he saw to meet in the chapel straightaway. By the time Sabas and Odilia had made their way around the city and then to the chapel, most of the townspeople were already there. Several men, members of the militia were armed. They stood in a group talking loudly, not even trying to disguise the fact that they were ready to go to war.

Sabas surveyed the group and stood behind the pulpit, where Father Rawley had preached his last homily no more than an hour earlier. As he observed the crowd, noting who had been taken and who was left, that same anger that he had in the hidden chamber returned to him.

"Quiet, everyone," he said. "Let me have your attention."

"Why did they do this?" A man cried out from the crowd.

"It's that new rescue. They came to get him," one of the militia men shouted. "We need to get rid of him and get our people back. Make a trade."

Sabas may have agreed, but with Father Rawley gone, he felt it was time for him to be mediator. "Please, settle down."

The crowd began to quiet down. A baby was crying, but his mother hardly seemed to notice that the baby was sitting in her lap.

Sabas nearly broke down in front of everyone. "Someone needs to take care of Father Rawley's body," he said, gazing out at the citizens of Mainz. But the nature of Father's death must have made everyone recoil at the thought. No one volunteered. There was only a hush across the crowd. Only the baby was heard still whimpering.

Sabas nodded. "Right, then. I'll do it. I can't stand the thought of him lying there like that."

"I'll go," one man stood up. A lady volunteered as well and said, "You stay here and talk to everyone, Sabas."

The two volunteers left to perform the sad task of putting Father's body into a coffin. A casket had already been prepared recently for a guard who was suffering from cancer.

Sabas cleared his throat many times and finally said, "We know that they came for the new rescue. This is true, but it was Father's last wish to spare him. I do not know why. Father tricked me and Odilia into the hidden room with the rescue and locked the door. Otherwise, I could have maybe protected Father."

"Why did you agree to rescue him? You said yourself it was too risky?" someone asked.

Sabas scanned the back of the church. The doors had small windows at about eye level, and Sabas thought he saw Jutta peeking through one of them.

"We didn't want to," Sabas said. "But Father felt something. He kept saying, 'This one is worth the risk.' Now, Father is dead, and many of our people have been taken. And there's one more bit of bad news in case you haven't heard," Sabas added. The crowd looked up at him so full of sorrow that he didn't know whether it was right to tell them. He cleared his throat, "I'm sorry to tell you this now, but...the Avogo." Sabas had to stop here. His voice broke, and he cried out, "They discovered Abaidus. He's dead, too." The whole crowd moaned together. Shortly, Sabas collected himself and said, "He might have gotten caught after helping us rescue Jutta."

"Jutta? That's his name?" an incredulous voice came from the group of men still standing. "A woman's name," he said disdainfully. "Let's give him back. They came for him. Let's trade him for our people. Surely they'll do that."

"It's possible," Sabas said. "I'm sure that's why they took them. But we have to be careful. What if they trick us and just take Jutta and not return our people? Then what do we have? Nothing. They'll just kill Jutta like they were planning to already. They certainly can't reintroduce him into Volmar now that he had his refreshing ceremony."

"We don't have nothing anyway," the man responded. "Just one lousy rescue. Who cares if he lives or dies?"

Jutta stood outside the doors listening to what they were saying.

"Yeah," a second man said. "We've got to try it. Make the trade."

"The thing is," Sabas said, hesitating. "Father Rawley said that Jutta might be able to write the program that would get rid of the Avogo."

A few of them scoffed at the idea, but someone asked, "How?"

The rescue attempt, like always, had been kept a secret from the general public, so they didn't know that Jutta was a Sasjovian, programmers who wrote code to help calm minds. The less the people knew, the better because the Avogo were masters at extracting information; anyone who knew about the plot could give away the secrets. That's one reason they scanned Father Rawley's head.

The same man who'd just shouted to get rid of Jutta then said, "If they don't trade for the kid, we have to be ready to fight. We might not defeat them, but I'd rather die than live without trying to save our people. This is a just war if there ever was one."

After a good deal of discussion, the front doors of the chapel opened, and the two volunteers wheeled Father's coffin to a place near the altar, and reality sat heavily on everyone's chest. Sabas felt ill-equipped for the moment and asked if anyone else would take over, but no one did.

As if in answer to Sabas' prayers, the same doors opened again, and the lady with the baby said, "There's Fargus." Jutta peeked through the high window in the back door and could see a tall, skinny, bald man. Shoulders hunched, he walked up to the podium and gave Sabas a brief hug. Sabas went to sit with Odilia, leaving the podium to Deacon Fargus.

* * *

Jutta pulled open the door carefully and slid quietly into a back pew. It was darker in the back, and everyone was facing the altar. He leaned back in the pew and listened to the deacon.

"Brothers and sisters," Fargus said, "I have been consoling Yaro's wife and child. She is too distraught to be here. We did not deserve this. And with God's help, we will overcome. But I just started thinking, maybe we should try to follow the Sogmols to find out if they took them back to Volmar. I've had a bad feeling that they might take them to CHAI."

Sabas stood up and said, "I'll go with you."

Odilia also stood up and took her place by his side.

"No, Odilia," Sabas said. "You stay. You heard what they said. You're the one they want the most. You and Jutta."

"Don't tell me to stay. I'm not a dog. I'll be fine," Odilia said.

"But I need you safe," Sabas said.

"We'll be together," Odilia said. "Let's go." Some of the other militiamen wanted to go, but Fargus, apparently content with Sabas and Odilia, said, "Okay, the three of us will try to track them down. Pray for us, everybody. Pray for the return of our loved ones. When we get back, we will discuss a course of action."

Fargus said a quick prayer over the group and then left with Sabas and Odilia.

Some of the crowd slowly began to leave through the back doors, and Jutta bowed his head low, like he had seen others doing during Mass earlier. A young man spotted him and went to tell some of his friends.

"Guys, the new rescue is here, hiding in the back pew." The boys walked to the back of the chapel and confronted Jutta.

"Hey, man," one of the boys said. He turned to one of the younger boys standing next to him and asked, "What's his name? Jutta?"

Jutta lifted his head a little but didn't make eye contact. After some prodding, he finally said, "Yes. I am Jutta."

"Can you do it?" the boy said.

"Do what?" Jutta asked, aware that nearly the entire crowd was now surrounding him.

"Write the program, the one that will get rid of the Avogo!" he said.

"Why would I want to get rid of the Avogo?" he asked.

"Why? Didn't you see what just happened?" the boy said. "They're evil. They don't care about anyone but themselves."

"They care about the citizens of Volmar," Jutta said unconvincingly. "They take good care of us."

Many of the Dicarers were visibly disappointed. Some shook their heads and walked away.

"They do not. They're evil, and anyone who defends them ought to be thrown out into the heat for a few days," said the boy.

"They take advantage of you people," said an older boy who seemed a bit testy. He sat down on the back of the pew in front of Jutta and put his feet on Jutta's pew. "Let me ask you a question. Do you want to be a daddy?"

Jutta laughed. "What? Weird. No!"

Some in the group of boys chuckled at his answer.

"Just a minute." The young man walked away, grabbed a woman by the hand, and brought her over to Jutta.

"Jutta," he said. "This is Anna. Anna, show him your belly." She turned sideways to reveal a grossly large stomach. Jutta was visibly disturbed by her deformity. His face grew troubled.

"Guess what's in there?" the boy asked, putting his palm gently on the girl's belly.

Jutta shook his head in disgust and didn't venture a guess.

"My son," he said. "I'm going to be a father, and if this little boy is going to have a good life, he's going to need your help. So, you'd better get a clue about what's going on. We're not the bad guys here. We're telling you the truth. The Avogo are bad. They don't even tell you how people are created. Well, this is how people are created," he touched his wife's belly.

"In a woman's belly. We are born, we live, and then we die. We are not refreshed. We die and go to one of three places: heaven, hell or purgatory." He stuck his hands in his pockets, and apparently unable to finish, he looked down at the ground. Then, he turned to look at his wife, who gave him a gentle, approving smile.

After a moment of silence, Jutta said, "I'm not sure I understand what he meant by father and son. I don't think you're using those words the way we do in Volmar."

"What would it take for you to believe?" asked the boy who had discovered Jutta sitting alone.

Jutta thought about it a few minutes while the others sat quietly. Finally, he said, "I guess if I saw someone I knew from Volmar who you rescued. Maybe that would help."

The expectant father said, "You probably haven't been away long enough to know what's going on. You're still brainwashed. But tell me, if we showed you someone who you recognize and you come around and agree with us... could you write such programs? I mean something that could make the Avogo change?"

Jutta responded. "I'm a Sasjovian. I'm supposed to write programs like that for the Vaipwo. I don't think I could write a program to change superior beings. That would go against my training."

The expectant father sighed. "They're not superior beings. They're just really, really old people who set themselves up as gods. What a waste of Father and Abaidus' lives," he said as he walked away with his wife. Many people turned and left Jutta alone.

But others were not ready to give up. "You're going to do it," said a tall skinny boy with pimples and straight brown hair. "Somebody get him a computer. We'll lock him up in a room and make him work night and day until he does it."

"Let's take him to see Michelina. She has all the computers and equipment he would need. If we don't have it, she'll know how to get it," said another young man named Chester.

The young men pulled Jutta out of his seat and began to drag him out of the chapel, but the back doors swung open: Fargus, Sabas, and Odilia were back.

The boys let go of Jutta.

"Everyone, gather around," Fargus said as he made his way to the podium.

"We have some good news. Gather round, everybody. It's a lucky break." Fargus got up to the podium and waited a moment for everyone to get settled.

"Here's the good news. Yaro escaped from the Sogmols!"

The door in the front opened, and a man entered through the doorway among the cheers of the people. "So it looks like they only have ten of us instead of eleven. Now Yaro says he saw Gangry put the scan of Fr. Rawley's last memory in his pocket. There's probably no way to get that back, and we have no idea what his last thoughts were. I can't deny that the scan could reveal secrets like who we've rescued over the past and other sensitive information. But, at least Yaro is free, and we know the others were taken to Volmar and not sold to CHAI. I'll let Yaro say a few words."

As Yaro approached the podium, Jutta started shaking and leaned forward as if someone had just punched him in the stomach. "Yarosky?" he whispered under his breath. "Sky?"

Chapter 11

The Elephant Ears

When Gangry returned to Volmar after unexpectedly killing Fr. Rawley, he couldn't push away the image of the head dropping at his feet. As he watched the Sogmols take the prisoners and lock them up in the Vauller, he was on edge, waiting for Volspat to shout inside his head about the mistakes he had made. He surveyed the prisoners again, hoping to somehow see Jutta among them, or, better yet, Odilia, whom Volspat had been eyeing for years.

Even before this botched mission, Volspat had been threatening to demote Gangry, and Gangry shuddered to think what the term "demote" actually meant in Volspat's vocabulary. Now that he had screwed up so badly, he would soon need a way out. But planning an escape was nearly impossible with elephant ears in his head.

Gangry started calling the device in his head "elephant ears" two years earlier when Volspat told him the story of the Kingdom of Kandy. One of Volspat's favorite episodes in history had to do with the Sri Lankan kingdom of Kandy in the 1600s. The King of Kandy had a palace, a kind of labyrinth that was called "The Woodstock Bower," with many turnings and windings and doors.

Volspat had told him: "The king himself had contrived all these turnings and windings. By means of those contrivances, it was not easy to know where the King was, and he didn't want them to know. He had strong watches day and night about his court...at night, they all had their set places within the court where they could come to the aid of the king. There were also elephants which were appointed all night to stand and watch, lest there should be any tumult; which if there should, could presently trample down a multitude. My dear Gangry," Volspat had paused and put his hand on Gangry's shoulder. "You are my strong elephant. If there be any tumult, you shall trample it."

"And you are my king," Gangry had said fawningly. He now cringed thinking about that first time he called Volspat his king.

But he tried hard not to think any negative thoughts about Volspat. Those "elephant ears" not only allowed Volspat to speak directly into Gangry's mind. They also allowed Volspat to hear some, but not all, of Gangry's thoughts.

The Sogmols finished moving the kidnapped Dicarers into the holding area of the Vauller, where prisoners and prospective citizens stayed while being vetted. Gangry hoped he could go back to his own chamber and be left alone, but as he drew near to his room, an obsequious Sogmol approached him.

"Grand Comrade," he said, bowing low. "The one they call Yaro has escaped."

Gangry immediately went into a rage, slapping the Sogmol in the face. The disgraced minion held his stinging cheek and bowed his way backwards out of the room.

Gangry waited for that fearful voice to pop into his head. But Volspat remained oddly silent. He certainly knew about all that had happened. And now, because the Sogmol had verbalized the news about the escape of Yaro, Volspat surely knew about that, too. It was just a matter of time before the clear bug of a voice began pestering him about the mishaps of the day.

Gangry decided he had better appear to be doing his job, so he chased down the Sogmol who had delivered the news about Yaro. Finding him among the others in the large room where the Sogmol minions bunked, Gangry grabbed him and yelled, "How did the prisoner escape?"

"Sorry. I do not know, Grand Comrade. Perhaps your highness could ask Flator. It was his prisoner." Flator happened to be standing nearby.

Gangry turned to Flator and said, "When will you fools learn? I can't trust any of you worthless Cretans. One simple job and you screw it up."

He stepped forward and punched Flator in the face, knocking a tooth loose. When he lifted his hand to punch the Sogmol again, the voice of Volspat finally spoke: "Enough, Gangry. This is your fault. You failed."

Gangry fell silent, and his hand dropped to his side. No one else had heard Volspat's voice. None of them had watched him punish the Sogmol for fear of being next. But when they didn't hear a face being punched, some of them glanced up and saw Gangry slumping over.

When Gangry saw that a few eyes dared to meet his own, he shouted, "Out!"

Several ran away immediately, but a few walked slowly out of the room. Some, including Scullion and another named Skyte, chose to be defiant by remaining in the room, sitting down on their beds.

When Gangry saw Flator leaving the room with the others, he picked up a knife and threw it at him. The blunt end hit him in the leg, and he shrieked as he ran through the door.

"Is that how you treat your men, Gangry?" said Volspat. "I suppose that's how I should treat you as well. Don't you know the Golden rule?"

Gangry didn't answer. He squatted down and put his head in his hands.

"One simple mission."

"We did what you requested," Gangry replied flatly.

"You came back with ten captives when I only wanted two, and none of them are the two I asked for. And to top it off, you killed that infernal priest. Don't you know what happens when you kill the leader?"

"When you cut off the head of the snake, you kill the snake."

"No. Fool. The snake lives. New heads pop up with new brains and new ideas. We can assume those ideas will not be peaceful, like the ones that floated around in Rawley's head. That Sabas, for example. We won't know what he's thinking. Speaking of that, bring me the scan of that priest's final thoughts."

Gangry rose to his feet, trying to focus on anything besides the scan that he knew was in his pocket. "Let me find it. Scullion!" he shouted at the Sogmol, who was lying on a bed. "Scullion! Give me the scan," Gangry shouted.

But Scullion said, "I gave it to you, sir comrade."

"You did not," Gangry retorted. "You had better find it, Scullion."

"I distinctly remember..." When Scullion saw the look of anger on the face of Gangry, he must have changed his mind. "Maybe the prisoner who escaped took it?" he suggested.

Volspat suddenly started shouting inside of Gangry's head. "You idiot. I'm going to start over with a new Grand Comrade. Maybe I'll find your replacement among the prisoners you brought me!"

Don't you know the Golden rule? Gangry thought, but then he quickly tried concentrating on his shoes, hoping that Volspat had not heard that thought.

"There will certainly be no pleasure with the prisoners for you or your kind," Volspat said. "They are all mine. You will not touch them. Leave them alone and await my orders."

"Yes, sir," replied Gangry.

"And what?" said Volspat.

"Bless the Avogo. Thank you, king."

Chapter 12

An Old Friend

Yaro reached the podium, and Jutta grabbed his stomach and began shaking. Jutta tried to focus his attention behind the podium on the cross where a man was hanging by way of nails in his hands and feet. When Yaro said, "I'm okay, everyone," Jutta stood up to run. Instead, he tripped and fell to his knees in the aisle and made a gagging sound as though he would vomit.

The boys who had been ready to drag Jutta back to their room and chain him to a computer nearly fell over each other trying to get away from him. Yaro noticed the commotion and said, "Just a minute, everyone. I had hoped someone would break the news to Jutta first."

Yaro had been the head of Jutta's group unit in Volmar seven years earlier, and this recognition felt to Jutta like a punch in the gut. Jutta found himself kneeling there in the chapel with hundreds of eyes fixed on him. Yaro was coming towards him, and the man was still hanging from a cross in the background. Yaro knelt beside Jutta, whose gagging intensified, but nothing was coming out.

"Oh, Jutta. I'm so sorry. I had hoped to meet you again under better circumstances. We had planned to break the news quite differently."

Jutta recoiled from Yaro. "No," he said, waving him off as if Yaro were an apparition.

Yaro had been close to Jutta in Volmar. But because he was in his mid-forties at that time seven years earlier, the Avogo announced that he would be refreshed into a girl named Bibiana, the six-year-old who had held onto Jutta's leg and swore she wouldn't let him go.

But Yaro was still there in his old fleshly presence, kneeling right beside Jutta, who crawled a few feet away from Yaro and started to heave. This time, he really did become sick and threw up all over the floor.

"Let's get him to his room," Yaro said to a couple of boys nearby. "He's had too much for one day."

An older man helped Jutta stand, but Jutta waved him off. Yaro held out his hand, but Jutta pulled himself up by the back of a pew and stood unaided.

"This way," Yaro pointed to the doors at the back of the chapel.

As the chapel doors closed behind them, the congregation erupted in conversation. In the hallway, Yaro cleared his throat and said, "I'm sure this all seems incredibly strange, Jutta. It must be a real shock to see me again. I can imagine how you're feeling. It was really hard for me at first, too. But I've come around. You will, too. I know you too well."

They ambled in silence for a moment until Jutta said, shakily, "Where are we going?"

"Have you been to your own room yet? Let me show you to it. You must be exhausted." After a pause, he said, "I know you're still freaked out, but it is so good to see you, Jutta. You don't know how happy I am that you're finally here. It'll take some time, but eventually, I think you'll adjust." The two arrived at the doorway of a small room near the infirmary. "Here we are. This will be your room for now. Come in and rest awhile. And I'll try to help you make sense of things."

Jutta sat on one side of the bed, examining the rock walls of the tiny room. He felt a chill and crossed his arms to warm himself up.

"Do you need to lie down?" Yaro asked.

Jutta shook his head to indicate he'd rather sit. He felt color was beginning to return to his face, and he took a glass of water that was sitting by his bedside.

Yaro turned on a light on the nightstand and smiled as he watched Jutta take a drink. "I remember one time you and Mistique got into a fight over a water bottle."

Jutta almost choked on the water. Until that moment, he had hoped that maybe the person in front of him was some sort of fake, some cloned copy of his former group unit leader. But he remembered that fight with Mistique well, and Jutta lost hope of denying who was standing in front of him. He began to cry.

Yaro patted his back, but that only made the crying worse. He tried to stop, but just when it seemed like he had control over his emotions, he would look at Yaro and begin crying again. He couldn't stop crying long enough to speak. And he felt embarrassed by his lack of control.

Yaro seemed to be at a loss for words. He sat down in a chair next to Jutta's bed and, soon, started to wipe his own eyes. Eventually, Yaro said, "Come here, Jutta. Give me a hug, old friend!"

Jutta jumped up from his bed and threw his arms around his former group unit leader, who had been roughly equivalent to a father for Jutta.

After a few more minutes, Odilia knocked on the door of Jutta's room.

"Sorry to interrupt you guys," she said. "The congregation is kinda getting out of hand. They want to hear from you, Yaro."

"Of course," he said. "Of course, sorry. We got wrapped up, didn't we, Jutta?"

"We did," Jutta smiled, still wiping tears from his bloodshot eyes. Odilia smiled compassionately, and her eyes locked on his for a brief moment.

Yaro stood up. "Will you go with us, Jutta?"

Jutta felt discomforted by the suggestion.

"Never mind. You stay here and rest. Maybe Odilia can get you

something to eat? You must be starving since you lost your lunch."
They all laughed. "Okay. See you in a bit, Jutta. So glad you're
finally here!"

Odilia asked if she could get him something.

Though he didn't feel like eating, he felt like he needed something
to settle his stomach. "Do you have any of that green stuff you gave
me in the safe hole?" he asked.

She smiled. "Of course. Do you want to come with me, or should I
bring it to you?"

"Uh, I'll go," he said.

"Okay. This way," she said. "You can come anytime to get your
food. We don't always have enough, and we're kind of rationing
right now. But I think you should eat all you want, Jutta. And since
we lost eleven people today, we probably have plenty." Her tone
grew somber. "You need to regain your strength. And I'm sure you
are in shock. You've been through a lot lately."

"So have you," Jutta ventured. But he did not know what else to
say.

Odilia stopped and gazed into his eyes as if she were searching for
something. "Thank you," she said.

Jutta smiled at her awkwardly and wished Redhing were there to
tell him what to say.

In the kitchen, Odilia opened a cabinet and pulled out the
survival food used for excursions outside the city. "Here you are.
One broonscake! It's quite a delicacy, you know," she said
teasingly, but Jutta could see the sadness in her eyes.

"I don't need a whole one. Just enough to calm my nerves. Thank
you."

"Sure." She grabbed a knife and cut the broonscake in half. "Must
be quite a shock to see Yaro again."

He didn't respond. As he ate, Odilia watched him discreetly.
"Want some water?" she asked.

"Yes, please."

As she poured the water, Jutta studied her closely. He wondered how this could be the same girl who had driven him through the desert on the traverser the night before. She had seemed so tough and so knowing then. Now, she seemed worried and unsure of herself.

She handed him the glass and said, "Well. If you don't mind, I think I'll get back to the chapel. I'd like to know what they are talking about. You're welcome to come."

Jutta turned red thinking about how he had just thrown up in front of everyone. "You, you don't think they'd be mad to see me?" he asked.

"Of course not," she scoffed. "You might give them hope now. Father Rawley put a lot of hope in you, but I don't want to put too much pressure on you. You just do what you want. Maybe get some rest?"

He looked away from her without answering.

"Seriously," she said. "It would be good to have you there, but I understand if you're not ready. I'll let you decide. I trust you can find your way back to your room or to the chapel?"

"Yes," he said.

"Well, then. I'll see you soon."

"Odilia?" he said.

"Yes?"

"Thank you."

Odilia smiled and walked away.

Sitting alone, he thought about Yaro and felt like crying again. Seeking the familiar, he reached for Redhing, but the bot was gone. The kitchen was empty and quiet. In the distance, the congregation could occasionally be heard arguing about something.

Growing lonely, Jutta decided to return to the chapel. He pushed the door open just when the crowd had grown silent. It creaked, and Yaro paused while everyone turned to see Jutta. Hundreds of eyes were on him, and none of them appeared angry. Rather, they all seemed to be waiting for him to say something. Someone had cleaned up his mess, he noticed. He nodded at everyone and took a seat in the back. The congregation turned back to listen to Yaro, who smiled and nodded back at Jutta.

"My friends, I think we are not making very good progress right now. Our emotions are so raw. I know we're all worried about our loved ones, and we're devastated by the loss of our beloved father. He cannot be replaced. Who can replace him? We had hoped the rescuing of Jutta would be smoother. But we cannot blame him for this catastrophe that has come over us. All of us knew the risk involved. Father knew better than all of us what risk there was, and he paid the ultimate price for it. But let me be clear. No blame is on Jutta. No blame at all."

The congregation all nodded. Someone said, "Amen, that's right. We don't blame you, Jutta."

"It's that damn Volspat," an older man yelled.

"Sirus, please," Yaro said. "This is still the house of the Lord. No profanity, please."

"Sorry, father. I mean, deacon." Sirus hung his head, and the woman beside him gave him a scowl.

Yaro continued. "We know we have one enemy. And it's not Volspat or the other Avogo, although they are, of course, the face of the enemy right now. It is the enemy of old. It is the one who has caused humans throughout history to argue, to go to war, to cheat and to steal. It is the one who has caused untold harm to humanity."

Bettrily stood up to address the crowd. "It would be appropriate to pause a moment for prayer," she said. "Could we maybe review the readings for today's Mass since many of us, myself included, weren't able to make it? Would that be okay?"

There was a collective sigh of disappointment. But a few adamant "yeses" from some women brought a hush over the crowd. Bettrily walked to the podium and opened the book lying on it. She took some time to find the passage but eventually began to read in a loving voice, "A reading from the Acts of the Apostles: 'Repent, therefore, and turn again, that your sins may be blotted out, that times of refreshing,...'" She paused, and her voice started shaking. "...may come from the presence of the Lord, and that he may send the Christ appointed for you, Jesus....'"

After she finished reading the passage, Jutta felt a hundred eyes on him, but he could only wonder what repenting was and what it had to do with the refreshing.

Chapter 13

I am Godlip

Gangry made it to his room and closed the door behind him. Alone, he racked his brain, trying to remember the meaning of the Golden rule. Eventually, he recalled that it meant something like, "Whatever you do to someone else, that will be done to you." He recalled throwing the knife at that Sogmol and assumed that Volspat would soon take a knife to him as well.

He had been the Grand Comrade for almost three years now. No one had held the position quite as long as he had, but seniority didn't mean much in Volmar. The mission to retrieve Jutta had been a miserable failure, and Volspat had no tolerance for failure. Gangry came to realize he had only two options: he could sit around and wait for the knife. Or, he could run away.

Gangry had not made his own decisions for many years, and the chance that he could pull off an escape seemed slim. Volspat's elephant ears had taken over many of his thoughts, and to cope, Gangry devoted his time to physical exercise and pleasures of the flesh, which helped drown out some primordial voice deep inside of him that spoke in a strange tongue sometimes and brought about odd dreams. The voice seemed to be speaking at that moment in his private chambers, and what was left of a spirit inside of him tried to listen.

He closed his eyes to focus, and he thought he heard the voice say, "Run." But he was doubtful. He lay down on his bed, trying to visualize a means of escape while at the same time trying not to set off the elephant ears. Volspat could be listening. When he first became a Sogmol, he would sometimes lie awake wondering what life would be like elsewhere, what else there might be in the world.

But after the implant and the voice of Volspat, he had grown afraid to think of such things. Even now, he waited for Volspat to intrude and break his thoughts of freedom.

Volspat did, in fact, call him, but the command was short. "Gangry. Report to the Aspodt."

Gangry had not had time to plan his escape, but he knew what would happen if he showed up at the Aspodt. He remembered what happened to his predecessor, and he had heard rumors of the ones who'd come before him. None of those rumors particularly appealed to him.

"Run," the voice said again, this time more clearly. Thinking on it further, running seemed his only option. But where would he go? He searched the recesses of his mind to find memories of the outside, of freedom, of where he might go.

He sat up in his bed, and a few vague memories came to him. There was a town many miles away from the verdant city of Volmar, called Bandondery. His family had lived on the outskirts of this town. Only memories of the hard times came to him, but he kept searching for the good. Gangry heard his mom crying, and he wondered if Volspat could hear her too.

He remembered one night, during a heated argument with his mother, his father grabbed Gangry and left Bandonderry. His mother tried to stop him, but she was weak and pregnant. Gangry and his father walked for what seemed like weeks, all the way to the gates of Volmar. That was the last he ever saw of his father. They were separated at the entrance and, from that point on, everything from the past started to be erased.

Now, years later, it seemed death was at the gate. He had seen so much of the violence of Volspat.

"Gangry?" the King of Kandy spoke again into his brain. "Where are you?" Volspat sang as if he were a child playing hide-and-seek. "I can see you!"

Gangry delayed. How long had he been in Volmar? Ten years?

When he had entered Volmar, his muscles had already started to develop, and everyone knew he would be a strong man. He would have been even stronger if he had not been starving. Most of his life, he'd eaten very little. A day when he had a full meal was a good day. It was this strength that had attracted Volspat's attention and put him in line to be a Sogmol.

"Gangry? Come, Gangry. Here, boy."

Gangry put his hands to his ears and cursed his good luck at having been born strong.

During his first few weeks in Volmar, the Avogo, especially the King of Kandy (Volspat's preferred nickname for himself), lavished attention on him. He accepted all the attention eagerly and barely protested when the portal was installed. He was invited to Disibodenberg, even the Woodstock Bower. The King of Kandy began calling him his own child, and so it was natural to say yes to everything that Volspat asked.

Nourished on the food of Volmar, Gangry had grown in strength. One day, the king held the young man's hand and promised unimaginable glory. But the price was high.

Gangry shook his head with his hands still pressed to his ears, trying to dislodge the memories of what he had done. When he did, a vision of his mom came to him. A fond memory.

One day, she brought home a large piece of meat. She was laughing, and the two of them were singing. He helped her prepare the fire for cooking. She stopped and caressed his face and smiled into his eyes. Then, they both laughed for no reason, and she went about the task of cooking.

"My little helper," she said.

The aroma was still fresh in his mind. He could hear the sizzling of the squirrel, or maybe rabbit, meat. It was a nice change from the rat meat that they usually had, if there was any meat. The water boiled, and his mom put in a few scant wild greens that she had scavenged. His stomach ached then, but now his heart seemed to ache even worse.

When the meal was ready, they sat at a table, nothing more than a piece of wood thrown on top of two cinder blocks. His mother grabbed his hand and prayed.

"Gangry? Are you coming? Report please," said the King of Kandy sharply. The "please" was not a real please. It was the period on an impatient command.

Gangry stepped out of his personal chamber and looked around the Vauller. He knew every inch of it and could probably get away. But how long could he last out there in the heat? He still had not thought of any place to go.

And what if Volspat's voice continued to follow him? How could he ever be free of that? The King of Kandy would never let him leave in peace. He would sic the Sogmols after him. Some of them, like Scullion, would revel in hunting him because Gangry had enemies. He had inherited his father's short temper, and he had used it for his own benefit. He grew to be hated like he had hated his father. The memory of his father tearing him away from his mother and then sending him here to Volmar made him angry.

"What is my name?" he found himself asking.

"What?" was the short and angry response.

"My name. Before I came to Volmar. What was it?" he asked again.

"The old you is gone, Gangry. You belong to Volmar, and you know that. Now come to the Aspodt."

Gangry touched his pocket to make sure the scan of Father Rawley's last memory was still there. He didn't know why he wanted to keep it. He just wanted it. Though the scan had no use to him, he just felt like keeping something from Volspat.

"Of course, my king," Gangry said. "Silly question. I belong to

Volmar." He recited the Sogmol pledge and then said, "I will be there soon. Just need to check on the prisoners."

Gangry walked to the holding chambers where the kidnapped Dicarers were being held. He observed that some of them were on their knees, fumbling with a necklace of beads and mumbling words that he couldn't make out.

A vision from the past or perhaps a dream came to him. As a child, he had stood next to a mulberry tree in full bloom. Filled with bees at work, the tree itself seemed to be humming. The longer he looked, the louder the humming became, and a fear inside began to grow. The fear approached him slowly, like the noise of a traverser coming down a lonely stretch of desert. He could hear it approaching a mile away, and as it gradually got closer and louder, he wanted to run.

Many of the prisoners cowered when they saw him, their terrified eyes fixed on his tattooed hands and scarred arms that were resting on the bars of their cell. But Gangry said nothing. He only stared at them. After a few moments, he turned and left them alone. When he opened the door, heat from the outside rushed into the Vauller.

"Where are you going, Gangry?" Volspat shouted.

Gangry did not answer. He started running at the sound of Volspat's voice. He ran to the traversers sitting beneath the Vauller and shut off the sensors that might detect him.

"Gangry, report to me now. I am growing impatient," Volspat said. But Gangry did not respond. He jumped onto a traverser, and as he drove through the heaps, Volspat shouted threats, increasing the volume of the voice in Gangry's head.

Gangry heard Volspat calling his minions. "Gangry is defecting. Catch him and bring him back." There was a pause. "Dead or alive."

Gangry fled from the city of Volmar – that perfect, beautiful city where no one suffered, and everyone had everything they ever wanted.

"Gangry," Volspat called. "Why are you doing this? Didn't I treat you well? Didn't I give you everything you ever wanted? Treated you like you were one of my own."

Gangry momentarily questioned his decision. But remembering what had become of the other Grand Comrades before him, he pulled the throttle back all the way and fled quickly. His mother's memory came back, and he could almost smell the wood burning in the stove, and he could almost hear the rabbit meat sizzling in the pan. He saw her face smiling at him. She continued caressing his cheek, and he saw for the first time, the deep sadness in her eyes. She kissed his forehead, "Eat up, Godlip, my dear son."

Volspat shouted, "You'll never escape, Gangry. My desires will always reach you."

The road ahead disappeared into sand, but he plowed straight through in the direction of Mainz, not knowing where he would end up or how he would survive.

"Remember all you have done, Gangry. You belong to us. Your promise was given."

He rode faster than he had ever ridden a traverser before. He hadn't realized the machines could go that fast. He looked back to see if anyone was following him but didn't see anyone yet.

"I will kill you, Gangry!" Volspat shouted.

"Godlip," Gangry shouted back. "My name is Godlip!" Just then, his traverser hit something. He lost control, and the traverser went one way while he went another. The vehicle flew about thirty feet before sliding off a steep embankment. Gangry landed in a soft patch and rolled until his head hit a rock. The world began to vanish along with the voice of Volspat in his head.

"I am Godlip," he thought as the world turned to black. "I am Godlip."

Chapter 14

A Plan

After Bettrily read the passage about repenting "that a time of refreshing may come," the conversation in the chapel returned to how to respond to the attack from Volmar. Sirus, undeterred, stood up and said, "We can't just sit here and wait while our loved ones are being abused. You know they are probably already doing horrible things. I don't even want to think about what they could be doing to them, especially the women, right now. You know the Avogo will use every one of them, and it sickens me to think how."

Yaro said sadly, "By now, they have been injected with their nanotrack IDs. Mark my words. They will be used as bargaining chips. Soon, we will receive a demand to give up Jutta, and probably...others."

"Do it!" Sirus shouted. "Give 'em Jutta. Make the trade."

There was an uncomfortable murmur among the crowd. But Yaro held up his hand. "We will not give them Jutta or anyone else. It would mean certain death for Jutta. You know that. Volspat can't allow him to be seen in Volmar again. Jutta," Yaro said directly to him, "there's no going back for you, my friend. Makes me wonder why they wanted to kidnap me. Maybe they didn't realize who I was at the time."

Sirus's wife stood up, even though her husband was pulling on her arm, trying to get her to sit back down. "What have you told the Council?" she asked. "You know we have to appeal to the Council before we take action."

Yaro responded, "We have not been able to contact them because of the EMP that destroyed our communications devices last week. Most of the electronic equipment that wasn't in Michelina's Faraday cage was fried. We can only contact Bandonderry through the hardline, and I don't think we have called them yet. But we will. Fargus and I probably need to go to the council to make our case. I'm not optimistic they will help."

Sirus said, "That's an understatement." His wife gave him a drop-dead glare and sat down with her arms crossed and face red.

Sabas stood up and said, "While you and Fargus make a trip to the council, I can get the militia ready. But, what should we do? You know how fortified the city is. They've got the Sogmols on the bottom level in the Vauller. The ground outside around the city has motion sensors. At the top of the mountain, they've got sogs watching over their precious Disibodenberg. We can't exactly stroll in and start shooting."

"What about the glass that keeps the city cool," asked Chester, a red-haired teenager with a patch of freckles across his nose and cheek sitting next to Jutta. "Can we put a bomb or something to destroy it?"

"Nah," Sabas said. "Structurally, it's too sound, and we don't have the supplies to make the kind of bomb it would take to destroy it. Even if we did, we couldn't control it well enough to protect the innocents inside."

"They're not innocent if they're inside Volmar," Sirus insisted.

Yaro spoke up, "The Vaipwo, for the most part, are innocent. They really don't know what's going on. Very few of them sense that anything is wrong. Those who do just drown their doubts in constant entertainment. "

"Jutta must have known something was wrong," Chester said. "Why else would he volunteer for the refreshing? Why did you volunteer for the refreshing?" Chester asked.

The whole town turned to Jutta and waited for an answer. Jutta stood up slowly and looked at Odilia as if he was seeking moral support. She was sitting next to Sabas, who put his arm around her and pulled her close.

He almost said, "Bless the Avogo," which was customary in Volmar before addressing a large group like this. But instead, he said nervously, "I volunteered because, I don't know, I guess I was just not interested in anything there anymore. I felt...alone there. I mean, I had a lot of friends. My group unit was great; just ask Yaro. He knows most of them. But something inside just didn't feel right. I didn't know what it was. But, I think I'm starting to see. Um. I just felt like deep down inside, there had to be more to life than just the Volmar games and all that."

Many people were nodding as if they understood. He felt a sense of guilt rising up in him all of a sudden. "Look," he said, "I don't want to be any more trouble. If they offer to trade for me, just do it. I'll go. I don't mind."

"Nonsense." It was Bettrily, the little old lady. Jutta had not noticed her sitting behind him. "You'll help us. Father Rawley told me about you. You'll help us."

No one in the crowd seemed ready to argue with the lady, not even Sirus, who just a minute earlier had nearly demanded they make the trade.

"Go on now, Jutta," Bettrily said. "Tell us more about why you chose the refreshing."

Jutta nodded and turned back around to face Yaro. "Well, one time, I was working on a program for the COGOPT—that's what we call the Controller General of Prescriptive Thought. It was a program to help people who had headaches. I'm a Sasjovian, as you know. That means I get a bit more access to information than other people. One day, I was allowed into the library in Disibodenberg for a short time. I had never really seen books before. That was my first time. Anyway, I read something that the King of Kandy—um, that's Volspat—wanted me to look at. When I was done, I found out I was still alone. I thought no one was watching, so I peeked into one book, and it said the same thing that I heard you all read yesterday. Something about people doing wickedness and not even regretting anything. I remember it saying, 'A horse rushing into battle.' That phrase stuck with me. I don't know why. I just... I don't know."

"This is a sign!" Chester said. "What Father Rawley said is true. Jutta can do it. He can write the program. He will be our horse rushing into battle!"

Yaro smiled and held up his hand. "Just to clarify, the meaning of the 'horse dashing into battle' is that a horse doesn't know what it's getting itself into...the rider does. It's the horse's job to be obedient. It must take its cue from its master. Likewise, we must pray for guidance. But I have to admit, this does seem to be a good sign."

The crowd started murmuring excitedly. Jutta saw many of them glancing at him hopefully. The hopes and expectations of others are frequently the greatest burdens of life. Jutta had never felt such a heavy burden placed upon him. He saw that Odilia and Sabas were talking intently, and he sank back heavily into his seat. Chester patted him on the back.

After a moment, one girl in her early twenties stood up and asked, "So, what kind of program is Jutta expected to write? What is it? I mean, how would it work?"

Yaro spoke falteringly, as if he didn't really want to get into the topic. "Yeah. Okay. So...as everyone knows, if you want to move into Volmar, you have to agree to the implant so that programs can be installed directly into your brain. For citizens, it's really a quick way to say, learn a new language or calculus. I dare say that our friend Jutta here can speak three languages and do advanced calculus. Am I right, Jutta?"

Jutta shrugged awkwardly as if to say, "Can't everyone?"

"He's a Sasjovian. Selected early on for his aptitude and given a good deal more programs than are given to the average

Vaipwo...who really don't need anything but a strong capacity to fool around. I made a pretty good Vaipwo," Yaro said with his self-deprecating humor. "But uh, what few people realize is that the Avogo also have a portal in their brains as well. It's part of their secret to eternal life."

"Indefinite life," Sirus corrected.

"Yes. Indefinite life," Yaro said. "Father Rawley's theory was that a program, a virus, I suppose you might say, could be written to cause the Avogo to essentially have a heart again. It would, in Father's mind, revive the consciences that the King of Kandy and his cohort had numbed over the years. He thought that if their consciences were reawakened, they would stop what they were doing, and there would be a boon to humanity."

"A virus that makes people repent," Sabas said somewhat incredulously. "If Jutta can do it, more power to him. But it's urgent that we get our militia together and do our best to take them down. If we don't win, it'll be better than living like this."

Odilia stood up to speak. "Father Rawley believed that if we fought a traditional war, the result would not be good, even if we won. Let's say we actually kill the King of Kandy and his evil trio. What would happen? It's likely that we'd destroy much of the city and many of the people in the process. The survivors would have a really hard time adjusting to life like we live."

"And I always said," Sabas interrupted, "that we could take over their city and manage it. We could tell them all the truth and run the city as well as the Avogo did."

Odilia sat back down in her seat and turned her face away from Sabas.

"And Father Rawley said that the people would resent us," Yaro said. "They would never come around like they would if they saw their blessed Avogo 'repent' as you say."

It was clear from Yaro's tone that he didn't want to continue the debate.

"I think we should keep all options on the table," Yaro concluded. "We should, like always, pray and work for peace but be prepared for war. Sabas, get our militia activated and ready while Fargus and I make our case to the Council. Chester, get with Michelina and Jutta. And take Chaney, too. Get Jutta anything he needs. Computer parts, whatever he needs. If we don't have it, get it somehow. We all have a job to do. Pray without ceasing. *Ora et Labora!*"

Yaro left the podium, and everyone started talking at once. Chester threw his arm around Jutta as if they were suddenly best friends and guided him to Michelina's office to begin plotting the virus of repentance.

Chapter 15

The Virus of Repentance

In the room, a man named Chaney introduced Jutta to the Dicarers, who would help with the virus to infect the Avogos' minds. First, there was Chester. Chaney joked that Chester loved video games and code so much that he spent nearly all of his free time sitting in front of a computer.

Then there was Michelina, a heavyset, 24-year-old woman with straight black hair and glasses. Chaney put his arm on her shoulder and said, "When Michelina was thirteen, she was already good with code. She wrote a program for the computers that control the lights and pumps in our hydroponics systems. I believe our yields increased by something like ten percent. And we saved a lot of electricity. She was thirteen!" He patted her on the back, and a young boy walked into the room. Jutta recognized the child as the one who had stood holding the carrots right after Father Rawley's murder.

"Mommy," the boy ran up to Michelina.

She gave him a kiss and urged him to go with a lady who was standing outside the door. "Mommy's busy now, sweetie. You go with auntie Meriod, and I'll see you soon." When the boy left, Michelina wiped a tear from her eye and said, "Glad you're here, Jutta. I can't wait to find out how to make those bastards repent."

Next, Chaney introduced himself. The wiry man with long thinning hair and uneven patches of facial hair appeared to Jutta to be in his forties. His voice was kind and gentle, but it still carried authority somehow.

"I know nothing about computers or programming. My expertise is more in spiritual matters, I suppose. When I came to Mainz twenty years ago from Bandonderry, I had been seeking a meaningful life of the spirit. I thought about going to Volmar, but I just couldn't agree to the implant, and the thought of someone telling me what I could or couldn't read wasn't going to happen, you know? So I came to Mainz, where I heard that freedom of thought was still valued.

"In Mainz, I found the perfect environment. I could meditate as much as I wanted. Of course, I had to work really hard with my hands. But I was not distracted by a constant barrage of sensual input. I spend most of my mornings reading, attending Mass, and writing...all of which would have been impossible in Volmar. God isn't known there. I spend my afternoons and evenings growing food and fixing anything that is broken. So I guess the reason I'm here is that Yaro thought you might need some spiritual guidance in addition to technical expertise. After all, we are trying to find a way to get people to repent, right?"

Jutta nodded, and it seemed to him that Chaney might finally be through with the introductions. He greeted them all with a curt "Hello, everyone" as he scanned the room at the outdated equipment that he was expected to work with. Wires were strung from one computer to another. In one corner, piles of wires seemingly going nowhere resembled a bird's nest. It was a far cry from the streamlined wireless system used at Volmar. Jutta learned that Michelina did most of the work to keep it all running. She could fix a computer as quickly as Chaney could repair a broken door or a leaking tank.

Jutta and the others gathered into a circle and sat on rickety office chairs. There was a moment of awkward silence as if no one knew where to begin. The computer fans whirred, making it hard for Jutta to concentrate on the task they had at hand.

Chester finally started the conversation. "So, anybody got any ideas where to start?" Everyone looked at Jutta, but he didn't say anything.

Michelina offered an idea. "I think first we have to just consider the situation and see what we have to work with and what is possible. Maybe work our way backwards. For instance, let's assume we are able to write the virus of repentance. I guess that's what we'll call it. How can we deliver it to the Avogo? How could we get it to them and have them install it?"

"Yes. That's a good place to start," Chester agreed. "I don't know much about Volmar. Maybe Jutta will have some ideas. Jutta?" Jutta, who seemed to still be assessing the computer room, felt the weight of their expectations might be too much.

Chaney enjoined. "That's a tough one. They don't share their secrets too much. We do know they have ports like everyone else in Volmar. If we could figure out a way to get to them and insert the virus into their ports...maybe Sabas's group could just focus on capturing Disibodenberg instead of attacking Volmar. We just go straight to the leaders and skip the city itself. Then tie down the Avogo and force it on them?"

"Okay," Michelina said. "So if we are able to capture Disibodenberg, and if we are able to subdue the Avogo without killing them, how do we install the virus, and what does it do?"

Jutta's palms began to get sweaty, and he stood up, turning his back to the others, pretending to survey the equipment in the room. The others appeared to notice his discomfort and were silent for a moment.

"What's the matter, Jutta?" asked Chaney.

Jutta still did not reply but paced around the room, running his hands along the old computers and monitors. There was a broken tactile VR device that must have been fifty years old. He picked it up carefully and asked, "Does this thing still work?"

"It's missing a chip," Michelina said.

"This was the basis for the pleasure crafts in Volmar," Jutta said. "A real antique. I don't think I've ever seen one with my own eyes, or computers this old. I'm surprised any of it still works, especially down here, in the caves."

"We keep the moisture levels steady and guard the temperature quite well," she said.

"What's the matter, Jutta?" Chaney repeated. "Are you worried about something?"

"I... um. I guess I don't know. This is hard, you know. I was born and raised in Volmar. I grew up believing everything they taught me. Only a couple days ago, I was still there about to get refreshed and expecting to come back to life in a different body. Now, suddenly, I'm in a different world, still me, same old Jutta, but with a totally different life. It's just hard to take in. That's all. Now you're asking me to write a program to infect the ones we used to worship. I guess it's not that easy to turn against something you've believed all your life."

"Of course, Jutta. It's not easy at all. 'Had we but world enough and time,'" Chaney said. "But we have some time. Sit and tell me your doubts."

Chester and Michelina exchanged disappointing glances. They obviously were ready to get started programming.

Jutta sat down and, after a moment, spoke. "It's just, the Avogo are my—or were— my protectors. You see? I thought they gave me life. And now, I'm supposed to turn on them, just like that?"

"Tell me, Jutta, does your arm still hurt?" Chaney asked.

Jutta stared at his arm and touched the bandage covering the mangled skin that Redhing had left.

"Yes."

"That pain in your arm should be evidence for you. They were going to kill you. But more seriously, they were killing your spirit. Did they encourage you to read? Or did they keep books locked away from you?”

“I could read anything I wanted.”

“But you were a Sasjovian. And you could read only what they made available to you. You said yourself you got in trouble for reading part of the Bible. Have you seen our library yet?”

“You mean, you have books? Real books?” Jutta asked somewhat excitedly.

“Of course,” Chaney said. “Michelina, shall we show him?”

Michelina and Chester both shrugged.

Michelina wheeled her chair over to her desk, where she got a key that she used to unlock a safe hidden in the wall. Inside that safe was another key. Then, she opened a secret panel behind a shelf full of old hardware and pushed the door open.

Michelina stood back and let Chaney and Jutta go into the library alone.

Chaney said, “We keep everything in this room on multiple backups, but these originals are precious. They have helped combat the rewriting of history. When everything is digital, all it takes is a quick ‘search and replace’ and our history is changed. Plus, there’s just something special about being able to read an actual book. Of course, we don’t use them often. They’re for security, but everyone in Mainz has a digital copy and has access to all these books from the Bible to the Quran to the Sutras, the Bhagavad Gita. There’s all the great classic literature from thousands of years ago. Works by T.S. Elliot, Shakespeare, Chaucer, Bradbury, Tolkien, Chesterton, Moore, the Sufis...right on up to the cataclysm. And still, some pretty good work, I think, from more modern-day writers, like our own Father Rawley.”

Jutta pulled one off the shelf and held it carefully. “*The Catcher in the Rye*?” he asked, and he skimmed over a few pages.

“Salinger,” Chaney said. “Yes. Interesting novel.”

“Some of this is hard to follow,” Jutta said after skimming a page or two. "English certainly has changed."

"Languages change or die. We have phrases that a person in the 1900s or early 2000s wouldn't recognize. And they had terms that we hardly recognize anymore. For instance, the words for mother and father used to be really positive. But, as you know, in Volmar, those words and even the term family is prohibited. That's why you use 'tribe' or 'group unit.' But here, we still say family and mother and father."

"I see," Jutta said, placing the volume back on the shelf and looking around the room in awe.

"Want to see some really tough English?" Chaney asked as he pulled out a thick book. "Try Shakespeare." Chaney let the volume drop loudly onto the table. He opened it and casually flipped through the pages. "It's good stuff but hard to understand. Hard to believe sometimes that it's even English. Go back another couple hundred years from Shakespeare to Chaucer, and you'll understand even less. Then, go back another few hundred years to 'Dream of the Rood,' and you won't understand a thing."

"Dream of the Rood?" Jutta asked.

"Probably the oldest poem in the English language. It's about a vision that a guy had of the cross. You know, like the one you see hanging in our chapel?"

"You mean, with the dead man hanging on it?" Jutta asked.

"Yes. Well. That's before he was resurrected. Anyway, in the 'Dream of the Rood,' the cross comes alive and speaks to the author. It tells how the cross itself had suffered along with Christ."

Jutta wanted to ask who Christ was, but instead, he asked, "Resurrected means, like refreshing?"

"Yeah, sort of," Chaney replied. "Only you don't get a new body. The old one is raised again and made new, glorified we say."

"So I'm stuck with this one? I thought I'd be a girl by now," Jutta said disappointedly. "So do people resurrect each other? Your science would have to be pretty advanced to do that."

"No. It's not science. It's God."

Michelina, who still stood in the doorway of the library, asked, "Can we just talk about the virus and deal with the philosophical issues later?"

"I think this is important," Chaney said. "Obviously, this is why Yaro wanted me here. You know I'm useless with computers. Please. Just indulge me a bit here."

Michelina threw up her hands and said to Chester, "Let's talk by ourselves while these two figure out the meaning of life." Then she and Chester sat at a table.

Chaney turned back to Jutta, who asked, "And what is God?"

"God is the beginning and the end, the entity that created us...you, me, the world, the stars, the universe, the Avogo. Everything."

"Where is it?"

"Where is what?"

"The entity. The God. Where is it?"

"Well. He is outside space and time. He spoke, and suddenly, there was a huge explosion, and everything, all that exists, came into being. Then, he sent part of himself into space and time to arrange things. He arranged them perfectly, and he made the Earth spin around the sun, etc. Most of this can be found in the book of Genesis in the Bible. You're welcome to read it yourself and see if it makes sense to you. Anyway, he created people, and they were very happy. They walked and talked with Him face to face. But then something happened. God had made a rule. He said that they could eat of any tree in the garden where they were living except for one tree. Do you know what that tree was, Jutta?"

Jutta shrugged his shoulders and said, "Lemon?"

"No," Chaney laughed. "But good guess. It was the tree of knowledge."

"Wait. Knowledge grows on a tree?"

* * *

Chaney gawked at him incredulously. "It doesn't grow on trees. It's just a metaphor. You know, figurative language?"

Jutta nodded as if he understood, but Chaney apparently could tell Jutta was not following.

He sat down and said, "Figurative language is just a way of explaining something that's difficult to understand, usually by making a comparison. Anyway, it wasn't just the tree of any old knowledge; it was the tree of the knowledge of good and evil. We were not supposed to eat of that tree."

"Why not?"

"Well, the serpent said it was because we would be like God, knowing the difference between good and evil. I've often wondered if the serpent was lying there or telling the truth. When evil tells the truth, it is for evil purposes, often truth that should not be shared at that time. Sort of like, let's say a person is hiding from an enemy, and the enemy asks one prisoner if the person is hiding in that hut over there and the prisoner doesn't like the person who is hiding, so he says, 'Yes.' It is the truth spoken with evil intent. And you'll see, Jutta, it's the intention that is important...yet so unimportant."

"I'm confused."

"It's okay. I'm not finished. You'll be more confused soon."

Jutta flipped through the pages of Shakespeare, wondering whether this man, Chaney, had gone crazy. He was, after all, in his forties. Maybe refreshing people in their 40s was the right idea, after all. The Avogo may have had a good reason for it. Maybe old people had really lost all their usefulness, like a piece of tape that had already been used and could no longer stick to anything.

"Don't worry, Jutta. I am not crazy. You'll see. Bear with me a while longer. Where was I? Oh. The serpent said that if we eat of the tree that God told us not to eat, we would be like God, knowing good and evil. Well, we did. We ate of it. In other words, when we say we ate of the tree, it really means that we did it. We reaped the rewards of an action. We started to distinguish between good and evil. You see, as soon as we ate of that tree, our eyes were opened, and we realized one thing."

"What?" Jutta asked, gazing back into his eyes.

"That we had been evil at times." Jutta turned away, thinking of Father Rawley's death. "We realized that we had done evil. We put clothes on and hid from God. Why would we do that if we had not suddenly become aware of our nakedness? Before, we were naked in front of God. We had great closeness with God. We did not hide from him. But then, after we 'ate of that tree,'" he said using air quotes, "God came searching for us and could not find us. We were hiding from him, because we realized that we were naked, and we were embarrassed."

Michelina must have overheard this last bit and interjected from outside, "There's always room for interpretation, Jutta."

"It's the version that makes sense to me," Chaney continued. "Maybe it's not straight from the Catechism, but it makes sense to me."

"Okay," Jutta said. "So we realized we were evil, and we hid from God. What happened then?"

"Well, the rest of human history is really all about God trying to get us to stop hiding from him."

"Why do we hide from him? Is he cruel?"

"No. That's the funny thing. The message is that he loves us. You know what the cross means? That God came back down to get us to stop from hiding...you know we do a lot of really bad things when we are hiding from God's presence. The further away from God we get, the worse our actions are, even when they are well-intentioned. That's what I meant earlier. But we hide from God because we think we know better, or we are attracted by things of this world, like lust and drunkenness, etc. And when we are hiding from him, anything we do basically ends up being harmful. It rots. It's sort of like cleaning a floor with a dirty mop. Or wiping a table with a dirty wet rag. We make things worse despite our good intentions. So the cross reminds us that God came down to say that he loved us and wanted to be with us and wanted us to stop hurting each other and to live with him and stop hiding from him. The people who were alive in those days didn't believe him. They wanted him dead, so they killed him."

"That's stupid. Why would they kill God?" Jutta asked. "He created everything. He couldn't really die, could he?"

"He did. His soul separated from His body, joined the souls waiting for a savior in the Land of the Dead. Then, he was resurrected. He came back to life, then went back to heaven."

"But why did he go back to heaven? Why didn't he stay here to help us?"

"He did, in the form of other people. At that time, they were called apostles. They were given authority, and now they are called priests. That's what Father Rawley was. He was a priest. That's why, as you can imagine, it was such a tragedy for all of us. To lose a priest is a difficult thing, especially in this time when there are so few. Of course, we can all still talk directly to God. He hears our prayers."

"I never heard this story before. I don't know what to make of it. It seems like good news, but yet it is so sad. The world is still messed up, even after God did that. Do you think the Avogo know this story?"

"Of course. They heard it. They're old enough to remember a time when the story was told over and over at churches everywhere. But they don't like it. Their hearts are very hard. I really don't know what could possibly make them change. Only a deep experience of God, I suspect."

Michelina piped up again before Chaney had a chance to start. "That's a nice segue into talking about the virus and how this is all going to work."

"Right," Chester said. "We decided that if we can actually write a virus, we needed to figure out a way to insert it. I was thinking we might...well, Jutta, do you know if the ports in the Avogo are the same as the ones in the Vaipwo?"

***

The group left the library and returned to the computer room. Jutta ignored Chester's question as he was lost in thought. The others went on talking loudly, but he massaged his arm and looked around the room. As he did, his eyes fell on something that looked very familiar, a flat, white object that appeared to be a PASbot. He inched closer to find that it was not just any old PASbot; it was his own Redhing.

Jutta could almost hear it hissing at him. He remembered the voice Redhing had used in the safe hole, "I am your PASbot. I am here for your protection..." He took a step back and stared at the lifeless bot from a safe distance. The voices of the others were just background noise to him when he raised his hand to silence them. He stepped forward and picked up the bot very carefully with his thumb and index finger, handling it as if it were a dangerous insect that might bite him. He turned to the group and, holding Redhing at arm's length, said, "I think I have an idea."

Chapter 16

In the Cleft of the Rock

Godlip (Gangry) awoke to water being splashed into his face. As he tried to turn away from the water, his head felt like it had been pounded in by a steel hammer. Instinctively, he grabbed the back of his head and felt the bump apparently left by the rock he'd landed on. After a moment, he heard the noise of some sort of electric motor. He saw that it was one of the Dicarer's boxbots, scooting away from him and digging itself back into the sand.

The Sogmols knew about the boxbots and the safeholds of the Dicarers, but since they were both fairly harmless, they seldom destroyed them except for fun.

Sitting up slowly made him feel dizzy, but he was aware enough to realize that he had fallen into a small crevasse that would be no problem getting out of if he were feeling normal. But he was feeling anything but normal.

As he lay there trying to recuperate, he heard the sound of traversers coming from a distance and getting louder. Soon, the familiar voices of those he used to command were clear. Volspat was searching for him. But somehow, he could not hear Volspat's voice anymore. Godlip lay back down where he was and rolled under a rock cleft to hide as much as he possibly could. He felt a stabbing pain in the back of his head below his ear and realized that there was a bandage covering a wound. *The bot,* he thought to himself. *Why can't I hear Volspat?*

The traversers stopped not far from him, and the voices became quite clear. The Sogmol search party was standing nearby, apparently peering over a steep cliff.

"There!" Someone shouted. "He's down there. There's his traverser, can you see it?" Godlip recognized many of the voices that shouted that they saw it. There were probably ten or twelve in the search party.

"Let's go down and get him," one voice said.

The Sogmols searched for an easy place to descend the cliff, but it was apparent that the job would not be too easy. There was no obvious place to descend.

"Look, there's blood. I see blood. Gangry is dead." Others saw the blood as well, though they could not see a body.

A short scrawny Sogmol with a long beard and vacant eyes jumped down into the crevasse where Godlip was hiding. Godlip could see the boots of the Sogmol and could have reached out from under the rock and touched them, but just then Volspat called over the radio.

"His tracking device is down there with the traverser and not moving. I think we can be quite confident that Gangry is dead. See what happens when you don't listen to me? Gangry disobeyed. Leave the traverser there. Let his body rot. Return to the Vauller. Looks like I need to select the new Grand Comrade from among you."

The boots disappeared, and Godlip heard the traversers fading off into the distance back towards the beautiful city of Volmar.

When he was sure they were gone, Godlip slid slowly out from under the rock and sat up carefully, taking in his surroundings. The crevasse was only a few feet deep, and the rock had provided the perfect hiding place for him. The sun was beating down, and he realized that he was parched. But he also realized that any water and food he had was down in the traverser. Traversers were always stocked with water and food rations in case the Sogmols were ever stuck out overnight.

He slowly stood up and scanned the area to make sure no one

was watching. Then, he stepped out of the crevasse, and only a few feet away, peered down over the cliff. It must have been more than a hundred feet down, a sheer drop with very little, if any, place to grab onto. If he had fallen alongside the traverser, he would certainly have been killed. But now, he was not only alive but also given the gift of death. No one would be searching for him. Obviously, he couldn't go back to Volmar. There was no chance of that. But there were other towns around, other places that might take him.

He saw no way to climb down to his traverser. With no water, Godlip could not last long, a couple of days at most. And he had no way to travel, only his two feet... and one was missing a boot. He searched the ground to see if he could find what had happened to the shoe, but there were no signs of it. Finally, he stared down into the ravine where the traverser lay, and he thought he could make out an image of a boot about three feet away from the vehicle. "Great. Everything I need is down there," he said.

As he stared at the wreckage, he noticed a trail of blood leading away from the crash site. An animal must have been hit but crawled off somewhere to die. Godlip wiped the sweat from his face and eyes but still couldn't see clearly what it was. His sight was blurry. He felt the bandage on his neck again, wondering where it could have come from. He swaggered a bit and decided there wasn't much else to do but crawl back down into the crevasse and hide under the rock until nightfall. Maybe around sunset, it would be cool enough to crawl down to the traverser, but right now, the rocks on the cliff would burn his hands if he tried it.

Godlip lay back down under the rock cleft, and the cool shaded area helped to calm his throbbing head. Based on the direction he had taken when he fled Volmar, the closest town would be the one where he had just killed their priest. He would certainly want to avoid Mainz, of all places. In fact, he thought that he would rather go back to Volmar to be executed than face the people of Mainz.

He grew agitated, and his thoughts went cloudy. His head throbbed, and he couldn't keep himself awake. He felt so tired, and everything was so confusing that he decided to let himself succumb to sleep.

As he faded out, he heard the motor of the boxbot humming and could tell it was approaching. Godlip lacked the strength to kick it away, and his eyes seemed to glue themselves shut. In just a moment, the noise from the bot faded, and Godlip was fast asleep.

Chapter 17

The Language of Love

Sabas was recruiting new volunteers for his militia when the message arrived. A young girl with large spectacles delivered it into his hands just as he was trying to persuade a mother to let her fourteen-year-old boy fight for the cause. He took the message absentmindedly because he was so passionately imploring a heavyset woman who would not be moved. She crossed her arms—standing in the doorway of her apartment—and stared at him intently, knowing full well that there was no way on earth or in hell that she would allow her son to join the militia.

"I'd sooner join myself," she said.

"That will work," Sabas said, desperate to recruit anyone. "We'll meet in the morning in the courtyard. Bring Cal, too."

She turned away without uncrossing her arms and shut the door behind her. Sabas was left holding the note that the young girl had given him. He glanced at it but didn't think it urgent. All it said was, "Message received from boxbot 12, please check receiver."

He had seen many of these messages before. Some were false alarms. One time, he received a picture of a dead pronghorn that a boxbot had mistaken for a human. Often, the messages simply indicated that a bot was in need of repair or its storage tank had run out of potable water. So, the message slipped low on his list of priorities, and when he saw Odilia coming towards him, he crammed the paper in his pant pocket and forgot about it.

Odilia and Sabas had grown up together. He was two years older and had known that he loved her when he was in fifth grade. Even as early as the age of eight, during Mass, he would dream about what life would be like if everyone else vanished from the earth, and he and Odilia were the only two people left in the world. He dreamed how he would take care of her in his own place. He could raise tilapia and vegetables and hunt, and they would build a life together. But as they grew older, in his early teens, he teased her like they were brother and sister. He often did mean things to her. He alone knew that he had done them out of immaturity, unable to show love. Finally, when he was eighteen, he had matured enough to start trying to win her over appropriately.

Now, at age twenty, he kept trying to decide how best to propose to her, even though deep in his heart, he felt a doubt that she could love him. In his pocket next to the note was also a small ring that he had been keeping for over a month now, waiting for the right opportunity. But with all that had happened recently, he didn't know when that chance might come. He assumed it was a long time off.

Mainz was a small settlement of 800. It had grown at one time to over 1,000, but the population generally hovered at 800. The resources could not sustain much more than that, so the options for romantic interests were severely limited. There were only three girls the same age as Sabas, and none of them had held his interest for long. Odilia was his first love. Most people in town assumed that the two would be married. Much of the gossip revolved around the pair.

"How many did you get?" Sabas asked.

"Two," Odilia said as she walked up to him with slumped shoulders and the edges of her mouth turned down.

Sabas kissed her cheek, but she turned away.

"Hey," Sabas said. "Don't worry. We'll get through this. We'll find a way. Yaro's gone to the Council. They'll help, too."

Odilia snorted.

"What? You don't think the council will do anything?" Sabas asked.

But Odilia said nothing. She just stared blankly at the ground with watery eyes.

"All in all, we have eighty people already," he said. "We have a chance. It's time the King of Kandy pays for what he's been doing. Look at me," he said, pulling on her chin to guide her eyes to his. "It's going to be all right. I'll make sure of it." Then he kissed her on the lips.

Odilia wiped her eyes and worked her way out of his embrace.

"It's going to be okay. Are you worried about me?" Sabas asked.

"I just miss Father Rawley. Why did he have to die?" she asked.

"I don't know," he said, sounding defeated. "Why does anything have to happen? Life is a series of minor troubles and difficulties interrupted by major disasters."

***

Odilia groaned. Sabas had a dark side that appeared out of nowhere from time to time. She herself was optimistic most of the time. But Sabas could bring her down with just a few words. She had already been crying. She did not want to hear him talk about major disasters.

"I gotta go. I'm tired," she said. "I'll see you in the morning at the courtyard."

"Odilia, wait." He held her hand and would not let her retrieve it.

After an awkward moment of silence, he let go of her hand and kissed her cheek. "I love you. I will take care of this."

She managed a nod and returned a peck on the cheek.

Odilia thought she would head back home, but as she walked, she felt an urge to pray. She changed course and headed to the chapel. After she entered, the quietness and stillness engulfed her, and she began to weep when she genuflected towards the altar. A red candle flickered in the front, and two old ladies were in separate pews, praying silently.

She knelt, uninterested in praying the Rosary but not knowing where to begin her prayers. Normally, she began with "Thank you God for..." but she felt nothing to be thankful for, except for one thing she felt she probably should not be thankful for, at least, not in the way she was thankful. But the words still came. "Thank you for bringing us Jutta, God. Thank you for Jutta."

As she continued to pray, her eyes fell, for the first time, upon the long rectangular box at the front of the church. She recognized it immediately as the coffin with her blessed father inside. The casket was closed, and Odilia could not bring herself to move near it. Her prayers were interrupted, and the mood was lost. She couldn't stand to be there anymore. Overwhelmed with grief, she could not bear to be alone. She left the chapel hastily.

On her way to her room, she passed Michelina's office, where Jutta and the others were still awake and working on the virus of repentance. She paused outside the door a moment, just to listen. But then she saw Jutta standing there holding the PASbot that he had torn off of his arm, examining it as if he were a kid studying a tooth that had just come out.

Chester noticed her standing in the doorway and invited her in. "Come in, Odilia," he said. "Jutta was just about to tell us about his idea for the virus. Who would have thought that making your enemies repent would be the best revenge?"

Odilia hesitated but entered. "Have a seat," Chester said, pulling up a chair for her.

She refused to sit. "I was just passing by. Sabas and I have got about eighty commitments for the militia. He will get them ready for the mission in the morning. How is everything going here?" she asked, glancing at Chaney.

"How about you answer that, Jutta?" Chaney said.

Jutta nodded at Odilia and said, "So the virus could be sent through my old PASbot. We could infect it and then turn it loose near Volmar so that it can be discovered. Then, the Sasjovian who retrieves it and starts to process it would find something odd and send it up to the Avogo. That's how we could get the virus delivered to them."

"Cool!" Odilia said.

"So, we've got a virus carrier," Michelina said. "Now we just need to figure out how it's going to work. What language do we use for the virus?"

Odilia stared at Jutta almost unwillingly. She heard an answer in her mind to the question, but she dared not say it in front of them. She kept quiet. Jutta returned her gaze, and she found herself unable to take her eyes away from him.

A little voice inside her head kept saying, *Sabas. Get back to Sabas*, but she had no resolve. "What language?" Michelina asked again.

The voice inside Odilia's head said, "Love."

Chapter 18

Sabas

After speaking with Odilia, Sabas had gone back to his room to rest. It was getting late, and most of Mainz had settled in for the night. There was not much more that he could do in terms of recruiting, so he lay down on his bed, and he began to reflect on his life and the loss of Father Rawley.

He hated the poverty of Mainz and felt that he and the others deserved so much more. He had never felt as if he belonged in Mainz. When he started dating Odilia, he felt better. She had a calming effect on him and made him feel like he was a part of things. And now that others were counting on him, he felt a duty to his people. Since Abaidus and Father Rawley were now dead, people seemed to be counting on Sabas as their protector, and to Yaro and Fargus for spiritual guidance.

He lay on the small mattress that took up the corner of his room, staring up at the ceiling. The room was sparsely decorated. A desk, some weights that he lifted to keep in shape, a punching bag he had made from leftover corn husks. He thought about how long it had taken him to gather enough husks and to get the cloth to use to hold it all together, and he felt the old familiar feeling of being abandoned creep back up into him.

His mother had dumped him off in Mainz when he was just a young boy. He lived most of his life not knowing why his parents had left him there. In grade school, some kid had started a rumor that his parents ran off to join CHAI. But when Father Rawley saw him crying one day, he told Sabas the truth. His father had died from liver disease, and his mother was too weakened by poverty to take care of him. He had one older brother somewhere, but Father didn't know where he was. Sabas's mother left Sabas at Mainz and promised to return, but she never came back.

The more he studied his room, the more he cursed his situation. "If it weren't for Odilia, I could just leave," he said to himself. "Go see the world. Stop at Volmar. At least there, I could eat anything I want." He thought about how he could live at Volmar. He could take showers anytime, play games, and of course, he could mess around whenever he wanted. What little attention he got from Odilia was not enough.

He stood up to wash his face and brush his teeth. Then, he emptied his pockets on his desk. There was the ring he had been holding on to. He examined it, a simple band of gold that had no diamonds. It was too bland for her, and he felt ashamed by it. But jewelry was hard to come by, especially for a young man who wanted to shop in secret so as not to spoil the surprise. Mainz was so small, and he knew people would talk. He had searched for months for any ring that might be available. An elderly lady had passed away a month earlier, and her husband gave the ring to Sabas. If it had been expensive, something with huge diamonds in it, Sabas would have asked Odilia to marry him by now.

He put the ring down and picked up the note and read it again. "Message received from boxbot 12, please check receiver." He tossed it on the desk along with his keys and a few pieces of string he had found on the ground earlier.

I'll check it tomorrow, he thought as he turned off the light. But even before he lay down, he realized he would not be able to sleep if he didn't check the receiver. He punched his bed, got up, put on his trousers, grabbed his keys, and walked towards Michelina's office, where the receiver was.

Sabas was already tired and cranky. He had wanted to hold Odilia, but she had said she was tired. He assumed that she had gone back to her room, so when he entered the office and found her talking with Jutta, he could hardly contain his hurt. Odilia opened her mouth and her eyes widened, making it seem like she had been caught stealing. Sabas stared at her quizzically and then glanced at Jutta, who would not return his gaze.

Chaney must have sensed the tension and spoke up. "Hey, Sabas. How are you? Odilia told us the recruiting is a bit slow, but eighty is not bad. You know the story about Gideon, right?"

"I'm just here to check the receiver," Sabas said rudely. "Don't really need a Bible lesson right now. I got a message earlier from boxbot 12. Probably malfunctioning again. Don't let me interrupt your fun," he said.

The room fell awkwardly silent while he checked the message. When the readout was printed, Sabas scanned it and said, "Holy crap!"

"What?" Odilia asked, coming to his side.

He held up a picture for everyone to see. "Is that who I think it is?" Sabas asked the others.

"That's the..." Chester said. "That's the guy who killed Father Rawley."

They passed the image around. "Looks like him," Michelina said. Chaney agreed. Finally, it went to Jutta.

"Yes. That's him. That's Gangry."

"Can anybody tell me what he's doing hiding out under a rock six miles south of us?"

"Is he alone?" Jutta asked.

Sabas apparently forgot about his anger in light of this new, more urgent issue. "I didn't get any information about anyone else out there. Normally, that would be in the report if they were with someone else."

Michelina piped up. "Let's scan the area through the bot. Which boxbot was it? Twelve, you say?"

"Twelve, yes." Sabas answered.

They all gathered around the back of Michelina's chair as she searched for the bot and attempted to manually control it.

"Are you sure this is a good idea?" Odilia asked. "What if it is in hiding and Gangry or the others discover it?"

"They already know about our bots. It's not top-secret or anything."

The bot's cameras opened up and panned the area. Michelina expertly moved the bot to the coordinates that it had sent. Sure enough, lying there in the cleft of the rock was the man who had brought terror on Mainz.

"What could he possibly be doing there?" Chaney asked.

"I don't know," Sabas said. "Look around to see if there are others."

Michelina surveyed the surroundings and found no signs of anyone else. "There are traces of blood here, but no other living person in the vicinity."

"Let's go get him," Sabas said. He didn't wait for others to agree or not. He didn't ask for a vote. He just headed for the door. "Anyone coming?" he asked as he stomped toward the door.

The five exchanged glances. Odilia was the first to jump up and follow Sabas. As soon as she did, Michelina, who was always ready for adventure, followed. Chester was close on her heels.

Chaney stared at Jutta then shrugged and said, "'St. Michael, defend us in battle.' Why don't you stay here, Jutta? We need you to keep working on this virus. You've got a good start." Jutta nodded in agreement.

* * *

As soon as Chaney shut the door, Jutta looked at Redhing, and in his mind, he could hear that horrible voice again that had come out of the now lifeless PASbot while in the safe chamber. He smelled the gas and felt the vibrations and the needles. After a moment of hesitation, he tossed the bot back into the scrap bin and said, "Screw this. I'm going." Then he ran to catch up with the others.

Chapter 19
Eve Jutta Duc

Above the city of Volmar in Disibodenberg, a young lady cried out in pain. The King of Kandy watched as the Avogo's doctors and nurses delivered the specially designed baby to replace Jutta. A nurse wiped the girl's forehead while the doctor shouted at her to push. She had been struggling for hours, but Volspat refused to give her anything to ease the pain. "Don't waste it," he had said when one of the nurses began preparing the epidural.

The young girl looked bewildered but pushed until she could bear it no longer. Finally, the doctor put his forearm on the girl's belly and leaned on her with all his weight, forcing the baby to come out. Soon, the newborn baby was heard crying, but the new mother did not see it. The child was carried away, and the young, sobbing girl was given a sedative.

Before the baby had even cried, one of the Avogo, Clauberg, broadcasted the news that Jutta's refreshing was complete. His new name was Eve, and she would be added to group unit thirteen, who had been lacking a member for quite some time. A party would be held soon to welcome Eve Jutta Duc. Volspat could see through the multitude of cameras and PASbot reports that the city suddenly grew abuzz with excitement in anticipation of the party and the handing-over ceremony.

The doctor examined the baby. He drew in a breath. "What is it?" Volspat asked.

"Look," the doctor said, pointing at her foot. "Lower limb reduction defect."

Volspat became visibly disgusted. He hissed, "How the hell could you miss that? Why didn't you see it in the ultrasounds?"

The doctor glared at one of the nurses, who quickly fled the room.

"Should I kill it?" the doctor asked, grabbing a pair of scissors.

The doctor placed the crying baby on a table and put the scissors at the back of the neck, ready to snip the spinal cord, but Volspat snarled, "Wait. Where else are we going to get a baby girl on short notice like this?"

The doctor withdrew the scissors. "Didn't you order a new one from the ghost?"

"No. That's just another play toy for Clauberg. We'll have to make due with this one. Just make sure she stays wrapped up during the whole ceremony. After a few months, when the excitement dies down, we'll get rid of it."

While the Vaipwo celebrated, the Avogo met in Disibodenberg. Volspat, who had been pacing back and forth, shouted, "Why did you have to announce it so early, Clauberg?"

"How was I supposed to know it had a deformity?" Clauberg said defensively. "The bitch can't even use an ultrasound, right," he said, referring to the nurse who had fled the room.

Vlospat continued. "Like I don't have enough to worry about. You know that Gangry betrayed me. Now I have to get a new Grand Comrade. And you guys let Jutta get rescued by those hypocritical Christians. What would happen if Jutta strolled up in the middle of the party, which you already announced, and presented himself to everyone? We have to find him and make sure no one ever sees him again, ever."

"Oh, calm down, Volspat," said Clauberg. "Your panties are in a bind again. You worry about nothing. Even if he's still alive, we needn't worry about him coming back. Let them have Jutta. He's harmless. Like Abaidus said, they took others. All this time, the others didn't come back. Why would Jutta be any different? Just double up on the watches a while. The Dicarers won't attack us. It's not in their religion."

"You forget we now have prisoners from Mainz. They'll come for them. Gangry turned out to be a real disappointment. This is all his fault."

"I think you had a little to do with it, didn't you, Volspat?" said Clauberg. "We could have just kidnapped Jutta secretly. But you just had to be extravagant."

"I don't have time for this crap," Volspat said. "I'm going to choose Gangry's replacement and find Jutta."

Volspat stomped out of Disibodenberg and went to his own bedroom, where he called in two Sogmols he had been eyeing for some time as possible successors to Gangry: Scullion, the one who had scanned Fr. Rawley's head, and another named Skyte.

As the two Sogmols stood before him, Volspat ogled them. Both were strong and burley, but Skyte was known to be the strongest, even stronger than Gangry. His arms were as big as most men's legs. Scullion, no runt himself, was known for his intelligence and quick thinking and had served as lieutenant to Gangry. As Volspat ran his hands across their chests, he knew who he would choose. The position required intellect, not brawn. Under other circumstances, he might have enjoyed watching them fight for this position.

"Shame," he said finally. "It could have been a big event, but Gangry's leaving screwed that up."

The two Sogmols appeared to struggle to stand still in front of him as his hands wandered around them. The old man stopped in front of Scullion and peered into his eyes. "You will be the new Grand Comrade."

"Praise the Avogo," Scullion said, his voice shaking.

"I have a pesky problem right now in Mainz. I should have wiped them out a long time ago, but you know me. I was being nice." As he said this, he caressed Scullion's cheek with his withering palm.

Scullion lowered his head, away from the lecherous eyes, and Volspat walked away.

"We will have a party in two days for the refreshing of Jutta, a young Sasjovian whose new incarnation is that of a baby girl. The one I told Gangry to get in Mainz claims to be Jutta, the original Jutta," he scoffed. "They're all crazy there, you know. They don't believe in the refreshing. It's really quite tedious having to deal with the primitives. Maybe one day, I will wipe them all out."

Volspat got lost in thought. After a moment, he continued. "Scullion, you are now Grand Comrade and Skyte is your lieutenant. You both know what to do. Find the one who claims to be Jutta. Kill him and dispose of the body. And bring me the one they call Odilia. Keep your troops here on high alert to guard the city. The Dicarers will try something."

The two bowed down to him and then headed toward the door.

"Scullion?" Volspat said.

He stopped and leaned his head toward Volspat, waiting.

"You'll be needing a comm-implant. Come. I'll take you to the medical room." Volspat put his arm around Scullion and led him to the clinic.

Chapter 20

Getting Gangry

Godlip had been lying under the cleft of that rock for several hours when he awoke to the sound of the boxbot motor whirring. He had a splitting headache and felt like he had just had surgery on his brain.

It was night, and the Earth could almost be heard cooling as he crawled out into the moonlight. He sat up a while, taking in the coolness of the night and breathing in the unfiltered air of the natural world. It was nights like these that he remembered as a boy, and as the fresh air started to revive his spirits, he recalled one of the last memories he had of his mother and father together. They had been out for a walk on a night like this. The three of them had found a place on a grassy hill and lay there barely talking, just absorbing the beauty of the stars that he now saw above him.

They are the same stars, he thought. The same yesterday as they are today. In his memory, his mom was gazing down at him, his head in her lap. He must have been four or five years old. "When your brother, or sister, is born, you'll make a good older brother, won't you?" She asked. "You'll watch out for him, right?"

It had taken him a while to realize what his mother was saying. "Wait, I'm going to have a brother?" he asked in a moment of revelation. "Really? A brother?" He sat up and stared at her with big eyes.

"Well, maybe a sister, we don't know yet," she said, laughing at his enthusiasm.

"Oh, wow! A baby brother. When will he be here?" He said, jumping up and down.

His father, who had been sitting quietly, got agitated. "Sit down and be quiet, you little," he paused. "This i'n good news. Why you wanna fill his head with things like that? We haven't even decided to have the kid."

"*You* haven't decided," his mother said.

"You already complain that I don't support the two of you. How am I supposed to feed another little twerp?"

His mom tried to bring the conversation back to the baby and asked Godlip, "What do you think we should name him? I was thinking of a few names myself. What about you?"

"How about..." Godlip was thinking.

"How about twerp two?" his father chimed in. "Twerp one and Twerp two," he said as he took a flask out of his shirt pocket and took a sip.

Coming out of his reverie, Godlip said out loud to the desert and the stars, "I'm not a twerp now!" Now he was grown and was sure that he had become tougher than his father. "I bet I've killed more than you," he said as if his father were standing in front of him. "I'm a bigger man than you! How do you like me now?" he shouted into the void. Then he broke into laughter as if what he had said was a hilarious joke. He thought of his situation. It seemed likely he would either die in the desert, get killed by Volspat, or waste away in a prison in Mainz. But all he wanted to do was yell at his dead father. "How do you like your son now?" He yelled, but the pain in his head came back and made him silent again.

His stomach growled. He stood up and squinted at the area around him. Flat desert stretched as far as the eye could see. A few feet away was a sheer drop off. At the bottom was his traverser, which probably had three days' supply of food and water, if it hadn't been spilled or ruined in the crash. Knowing he had to get down there, he began walking along the ledge, searching for an easy place to climb down.

The moon was at a height so that the cliff wall remained dark while the land around him was bright. He couldn't tell what was below, and he had no rope to climb down. After fifteen minutes of feeling his way along the embankment, he sat down and dangled his feet over the cliff wall.

A few clouds were beginning to appear overhead, and from time to time, the moon would go behind them. When it did, the Earth got dark, and he would start to think he should move on or go back to the rock where he'd been hiding. Maybe sleep the night away and wake up early in the morning to scale down the wall at first light.

He thought he heard footsteps behind him, but by the time he turned around, the clouds had already darkened the ground, and he could see nothing. The moon came back out, but he still couldn't make out anything moving. So he sat there and felt to make sure his knife was still in his pocket.

Again he heard a noise. Something was moving behind him, but he still couldn't make out anything. He thought maybe it was a wild animal, but what kind? Maybe Volspat had sent more troops after him to retrieve his body.

Frankly, he wasn't all that concerned. He resigned himself to whatever might be about to happen. If it were an animal, he could fight it. If it were Sogmols, he could probably take them, too. But he didn't have a plan for what ultimately happened, so he was caught off guard.

"Excuse me," a voice of a young woman came from out of the darkness. Godlip stood up and turned around, almost falling over backward to his death.

"Over here. Can you help me?" The young lady's voice sounded desperate for help and scared.

"Where are you?" Godlip said.

"Here, to your left."

"Who are you?"

"A citizen of Mainz who has gotten lost. I stayed out too late, and my traverser broke down. I was wandering around and heard you talking and laughing. Are you alone?" she asked.

"Yes," he said, somewhat embarrassed.

"Well?"

"Well, what?"

"Can you help me?"

Godlip thought about it a moment and decided that she might be a good bargaining chip if he were to end up going into Mainz. He could ransom her for supplies and another traverser.

He followed her voice, and as he approached, the moon came out, and he could make out her silhouette. He was taken aback, and for the first time in recent memory, he almost had to struggle to see himself taking advantage of this woman.

"What's your name," he asked, approaching her.

"Odilia. What's yours?"

He knew that name. Odilia was the one Volspat had wanted him to bring back. When he answered her, he almost said "Gangry" but caught himself.

"Godlip." The name felt strange coming off his tongue. He hadn't said it in so many years.

"Godlip?" she said incredulously. "Not Gangry?"

Before he could respond, something stung him in the back of the neck, and a net flew over his head. He struggled a moment, but soon, the world went totally dark.

Chapter 21

Freedom and Consent

Jutta woke up early the next morning and was unable to go back to sleep. He got up and wandered the tunnels of Mainz until he came to the chapel, where he heard people talking. He entered through the back doors and found an empty pew. Chaney was leading a small group of about fifteen in the liturgy of the Mass.

"Father Rawley only left a small supply of Consecrated Hosts," Chaney was saying. "Before leaving with Fargus, Yaro told me to save the hosts for adoration and times of extreme unction."

To Jutta, the mood seemed grim among the faithful there. "We don't know when we might once again be able to partake of the Eucharist."

Most of the small group of worshipers were kneeling facing the altar. Tears ran unchecked down some faces that were staring at the coffin in the front.

"I see your tears," Chaney said. "Tears for the one who had heard our confessions and absolved our sins, who had daily worked the miracle of transforming bread into the flesh of God. Now he is gone, and no one can do those things."

Jutta saw Odilia walk in through the front doors, kneel briefly at the man on the cross and then take a seat in the front. Almost as soon as she sat, everyone stood up in unison, and Chaney led them in a written prayer: "O God, who through the grace of adoption chose us to be children of light, grant, we pray, that we may not be wrapped in the darkness of error but always be seen to stand in the bright light of truth. Through our Lord Jesus Christ, your Son, who lives and reigns with you in the unity of the Holy Spirit, one God, for ever and ever."

Chester entered and stood beside Jutta, who had no idea what was going on. Chester pulled out an old book that had the words the people were saying so that Jutta could follow along:

"I confess to almighty God, and to you, my brothers and sisters, that I have greatly sinned in my thoughts and in my words, in what I have done, and in what I have failed to do; through my fault, through my fault, through my most grievous fault. Therefore, I ask blessed Mary, ever virgin, all the angels and saints, and you, my brothers and sisters, to pray for me to the Lord our God."

"That's what I'm talking about," Chester whispered. "The virus of repentance."

Jutta's eyes were tired. Capturing Gangry had taken them until 2:30 a.m., and he had slept fitfully for only a couple of hours the rest of the night. Nevertheless, Jutta kept reading that rite over and over again when the others had moved on to something else.

"I have greatly sinned…through my fault…I failed…pray for me…"

Jutta reflected that no one in Volmar ever seemed to feel bad for what they had done. They never sat around thinking of their own faults. The only "badact" (as sin was called in Volmar) was the one that went against consensus. There was no badact if everyone agreed that whatever act was being committed was, in fact, "rightact."

He thought about a friend who had joined the Volmar games. Before going, Jutta had talked with her. Her frightened eyes stared into his.

"I'm not sure, Jutta," she had said. Her PASbot had begun to light up.

"But think of what will happen if you don't go," Jutta had said. So she consented and going became rightact, and that was the last he ever saw of her.

As the daily readings were being read, Jutta began wondering how you could agree that a rightact was rightact if you didn't fully understand what the act was or you were pressured into it.

After Mass had ended, Jutta said goodbye to Chester and started the trek back to his room.

Chaney caught up with him and asked, "Everything okay, Jutta?"

Jutta shrugged and remained silent for a moment. Finally, he asked, "How do I know I agree to something if there is pressure to agree?"

Chaney said. "Good question. You have to have a well-formed conscience."

"A what?" Jutta asked.

"Well, let me back up and give you an example. In the past, before the cataclysm, abortion was very common."

"What's abortion?" Jutta asked.

"Oh. Right," Chaney said. "Remember Anna? The girl with the baby inside her?"

Jutta cringed at the memory of the shocking sight. "Yes."

"So abortion would be killing the baby while it is still in the mother."

Jutta tilted his head, disgusted. "Why would someone do that?"

"Well, sometimes babies were not wanted. People got pregnant by accident or sometimes by rape. We believe that the baby inside the womb should be protected. But many people claimed that the woman should have the right to choose whether to give birth or get rid of the fetus."

"So, Anna has a choice?"

"Well, I guess she could go to Volmar, and they'd gladly kill the baby. Anyway, in the old days, sometimes, women were pressured to have an abortion. When that happens, there's not really a free choice. For example, if a parent warned their pregnant daughter that if she didn't have an abortion, she would be on her own, was that free choice? The choice was either abort the baby or live a life without the support of your parents. Gain a baby but lose your parents. How can anyone say a woman had made a choice if society didn't do everything in its power to give her a really good alternative to abortion? Not much of a choice there. In Volmar, they do a good job of making you think you're free. Nobody judges you," he said in a mocking tone. "Be who you are, be who you want to be, you're perfect the way you are, don't let anyone say anything bad about who you are or what you identify as... and if you challenge any of these sacred ideas, the COGOPT will come for you. That's Volmarian freedom for you. When no one looks inside and sees his or her own fault, true freedom goes out the window."

"Doesn't seem right. How could focusing on our own faults make us more free?" Jutta asked.

"I think it's because in a society where everyone is willing to contemplate their own failures and realize that they are imperfect, it's less likely they will always be imposing their own will on others."

"But in Volmar, we don't impose our wills on each other."

"Don't you? What do you think Volspat is doing?"

"I used to think he was taking care of us."

"After what you've seen here these past couple of days, you don't still believe that, do you?"

"No."

"Someone once said, 'The opposite of love is not hate; it is use.' Hate is a short-lived, transitory, secondary emotion, not a primary emotion. It's like anger. Love, on the other hand, is selfless giving. It springs up spontaneously. A mother naturally loves her baby. A child naturally loves its pets and offers himself as their caretaker. When we use others to satisfy our urges, we are committing the opposite of love. And I think another word for the opposite of love is evil."

The two arrived at Jutta's room, and as they stood in the doorway, Jutta yawned. "It's a lot to take in."

"Of course. Like drinking from a fire hydrant."

Jutta narrowed his eyes and tilted his head, confused.

"Never mind. It's an archaic expression. It was a long night. I'm tired. You're tired. I'm not sure I'm even making any sense. You should get some rest. Thanks for your help with Gangry."

Before Chaney left, Jutta said, "Speaking of him, are we imposing our will on him? Isn't it evil to have him locked up in a cage there?"

"But it is likely he would have imposed his will on us, which may have been to kill us. In that case, we have the right to defend ourselves."

"I see," Jutta said.

"See you later," Chaney said.

"See you." Jutta stepped into his room, lay down on his bed, and tried to rest.

* * *

Unlike Jutta, Sabas had not slept at all. And he hadn't gone to Mass. He was too busy worrying about what to do with Gangry, and about getting the militia ready, and about Odilia acting distant.

Also, at seven a.m., when Mass was starting, he had gone to check the receiver in Michelina's office. There was a message from Volmar, as he had expected. They were offering a trade. Jutta and Odilia for the others.

Sabas crumpled the printout and went back to where they were keeping Gangry. The Grand Comrade was still sedated and securely tied down. Earlier, Sabas had examined Gangry's pockets and found a storage device. He now held it in his hands and pressed it to his heart. It had to be the scan of Father Rawley's last memories. Sabas searched for a safe place to put it, but finding none that appealed to him more than his own person, he slipped the disk into his pocket.

The murderer had carried nothing else with him. Michelina's scanners had found no tracking device that might have been on him or in him.

The bot must have gotten them all, he thought.

Looking over the rugged face of Gangry, Sabas felt there was something familiar about him, but he couldn't put his finger on it. His only encounters with Gangry had been violent, including watching him kill Fr. Rawley through the viewer. Sabas thought about torturing Gangry, but he knew Fr. Rawley would not approve. Father might have prayed over the ugly Sogmol comrade, but Sabas just wanted to punch him in the face multiple times.

He also wanted to punch Jutta a couple of times. Something about the younger kid just made him mad. Though Jutta had really done nothing to offend him—Odilia had been the one who lied to him about wanting to go to bed—Sabas felt angry every time he saw him.

"He's just a stupid, sheltered kid," he said to himself. "But I'd still like to pound his face."

Maybe he blamed Jutta for Rawley's death. That was it. That was why he hated him. But then he saw Gangry lying there and knew there was plenty of blame to go around.

"I would have killed you," he whispered to Gangry, who still slept from the injection he'd been given. "Father Rawley saved you when he locked me in that room."

As he stared at Gangry, he once again felt like he'd known that face in a past life or some distant land. For all he knew, maybe they could have been friends under other circumstances. He sat down and realized how tired he was. His eyes grew leaden, and finding no reason to stay awake, lay back in the armchair, and allowed himself rest a while.

* * *

Michelina had not slept either. She had returned to the computer room to work on a tracking chip to insert into Gangry in case he got away. She had finished preparing the chip and brought it to the room where Gangry, and now Sabas, were sleeping.

She entered the room and started to say something but, realizing Sabas was asleep, held her tongue and paused a moment to watch him. She was one of the girls who had hoped Sabas would be hers, even though she was several years older. But Sabas had never shown interest in her. Gazing at him asleep there, after all he had done that night, she felt that old feeling of lovesickness rising back up in her. But she knew she was not his type. His type was Odilia. Michelina carried some extra weight and had a bit of a rough personality, a bit manly, some people said.

She pulled her gaze away from him and turned to Gangry to find a place to inject the chip. Normally, she liked to put chips in the back where it would be inconspicuous, and the carrier wouldn't know about it and would be less likely to try to remove it. But he was lying on his back, and she was too tired to move such a big man; she opted to put it in his left shoulder as far back as manageable. She swabbed his skin with a disinfecting wipe and then pulled out the huge syringe and plunged it into him. Gangry's eyes opened, and he looked straight at Michelina after she had pushed down on the syringe, injecting the chip. His big hand grabbed her arm, and they stared into each other's eyes for a moment.

His eyes slowly closed, and Gangry went back to sleep. Michelina felt a flow of heat coursing through her body. Gangry slept as soundly as he had before, like nothing had happened. She scanned the room and felt flush and exhausted with excitement.

Unwilling to leave, she sat down on the sofa next to Sabas. Instead of watching Sabas, her eyes consumed Gangry, wondering what the look in his eyes had tried to tell her. The commotion of her sitting down next to him caused Sabas to wake up. When he saw Michelina there, he smiled, recalling the good news that he had recovered the scan. He held out his hand, showing her the DNI. She smiled and gave him the thumbs up. Then, the two just sat there next to each other. Sabas closed his eyes again, and after a few minutes, Michelina did too.

* * *

It was then that Odilia appeared in the doorway. She had been on her way back to her room after Mass and decided she had better make sure Sabas was okay. She stood outside the room and thought for a brief moment that maybe Sabas belonged to someone else. Maybe not Michelina but someone. Without a word, she turned and walked away.

Chapter 22

Scullion and Skyte

Scullion lay in bed recovering from the operation that had implanted the telepathic device in his head, what Gangry had called "elephant ears." It would take some getting used to, hearing another person speaking in his head. Volspat never gave a warning about when he would speak. The first time it happened, Scullion jumped out of bed and clawed at his ears to make it stop. Volspat was somewhat merciful, allowing him to calm down before causing a new panic attack.

Is this what Gangry was going through all this time? he wondered.

"Yes," was the answer. The telepathic device was working perfectly, and Scullion sat up in his bed sweating.

"Scullion, I've made Mainz an offer they can't refuse. A fair trade. Jutta and Odilia for the prisoners. But while I'm waiting for the trade, you and Skyte will go out to find them. First, go back to the scene of Gangry's accident. He may have carried with him the scan of that miserable Dicarer. It may contain useful information for me. Get the scan and then go to Mainz. Tell them you are from Bandonderry or some other crap hole. Snoop around until you find Jutta. I'll tell you what to do when you find him."

Scullion didn't have to answer. He got out of bed and rubbed at the pain behind his right ear canal. He went to the Vauller and found Skyte, whom he grabbed by the shirt and led to the traversers.

"What do you want, Scullion?" he said as Scullion lead him outside into the heat. "Where are we going?"

Scullion didn't answer. He just got on a traverser and gestured for

Skyte to do the same.

The two rode away from Volmar to the place where Gangry had had the accident. They dismounted and Volspat spoke inside Scullion's head.

"Report."

"I see the traverser down there."

Skyte, who was still not aware that Scullion had the elephant ears, said, "Yeah. I see it."

Scullion glared at him with a "not you, idiot" expression on his face.

"Turn on your camera," Volspat said.

"Oh, yes. Sorry. I forgot."

"Forgot what?" Skyte said.

"I'm not talking to you, dude. It's the King of Kandy in my brain now, like Gangry. I'm Gangry."

Skyte didn't say anything. He gave Scullion a look that blended pity, fear, and disbelief altogether.

"Yeah," said Scullion.

"Show me Gangry's body," Volspat said to Scullion.

Scullion eyed the bottom of the cliff. "Do you see his body?" he asked Skyte.

"No. Maybe the wolstarz got him."

"Go down there and examine more closely," said Volspat.

Scullion grabbed a rope from a traverser and had Skyte spot him as he scaled down the wall.

"Nothing, master," Scullion said, getting used to the voice being inside his head. "He's not here. It looks like the traverser hit some kind of animal."

He followed the trail of blood with his camera so that Volspat could see. When they found the animal about 30 feet away, Volspat said, "That's a pronghorn. Shit. How could you idiots have been so careless? He tricked you. He didn't go over the cliff with the traverser. He probably killed that pronghorn to use the blood to make you think he was down there. But obviously, you didn't look that close!" Volspat shouted.

Scullion kneeled down and put his hands over his ears.

"That means he's alive," Volspat said, his voice softening a bit. "He may still be hiding out there. Be on your guard. He will kill you if he gets the chance."

"Watch out for Gangry," Scullion yelled up to Skyte, still at the top of the cliff. "He may be around here."

"Go on to Mainz, and find Jutta and Odilia. I don't think they're going to come peacefully. Watch your back. Gangry is dangerous. You have no idea what I have done all these years to protect you from him."

Scullion examined the traverser that had crashed. "All the survival supplies are still here. He didn't take that with him. That's weird."

There was a pause. Volspat must have been thinking. "Just watch out for him, but get to Mainz, NOW."

Scullion climbed back up the wall with the help of Skyte and the rope. Then, they headed in the direction of Mainz.

* * *

Jutta was awakened about 1:00 in the afternoon with a light knock on his door. It was so soft that it barely woke him, and it took a while to orientate himself to his situation. Finally, he recalled where he was, and after the third knock, he drug himself out of bed.

Wiping sleep from his eyes, he opened the door and saw before him Odilia. His heart began to pound faster. He reached for Redhing, thinking the bot would be there to monitor his heartbeat and help him communicate with the girl. When he remembered

Redhing was disabled, he became self-conscious.

"Hey," he said, trying to act cool.

"Sorry to wake you," Odilia said. "Sabas just came and woke me up. He wants to meet everyone in the lockup where we're keeping Gangry. Can you come now? We can have some breakfast...or, I guess, lunch afterwards."

They spoke over each other. "Yeah. Sure. Let me just change my clothes..."

"I'll let you get dressed..."

They both laughed.

Odilia nodded and smiled. "Okay. See you in a minute."

"Yeah. See you there." Jutta closed the door and took a deep breath and felt as though part of him was melting into her.

He threw on a change of clothes that someone had left on his nightstand, hastily brushed his teeth and patted down his hair with wet palms. He headed to the lockup where Gangry was being held. Soon, he appeared in the doorway and saw Odilia and Sabas sitting apart from each other.

Sabas gave him a dirty look. "We're just waiting for Michelina and Chester," he said.

Jutta nodded and glanced at Gangry who, miraculously, was still sleeping, his arms now securely bound to the bars on each side of his bed.

Chaney stood up and offered a seat to Jutta and then tried to make small talk, but everyone seemed tired and irritable. Jutta picked up a piece of paper from the floor and fiddled with it. When he was sure Sabas wasn't looking at him, he stole a glance at Odilia.

When Michelina and Chester arrived, Sabas said, "Okay. Listen up. I have some good news and some bad news."

He reached into his pocket and pulled out the disk that he had found on Gangry. "First, the good news. Know what this is?" he asked, holding it up for everyone to see. "It's the scan that they tried to take of Father Rawley's mind after that beast killed him."

Odilia stood up and reached out to touch it as if it were some sacred object, a sacramental that was too holy for a sinful woman. It could have been a piece of the cross itself. But she seemed to snap out of the spell, and she sat back down without touching it.

"What's the bad news?" she asked.

"Volspat has offered to swap the prisoners for a couple people: Jutta and..." Sabas stopped and just stared at the DNI.

"And who?" Michelina asked. "Odilia?"

Sabas nodded avoiding eye contact with anyone, and no one seemed to know what to say.

After a moment, Chester said, "I wonder why Gangry was there last night."

"Maybe he got into trouble with the Avogo, and he had to run away," Michelina said. "We'll have to wait until he wakes up."

"Even then," said Sabas, "I don't suspect he'll be telling us too much willingly."

"What should we do with the memory scan?" Jutta asked.

"We must delete it," Chaney said. "It is only right. We must respect Father's privacy. Whatever is on that disk is between him and God."

Odilia concurred. "Chaney is right. We should destroy it. Anyway, it was recorded by the Avogo so that they could find out if Jutta was here and to get more information about us. They were probably hoping to find some dirt on him to trash our faith and call us hypocrites, like they're always doing."

"I think you're right. Everyone agree I should destroy it?" Sabas asked as he put it on the floor. He lifted his foot to crush the device when Chester spoke up. "But, it might also contain some good evidence for Yaro and Fargus to present to the council. It might be worth keeping just a while longer. Maybe we could let just Yaro see it and no one else. He's a deacon, and that's the closest thing to a priest."

Sabas shrugged. "I guess it wouldn't hurt to keep it a while. At least we know the Avogo don't have it, and they are still not sure that we have Jutta." He purposefully mispronounced his name, like the name of the old state, Utah. He put the DNI down on a table away from the bed where Gangry lay. "Okay. I say we wake him up and see what we can get out of him."

Michelina walked to the bed and stood over Gangry. She spoke softly. "He'll wake up soon enough. Let's let him sleep awhile."

Apparently, nobody wanted to wake him except Sabas, so Chaney changed the subject. "Jutta and I were talking about consent after Mass this morning, weren't we, Jutta?"

Sabas sat down alone on the couch and sighed. "God! Am I the only one here who sees the urgency of our situation?"

"I feel sorry for that man lying here," Chaney said, ignoring Sabas.

Sabas scoffed. "What? You can feel sorry for him all you want. But don't forget what he did to us. Father Rawley is dead, and ten of our own are now trapped in Volmar."

Chaney was silent a moment. "It is true. By most accounts, he is our enemy. But Jesus told us we must love our enemies."

"Shit," Sabas said as he sank deeper into the couch. "What about Jutta and Odilia? Volspat's going to come for them."

"If we don't love him, our faith means nothing," Chaney said, undeterred by Sabas. "The Bible is very clear on that. Love your enemies. A lot of people think that religion is about keeping laws. But Romans 13:8-10 says, 'Brothers and sisters: Owe nothing to anyone, except to love one another; for the one who loves another has fulfilled the law. The commandments, 'You shall not commit adultery; you shall not kill; you shall not steal; you shall not covet,' and whatever other commandment there may be, are summed up in this saying, namely, 'You shall love your neighbor as yourself.' Love does no evil to neighbor; hence, love is the fulfillment of the law."

"You must not have loved Father Rawley like we did," Sabas said. "If you had, you wouldn't find it so easy to forgive him just yet."

"That's not fair," Odilia said, coming to Chaney's defense.

Sabas stood up. "Look, I'm getting the militia ready while we wait to hear from Yaro and Fargus. We will march tomorrow. You guys talk all you want about love. I'm gonna love MY people by defending them."

"Right now, we need to wait on the Lord, Sabas," Chaney said in an authoritative voice. "We need to ask for discernment. Don't put the cart before the horse. God will show us what to do."

"That's fine and all for you, Chaney. But God helps those who help themselves. You all need to get back to work on that virus. I'm going to round up the troops. Tell me when he wakes up. If your virus isn't ready by tomorrow morning, I'm leading a charge."

"If you don't wait for God, at least wait for news from Yaro and Fargus. Maybe they will find more help at the Council meeting."

Sabas scoffed. "How much help have they been all these years? Huh? What have they done for us? Like Chester said, they've ceded any sort of power they once had to the Avogo and the other so-called immortals. No. Our only hope is, as you say, God...and this," he said, opening his shirt to reveal the nine mm pistol he was carrying.

"But, Sabas, pray for direction. Wait on the Lord."

Sabas stared at Odilia, who seemed to be pleading with him to concur with Chaney. Unable to answer and fed up with the whole religious line from Chaney, Sabas stormed out of the room. "One day, folks. You've got one day," he said as he left the room.

* * *

At about the same time that conversation was taking place, two strange men were approaching the gates of Mainz. A young man, temporarily filling in for his father who was in bed fighting an infection, was standing guard. He asked them who they were and what business they had there.

"We are friends from Bandonderry," one of them said in a raspy voice. "We heard you had some trouble recently. The Avogo sic'ed their Sogmol dogs on you, did they?"

The young man's eyes narrowed. "You don't look like Bandarians to me," he said. They both had scars and tattoos covering most of their skin. One of them had a fresh bandage on his right ear.

The one with the bandage said in a monotone voice, almost as if he were repeating something he was told to say, "We came to see what we could do. We've had problems before with them, the Avogo."

The bigger man spoke up. "We are here to offer our services and are asking to meet with Father Rawley."

On hearing the name of his beloved priest, the boy grew emotional. "I'm sorry. You're a little late. Father was killed two days ago."

"Oh. I'm sorry," said the same man sympathetically. Then, he carefully took out a couple of guns.

When the boy saw them, he immediately drew his weapon.

"Hold on! Hold on!" the man implored, holding his hands up. "Look. I'm going to take out the magazines and empty the chambers." He did so and then he put them down in front of the boy. "We're now unarmed. Could you take us to whoever's in charge?"

The boy kept his gun drawn and stared at the other man with the bandage behind his ear and said, "What about him? He armed?"

The other man also took out a gun and put it on the counter that the young substitute guard was standing behind. A little boy who liked to sit at the city gate and look out over the vast desert grew curious and approached them.

"Hey, little guy," said one of the men. "What's your name?"

"Wilton," he said shyly. "What's yours?"

"I'm Skyte, and this here's Scullion. He's pretty ugly, don't you think?"

The little boy laughed, and the guard said, "Got any way to prove where you're from?"

Scullion picked his guns back up and said, "Pastor Hylebos sent us. It's okay if you don't want to let us in. We'll just take our help and go on back."

The two turned around as if they were ready to leave, but the young guard stopped them. "Hold on. You know Hylebos?"

Scullion replied, "Of course, we do. He's our..." There was a pause as if he were searching for the word. "...pastor."

He let them in, and Wilton volunteered to help them find Sabas because the young guard was not allowed to leave his post.

* * *

After Sabas had stormed out, Chaney resumed talking. "Jutta, remember our conversation about us hiding from God?"

Michelina stood next to Gangry and rolled her eyes, making a groaning sound. Chester smiled and laughed at her.

Jutta said he remembered but, to Michelina, he didn't appear too interested.

"We all long to be loved. We are built for intimacy," Chaney said.

Jutta glanced at Odilia, and when their eyes met, he blushed.

"But that longing does not come from within ourselves," Chaney continued. "What we are experiencing when we long to be loved is actually God's longing to be loved by us."

When Chaney said this, Gangry slowly opened his eyes to see Michelina next to him. She caught his gaze but said nothing to the others. Gangry closed his eyes slowly and listened to Chaney.

"We hide from God, and any longing for love inside us is the pulling of him on our heartstrings. Imagine the love a mother has for a child or that a man has for a woman. Did you ever experience that, Jutta?"

Jutta shook his head and shifted in his seat uncomfortably.

"That same feeling is experienced for you by the one who created the entire universe. The one who, out of love, spoke and the primordial atom was split, and all things came into being. That's how we got here, and that's why we're here. To live in a loving relationship with the one who created us. That perfect town you grew up in? Is it really so perfect? Did you ever hear of God there?"

Jutta shook his head again.

"No. Everyone there is too wrapped up in having their own way and pleasing any lusts that come into their minds that there's no way they could ever hear the still small voice of God, calling to them to share life with him. God is all-powerful, but for some reason, his voice is heard in silence. Only in silence. There's a story in the Bible. A prophet named Elijah was told to stand on a mountain before God. Soon a strong howling wind came, but God was not in the wind. Then there was a crashing destructive earthquake, but God was not in the earthquake. And after the earthquake, a fire. But the Lord was not in the fire. And after the fire, a still small voice."

Just then, a knock was heard on the door, and a little child about six years old entered. "Odi'a!" the little boy said when he saw Odilia standing there. He ran to give her a hug, and she picked him up. As she did, two strange men stood in the doorway. Odilia was frightened and moved next to Jutta with the boy in her arms.

"These aw my fwiends," Wilton said. All eyes fell on the two men.

And everyone in the room stood up. Even Gangry tried to rise up in his bed, though his hands and feet were still bound.

"What are your friends' names?" Odilia asked.

"Dat one's Scuwon and dat one Skite," he said, pointing to them.

Scullion and Skyte seemed proud of themselves.

"Well, well. Who do we have here?" Scullion said.

"Jackpot!" Skyte said, punching Scullion on the shoulder.

"Gangry! It's good to see you're still alive," Scullion said, smiling. Then he looked at the others. "You must be the one pretending to be Jutta. Oh boy, have we been searching for you. And you must be Odilia. Oh, yeah. Now I see why the Avogo have their eyes on you."

"Glad to see you two cretans," Gangry said. "It's about time. Now, get me out of these chains," he said.

"What?" Scullion said incredulously. "You want us to help you?"

He glanced at Skyte and the two laughed together. "Yeah. Not gonna happen 'boss.'" Skyte said as he pulled a gun from its holster hidden under his shirt on his hip.

The little boy buried his face in Odilia's neck.

"I don't think these are your friends, little one," she whispered, and the boy began to sob.

Michelina moved over slightly to try to shield the little boy, but as she did, she remembered that Gangry was still strapped in bed. Below the bed was a release tab that could easily be stepped on to release him.

Gangry felt his straps loosen, and Michelina nodded at him, as if she were giving him permission to go free.

"I am a citizen of Volmar, a Sasjovian," Jutta said to the Sogmols condescendingly. "You are sworn to protect me and do as I command."

Scullion sniffed. "Ah, but you're an imposter. You're supposed to die." He lifted his gun and pointed it at Jutta's head. Michelina screamed as Chester jumped up and knocked Scullion's arm away just as the trigger was being squeezed. The bullet narrowly missed Jutta. Odilia fell to the ground, pulling Jutta down along with her and the child.

As Skyte reached for a hidden gun as well, Gangry jumped on him and wrapped the straps that had bound his own arms around Skyte's neck. Gangry pulled hard on the straps, and Skyte gasped for air, dropping his weapon, which landed near Michelina, who had rounded the bed to help Gangry.

Scullion pushed Chester backwards and shot him. Chester fell like a lead weight, hitting the floor with a sickening thud. Chaney tried his best to fight with Scullion, but he was no match for the new leader of the Sogmols, who soon shot Chaney as well.

Scullion turned and saw that Gangry was choking Skyte and using him as a human shield. Rather than try to help his fellow Sogmol, Scullion shot Skyte through the heart, knowing that the bullet would pass into Gangry. They both fell with that one bullet. Skyte was dead. Michelina had picked up Skyte's gun and shot Scullion between the eyes.

The battle was over in the now blood-drenched room. Gangry pushed the dead Sogmol off of him and crawled over to Chester.

"This one's dead," he said. But Chaney was still breathing.

"Get the doctor!" Michelina cried out. "Somebody, get the doctor!"

By this time, everyone in Mainz had heard the shots and many people came running, including Sabas, who was the first to arrive. He entered the room with his gun drawn.

Chaney lay on the cold ground beckoning Sabas to come closer. Jutta and Odilia stood up and hugged each other, apparently unaware that Sabas had returned. Sabas knelt down next to the injured man and asked tearfully, "What happened?"

Chaney whispered, "Next time, wait for God." Then he took Sabas' hand and groaned loudly in pain.

Michelina crawled over to Gangry, who was leaned against the wall, and asked, "Are you okay?"

He looked puzzled. "I don't think we've met. My name is Godlip."

Chaney squeezed Sabas's hand so hard that Sabas started to grimace. The doctor and a nurse arrived and were able to stabilize Chaney and then tend to Godlip's wounds. "It looks like the bullet just skimmed his side," the doctor said to Michelina, who was holding Godlip's head in her lap. "As long as infection doesn't set in, he should be okay."

Wilton begged for Odilia and Jutta to pick him up, so they stood there having a group hug. Jutta stared at the two dead Sogmols and at Chester's body now covered with a bag. "How could Sogmols do this?" he asked. "I thought they were our protectors."

Odilia's voice was shaking, but she managed to say, "Now you believe, don't you?"

"You were right," he said.

Sabas watched this tender moment with disgust. He put his aching hand in his pocket and pulled out the ring he had intended to give to Odilia. Then, he squeezed it in Chaney's hand and stood up. He leveled his gun right at Gangry's head and started taking a deep breath so that his shot would be more accurate.

Michelina yelled, "No! Sabas! He helped us," and flung herself in front of Gangry to shield him. Sabas lowered his gun and glanced back at Odilia, whose eyes he imagined saw nothing but fear and loathing of him.

Godlip grunted as he tried to get Michelina off of him. "It's okay," he said. "I deserve it. Let him..." But Sabas was gone.

Godlip switched his attention to the corpse of Scullion, noticing the incision where the elephant ears must have been implanted. To everyone's disgust, he pulled out a knife and dug into the dead man's neck.

"Oh," the crowd that had gathered at the doorway sighed.

"What's he doing?" Odilia said.

"Godlip," Michelina said. "Stop. He's dead already."

Godlip ignored her and kept digging in the dead man's neck and ear until he had extracted the elephant ears. He stood up slowly and painfully, wiped the blood off the device and put part of it in his own ear, and walked out the door. The frightened onlookers fled from him. About three steps outside the door, he waved his hand as if to silence everyone. "Shh. I'm listening to Volspat."

Suddenly he covered the device tightly in his hands and spoke softly but urgently to everyone. "It's not safe to stay here. Everyone must go. They are going to gas the city."

A panic ensued. Sabas was not there to take charge, Yaro and Fargus had gone out to talk to the Council, and Chaney was in no condition to take over, so Odilia handed Wilton to Jutta, who in turn, put the boy down in the chair behind him.

Odilia eyed Michelina. "Do you believe him?" she asked, referring to Godlip.

Michelina nodded, "Yes."

Odilia said to the onlookers who hadn't fled from Godlip, "Everyone, listen up. Go back to your rooms, grab only the things you need to survive a couple of days in the desert. Tell everyone else to meet at the adit in thirty minutes, or near the Vitex tree. We need to go to Bandonderry for a while." Then she turned to Michelina and said, "Let them know we're coming."

Michelina nodded and then went to Godlip, who leaned back on a wall and slid down against it.

"You rest," she told him. "Lie down. I will be back for you." Then, she went off to send the message to Bandonderry, the nearest settlement that also resisted Volmar's influence.

Chapter 23
Leaving Mainz

Gradually, the citizens of Mainz began gathering around the Vitex tree near the adit. They were well-equipped with broonscakes, water flasks, long pants and thick-soled shoes, hats and sunscreens and, of course, their cooling jackets.

Young and old spoke in worried tones. Jutta was there, holding hands with the boy Wilton. Odilia wandered about checking with the leaders of each group, asking if anyone had seen Sabas. No one had seen him.

Those who were missing included Chaney and Godlip, who were too weak to travel; Michelina, who had offered to stay and take care of them; Yaro and Fargus, who were appealing to the Council; and, of course, the ten who were being held in Volmar. The militiamen took their places around the group to protect them.

"Okay, everyone," Odilia shouted as she scanned the crowd. "We have a two-day walk ahead of us. Michelina has already told Bandonderry that we are coming. We have three traversers for those who get too tired to walk. You can take turns with them. Stay hydrated, help each other, and stay together. Let's go!"

"Odilia!" One young man's voice cried out, "How do we know they are going to gas us?" he asked.

And another added what everyone must have been thinking: "Yeah. What if Gangry was lying? What if he just wanted to get us out here so that they could kill us in the open and take our city?"

Odilia didn't have an answer. She stood there for a moment, her first big test of leadership, and didn't know what to say.

"He saved us," came a small soft voice from next to Jutta.

"Gangry saved us from dos mean guys."

"That's right, Wilton," Odilia said loudly so that everyone could hear. "Gangry defended us from the two Sogmols. Why would he do that if he just wanted to kill us?"

Everyone seemed to accept the explanation. "Let's hope you're right, Wilton," the young man said.

Odilia nodded.

"Okay, everyone. Let's move out," she shouted.

Jutta walked with Wilton, who very quickly began to complain that his feet were hurting. The heat was making him cranky, so Jutta bent over and picked him up.

"You're getting a little too big for people to carry you," Jutta said. "But I'll give you a ride a little ways. Then you can give me a ride, too, how about that?"

Wilton shook his head no and then buried his face in Jutta's neck. Jutta pulled the umbrella-like cape from his jacket over the two of them and turned on the refrigerated fan to cool himself and the boy.

After an hour's walk, the group came to a place where two Vitex trees grew not far from each other. They stopped for a bit of rest. Odilia made her way around the group, checking to make sure everyone was okay.

One lady, the one who had read the scriptures at Mass, was not doing well. Odilia asked for a traverser to be brought to her, and soon, a militia member took her speeding forward ahead of the group. She wouldn't make the long walk, so they rushed her on to Bandonderry.

Odilia sat next to Jutta and asked how he was doing.

"Fine. Except this little guy wants me to carry him everywhere. It's your turn to carry me, Wilton," he said jokingly.

Odilia said, "Don't worry, Wilton. Maybe some of the Bandarians will meet us halfway. Maybe they'll have some more traversers for us."

The day was getting on, so there was a mixture of gladness and trepidation among the people that, at nightfall, the temperatures would drop. They would be a bit more comfortable then, but cold is often as bad as hot. Just as Odilia was getting everyone ready to move out again, a loud explosion was heard in the distance from where they had come. Odilia peered through her binoculars and saw a cloud of dust hovering over Mainz.

"Oh, my God," she whispered.

A collective moan went up among the citizens.

"It's Mainz," one guy said. "They've destroyed our home." Another person responded that Gangry had been right, that he hadn't been lying. "Poor Chaney and Michelina," someone said.

Odilia put her binoculars down, and when she saw Jutta and Wilton, she melted into tears. Jutta walked over to comfort her, and she fell into his arms. He didn't know what to say. Others were talking. Some were swearing their revenge against the Avogo. The elderly were wondering what they were going to do. "Where will we live?"

Someone said, "I hope Sabas is okay. I hope he didn't go back." Odilia snapped out of her despair and pulled herself away from Jutta, and ran off.

Momentarily, she returned with three men and two traversers. "We'll go back and see about Chaney and the others," she said while looking at Jutta but intending for everyone to hear. "You all keep going. Don't stop. Follow the militiamen. You'll meet up with the Bandarians soon. Stay on the path we planned, and we'll be back soon. I have to see if they are okay."

Odilia and two men went to Mainz but could find no way into the city. Both adits, front and back, had been blown up and collapsed. There was no way to know how extensive the damage was inside. They called out for the three—possibly four, counting Sabas—who were last seen inside. No answer.

Odilia and the others did their best to remove the boulders that were blocking the entrance but realized that if anyone inside was still alive, the three of them could not help them get out. This project would require more than just their hands. Odilia gave one last pull out of frustration on one rock, and it moved, then fell to the ground. Out of the hole that was left, a toxic gas came seeping through.

Odilia covered her mouth and nose. "How did they do this?"

"Bastards," one man said. "It's useless. We are needed elsewhere, and the Sogmols could still be close by. We'd better get back."

Odilia yelled into the hole, "Sabas! Michelina! Chaney! Can you hear me? Michelina?" She kept calling, but no one answered.

"Come, Odilia," the oldest said after waiting for Odilia to tire of calling to those inside. "They can't hear you. They have masks. We have to get back."

Wiping her eyes, she nodded. "Okay. Let's get back to the others."

Chapter 24
Laudus and Camara

After the shooting with the Sogmols, Sabas had wandered back to the spot where they had captured Gangry the night before. He picked up a rock and hurled it down as hard as he could at Gangry's traverser, which still lay broken in the ravine far below. He didn't know how he could ever face his fellow Dicarers again. He certainly couldn't face Odilia, at least not at that moment. If he saw her again with that worthless rescue, he would likely hurt someone.

The sun beat down on him, and the sweat dripped into his eyes. "I don't have to go back," he said to himself aloud as he hunkered down under a rock to rest. "I can always become a ghost."

Ghosts were not spirits. Rather, ghosts were people who roamed around without any ties to a particular place. They were generally solitary and made their living any way they could. Some did it by collecting resources that different towns might need or by hunting. But others made their living by kidnapping people and selling them to places like Volmar or CHAI. Slavery was the most lucrative trade for ghosts. That's one reason that Mainz parents were always so careful not to let their children play outside unsupervised.

As Sabas lay down under the rock, he said, "Maybe I'll collect seashells by the seashore." He laughed deliriously for a moment, wondering what a seashore was. Eventually, he stopped laughing as he realized where he was: Under the same rock that Gangry had been hiding under when boxbot 12 had sent Sabas that picture.

He yelled loudly at God, "Why do you hate me!?" He crawled out of that crevice and made a bee-line for a nearby safe hole. When he found it, he pulled open the hot door, crawled in, and shut the lid over him then descended into the cool darkness.

He turned on a light to make sure he wasn't sharing the den with spiders or any other unwanted critter. When he was satisfied that he was alone, he turned off the light and lay down on the bare musty floor in the pitch black. He curled up into a ball and wished he could continue curling until he had caved in on himself, unaware of past or present and unconcerned about the future.

"It wasn't my fault," he said to the darkness. "They wouldn't listen. If Chaney had listened to me, I would have been there. I would have killed the Sogmols. But instead, he tells me it's because I didn't wait for God..." there was a long pause before he suddenly yelled at the top of his lungs, "Aghh!!!"

The word echoed up and down the safe hole, and when it had come back down to him empty and dissipated, he stretched out on his back. He thought he heard a clanking noise coming from above. He sat up to listen, his heart pounding. Nothing. It was quiet again. He lay back down slowly and cautiously, but soon he heard the latch overhead being turned, and light came pouring into the safe hole.

Sabas stood up silently and flattened himself against the wall in an attempt to make himself invisible. Who could this be? he thought. Certainly, no Dicarers would be about. Sogmols? Then, the craziest thought of all came to him. Maybe it was Odilia. Maybe she had come looking for him. She was ready to apologize and confess that Jutta meant nothing to her and that no one would ever come between them. His heart nearly stopped, remembering the ring that he had pressed in Chaney's hand. If it was her and she was about to confess her undying love, this would be the time to give it to her, and for the first time in weeks, he didn't have it on him.

There was a loud thud of a bundle hitting the floor next to him, and a voice above saying, "Go on. Get in there." It was neither Odilia nor the Sogmols.

It sounded like the other person didn't want to cooperate. Sabas heard a girl struggle, and some sand fell into his face. He pulled out his gun and held his breath as he waited for them to descend.

Peering up, he could see the silhouettes of two people. One appeared to be a slender female, another was a blob, apparently of a man. The girl soon let go of the last rung and dropped to the floor where she came face to face with Sabas. She gasped, but Sabas put his finger to his lips, imploring her to be quiet.

"What happened?" the gruff voice called out from above. But the man could not see anything below him as he descended the ladder.

"I thought I stepped on something."

The large man closed the latch above and somehow turned on a small light to guide his way down into the hole. As soon as the man's right foot hit the floor, Sabas turned on a flashlight and pointed his gun at the man's face, which was covered in tattoos.

"Move, and your brains go into the wall behind you," he said so convincingly that the man stood still. "Get your hands up against the wall," he said. Both of them did as he said. Sabas turned on a light and put down his flashlight. He noticed that the girl's hands were already bound.

"Who the hell is this?" the pot-bellied man said to himself as he put his hands on the wall and waited to be frisked.

Sabas searched the man and found a large knife and a handgun. Sabas then used his own belt to wrap around the man's hands since he didn't have anything else to serve as handcuffs.

Once the hands were secured behind his back, Sabas turned him around and had him sit down with his back against the wall.

"The better question is who the hell are you?" He glanced at the girl and indicated that she should sit down as well. She looked to be about Odilia's age, slender, with long straight brown hair. She smiled at him as she slowly sat down, leaving some space between her and the man.

"Don't you recognize me, Dicarer? I'm the Pope," the man said and then laughed so hard at his own joke that he began coughing.

Neither Sabas nor the girl found anything funny in that response.

"Don't listen to him," said the girl, who apparently had no idea what a Pope was. "He's got a lot of names as far as I can tell."

"The only name you need to know, sweetheart, is Sir," he said to the girl.

Sabas punched the man in the face and sent the back of his head into the rock wall. The man passed out.

"Shit," Sabas said, fearing that he'd killed him.

"Oh, that's awesome!" the girl said. "That's so awesome. Thank you! I could kiss you."

Sabas examined the man and, when he heard him groan, said, "I guess he'll be okay. He'll probably have a concussion, though."

"You are the best!" The girl said, leaning forward in an attempt to kiss him on the cheek.

"Just...hold on a second," Sabas said, a bit taken aback by her forwardness. "Who are you people? This your boyfriend?"

The girl laughed. "No. He wishes."

There was a pause. Sabas waited for her to continue, but she apparently needed some prodding. "Well?" he said impatiently.

"He kidnapped me a week or two ago. Was trying to make me his slave all this time. But now I guess he's decided to sell me to Volmar." She held out her bound hands to prove it. Sabas untied them. "Thank you," she said and quickly kissed his cheek.

"He's a ghost?" Sabas asked, wiping his cheek thoughtfully.

She shrugged her shoulders as if she didn't know. "A big fat ass," she said as she kicked the man in the shin.

Sabas shielded him from her. "All right. I get it. So he kidnapped you, and you're on your way to Volmar. I guess I've put an end to that plan?"

"Yes. Thank you!" she said. "You are amazing."

Sabas leaned back and said, "Not so much. Just relax a minute. I will get you to a safe place soon."

"Okay," the girl said, staring unabashedly at Sabas, who noted that she was quite attractive. "Do you have anything to eat?" she asked.

"I don't," he said.

"Fat ass does," she said, and she reached for his bag. "He's always eating something."

Sabas waved her away from the bag and opened it himself. He didn't know if there were weapons in the bag, but he didn't want her grabbing one until he had verified her story, and she had earned his trust.

He rummaged through the bag and found mainly hunting and survival supplies, only a few pieces of dried jerky, which he handed to her.

She took it disappointedly and said, "Dog jerky. That's all I've had for days. Guess it's better than nothing."

Sabas nodded in agreement but didn't take any of the jerky himself. The ghost began to stir.

"What are we going to do?" the girl asked, moving behind Sabas.

"I'll bring you back to Mainz, where you'll be safe. They'll take care of you there. You won't have to worry about him. We'll leave him here, and when I have time, I'll come back for him.

"What'll you do to him?"

"What do you want me to do to him?" Sabas asked just for fun.

"Kill him," she said.

He was a bit shocked by the request. "We'll see. I wonder how he knew I was a Dicarer."

"What's a Dicarer?" the girl asked as she took another bite of jerky.

"It's just a person from Mainz." Sabas made sure the ghost's hands were tied up securely. He left some water for him. He didn't feel the man needed so much food, so he didn't leave any.

When that was done, he put his gun in his left hand and extended his right hand to the girl: "I'm Sabas."

The girl just stared at the hand as if she didn't understand what was being asked of her.

"Your name?" he asked, lowering his hand.

"Camera, I think."

Sabas chuckled and then tucked his gun into his pocket. "You mean Camara?"

"Maybe," she said.

"Okay, then, Camara," he said. "Let's get you to Mainz."

Chapter 25

The Beatific Vision of Father Rawley

After a few more hours of walking, the Dicarers found a place to camp for the night. They all had a small dinner of some of the rations that they brought. Jutta found a place to rest and saw that Odilia was not too far away. She was resting on her mat and appeared to be praying when he waved at her. She waved back, and he spread out his sleeping bag and lay down on top.

As soon as he got comfortable, the little boy, Wilton, surprised him with a good-natured pounce right onto his stomach.

"Can I sweep here with you, Jutta?" he asked. "Pwease?"

"Ah, don't you think you should sleep with your growth promoter?"

"What's that?" Wilton said.

"I mean," Jutta said. "Don't you have a, um, what do you call it? A leader who is biologically female that contributes to your development?"

"Whaaaat?" Wilton said, laughing as if he thought Jutta was making a joke.

"Never mind," Jutta said. "I guess you can sleep here. But I must warn you, I snore, talk in my sleep, walk in my sleep, and sometimes, I wet the bed."

Wilton laughed. "No, you don't."

"You're right. But do *you*?"

"No," he said in a tone that included "no" and "of course not."

"Well, okay then. I guess we'll be all right."

The Earth slowly grew quiet. Jutta lay next to the six-year-old boy, who had quickly fallen asleep after a traumatic and exhausting day. Jutta's mind was wandering, but he tried to focus on the virus of repentance: what it would be and how it would work. He thought about the program he had written to cure chest pains. The Nasrup prize he had received for it gave him little confidence that he was up to the task this time.

He tried to understand why Father Rawley had so much faith in him? Was it Jutta's fault this disaster had befallen these people? If they had just left him alone and let him die in the refreshing, none of this would have happened. He felt a tinge of guilt, something that was not new to him; but without Redhing to report this emotion to the COGOPT, he was able to let it sink in and feel its true weight. He looked at the sleeping boy and wondered whether anyone in Wilton's group unit had been kidnapped because of him. "Family," he whispered, remembering the term they used in Mainz. "Where's your mother?" he whispered to Wilton. And for the first time in his life, it occurred to him that he too might have had a mother. He wondered who she was.

It was eerily quiet, so much so that he got the feeling that no one was sleeping. If they were, he would have heard heavy breathing or snoring. But there was no sound like that. A half-moon cast a pale light over the camp, and he sat up slowly, careful not to wake Wilton. Instead of the stars above, he saw eyes around him. Thousands of eyes peered out through their coverings. He saw two that he thought belonged to Odilia. They were uncondemning eyes filled with questions that welled up into tears, and as the tears dropped, the splattering asked, "Will you help us? Can you write it?"

"Yes," he said. "I will help you."

Wilton stirred, and he wondered if he'd said that aloud. Was he, in fact, talking in his sleep? Wilton moved again, cuddling up closer and throwing a leg around Jutta's waist.

Jutta lay back down, and as he tried to move Wilton's leg, he brushed against something in Wilton's pocket that must have been making the boy uncomfortable. He reached into the boy's pocket and found the direct neural interface that contained the last thoughts of Father Rawley.

"How did you get this?" he whispered. Ah. He remembered Sabas had put it on the table before the two Sogmols came in. Wilton must have picked it up.

He fiddled with it in his hands for a while, wondering what was on it. The others had thought they should destroy it, but Jutta had been curious. What would a dying man's last thoughts be? Here was the answer in his own hands. He had only to insert the device into the port in his neck, and he could easily find out.

He tried to remember the reasons they wanted to destroy it.

Privacy? he thought. There were no privacy rights in Volmar. In fact, the word privacy was one of the dirtiest words one could utter.

Jutta sat up again as if to ask the eyes what he should do. But they were all closed now. He looked to Odilia but couldn't see her anymore. The half-moon grew dimmer behind clouds passing high in the sky.

"What could it hurt?" he decided. *If there's something bad, I just won't tell anyone.*

He plugged the DNI into his neck and turned on the power, and lay back down as if he were about to watch a movie. But what he saw was no movie.

Almost immediately, Jutta tensed up, and he began mumbling to himself. He entered a world he never could have imagined. There were creatures he had no reference for and a light that kept getting brighter and brighter until it was truly unbearable. As it approached, he felt his heart might break in half. His arms flapped about, and he was unable to control them. He had already lost the consciousness required to unplug the device. He screamed at the encroaching, unbearable light, which he felt would fully rend him in two if it came any closer. He could not stand an inch closer, and just as he felt the end coming, he awoke.

He had been screaming. The entire camp had woken up. His heart was racing, he was covered in sweat, and he could hardly catch his breath. Wilton was crying, and Odilia stood over him holding the DNI.

"What did you see?" she asked, in a tone that indicated he'd just committed a great badact.

He was unable to speak.

"What did you see?" she asked again.

Jutta shook his head. Odilia put the DNI in her own pocket and zipped it up, and gave him the look a mother would give to a child after taking away something he had been told not to play with.

"It's okay, everyone," Odilia said. "Go back to sleep. Jutta had a nightmare." Wilton grabbed her hand, and the two went off together.

"Sorry," Jutta mumbled.

Odilia grunted. "Goodnight, Jutta," she said with a tone of finality.

"Sorry, Wilton," Jutta said, still trembling. "I told you, I talk in my sleep."

As he lay back down on the dirty sleeping bag, he gazed up at the skies. The clouds high up were gone, and the stars were out in their fullness. He wanted to stay awake to analyze what had happened, but a great abiding peace fell upon him, and he fell asleep knowing what had to be done.

Chapter 26

Gaining a Brother

Sabas climbed out of the safe hole as the sun was going down. He turned to help the girl he had just saved from being sold to the Avogo, and as he reached down to help her up, she smiled warmly. After Sabas closed the lid and covered up the hole, the man they left inside could be heard yelling, and the girl spat on the lid.

The sun was setting in the west over Volmar; Mainz lay several miles away.

"We've got over an hour's walk ahead of us," Sabas said, and he beckoned her to follow him. Observing her in the evening light, Sabas said, "I guess you must be from far away."

"I think so."

"Where are you from?"

"New York."

"New York? Really? But, I thought that was CHAI country. I thought anyone left in CHAI country would be fully owned by the machines."

"Pretty much," she said elusively.

"But, you're not."

"Well, I don't know, really."

"Wait. Did that guy take you from CHAI?"

"I think so," she said.

"You think so?" Sabas said incredulously.

"I mean, I didn't know what was going on at the time. It took me a while to figure it out."

The two walked along quietly for a few minutes. Sabas stole several glances at her. Finally, he asked.

"So how come you speak English so well? I mean, if you were a slave to CHAI all this time, how did you learn English?"

"Oh, I spoke it when I was a kid, before CHAI incorporated our village."

"How old were you?" Sabas asked.

"At incorporation? Probably four."

Sabas reflected on what he had learned in school about what had happened in New York and many parts of the world. Years earlier, AI had reached what some referred to as its singularity. When it did, it must have realized that it needed some way to fix its servers and maintain itself. It needed a body, and since no mechanical bodies were as efficient as human bodies, it began to take over people to use as its hands and feet. Starting in China, all the people began to get networked together, and the entity came to be known as Conglomeration of Humans and Artificial Intelligence (CHAI).

It didn't take over the entire world, though. Somehow, it seemed to have grown satisfied with itself and had so far left Mainz and Volmar and many other settlements alone. Settlements like Mainz and Bandonderry just tried to stay out of its way and made sure they did not threaten CHAI. And everyone Sabas had ever known was told to stay out of CHAI country.

But now, here with Sabas, was a beautiful girl who had been part of it.

"So, do you think you want to go back?" Sabas stopped and stared at her.

"To CHAI?" the girl asked. "No. At first, I did, but now. Mmmm, maybe not." She put her hand on Sabas's shoulder and began to massage it. He thought about pulling her close and kissing her beautiful lips. But he imagined Odilia's disappointed face and said, "It's getting late. We should hurry."

The two traveled along in silence for a few moments. Sabas wondered briefly if CHAI might be another option that he could take if he ended up leaving Mainz and the faith he had grown up with, which now seemed so useless. *Where is God, anyway?* he wondered.

After over a mile, he asked, "In CHAI, are individuals even aware of themselves anymore?"

Camara shrugged.

"Were you aware of anything while you were there?" he followed up.

"It was kinda like dreaming all the time. Sometimes the horrors came, but when they did, CHAI injected us with something that helped. You don't have anything like that, do you?" she asked hopefully.

"No," Sabas said, not quite sure what she meant. The two approached Mainz in darkness. Sabas immediately knew that something was wrong. The territory wasn't shaped the way it always had been. The entryway didn't sit dark in the nightscape. It reflected more light, and he soon realized it was because rocks were blocking its way.

He ran to it and frantically pulled away any stones he could move, but he couldn't get a grip on the larger ones that would have to go in order for him to enter.

"Hello!" he shouted. "Is anyone in there?"

"Is this Mainz?" Camara asked.

"Yes. I don't know what's happened. It was fine earlier today. Everyone was here. Help me move these stones."

"Hello, is anyone still inside?" He yelled again and again. He remembered a large walking stick that he had abandoned outside not long ago. He found it where he had left it. Using the sturdy walking stick, the two were able to move another rock to widen the hole that had been made earlier. Sabas stuck his head in and shouted. But there was no answer, and he could still smell the residue of a noxious gas. He finally sat down on the ground. Until then, he had not realized he had been crying.

He thought of everyone still inside. He cried for the loss of the entire town of Mainz. He cried for the children. For the elderly. For Wilton and his sister, the handicapped girl who loved playing Zalltilinger. For the cooks, the workers, the pious and the sinners. For the gardens inside that would soon be dead for lack of care. He cried, knowing that this meant the end of his faith in God. But mostly, he cried for Odilia.

Camara went a short distance away and sat down by herself.

After a while, a voice came from inside the cave. "Sabas? Is that you?"

He looked around and wiped his eyes. "Who's that?"

"Michelina. I'm in here with Chaney and Godlip. We're okay. Why are you crying? Did something happen to the others?"

"The others? What do you mean?"

"They all left this afternoon on Godlip's warning."

"Really? Everyone is okay?"

"Yes. They went to Bandonderry."

Sabas couldn't believe his ears. "Odilia is okay?"

"I think so. She led them herself."

"Oh, thank God!" he said. "Wait, who's Godlip?"

"Gangry. It's his real name. Sabas, we need to get out of here. We need to get to Bandonderry somehow."

He jumped into action. Though he was never much for the religion he grew up with, Sabas couldn't contain the relief he felt. "Oh, Thank God! Thank you, God. Oh, thank you, Jesus. Hold on, guys. We'll get you out of here. We'll get you out."

They worked together, Sabas and Camara, on the outside and Michelina and Godlip on the inside. They devised a way to budge one big boulder far enough that they could squeeze through. Michelina gave Sabas a big hug, and Sabas introduced her to Camara. Michelina led them to where Chaney was lying on a mat.

The interior of Mainz had been gassed but was still intact. The three had survived with gas masks. Only the entryways had been destroyed by the missiles. They gathered up supplies they would need for their trip to Bandonderry, but Sabas kept his distance from Godlip. Sabas had a hard time forgetting that this was the one who killed Fr. Rawley. In fact, it was a great struggle for him not to shoot Godlip. But it seemed that Michelina had grown fond of him, and Chaney had come to trust him as well.

Sabas described the ghost who had kidnapped Camara. "Weird looking guy. Has a high-pitched voice and a bunch of tattoos all over his face. The one in the center of his forehead looks like some Chinese word."

Godlip, who had listened intently to the description of the ghost, asked, "Was it kind of like a circle in the middle and something like two pitchforks crossing each other?"

"Sounds about right," Sabas said skeptically.

"I think we should go see this person before we go to Bandonderry," Godlip said.

"Why?" Sabas said. "Friend of yours?"

"I might know him," Godlip said.

"Well, that's no reason. You want us to waste time on you, Gangry," Sabas said with condescension.

"That's not fair, Sabas," Michelina said. "His name is Godlip. And he saved us from the attack. I know what he did to Father, but he regrets it. It wasn't him. It was Volspat. We owe him our lives. Actually, our entire city does, if he hadn't warned us."

"Listen to Michelina, Sabas. I trust him," Chaney said, beckoning for Sabas to come to him. Sabas knelt next to him and said, "What is it?"

"Open your hand."

"What?"

"Just open your hand," Chaney repeated.

Sabas opened his hand, and Chaney squeezed it hard. Sabas

could feel the ring being pressed into his palm. "Let's go see this ghost," Chaney said.

Sabas observed the ring a moment and teared up. "Okay. Whatever you guys say. Let's do it."

Michelina had already built a makeshift stretcher for Chaney from an old garden cart that had been used to pull vegetables. Once they got Chaney through the crevice, Sabas pulled the stretcher while everyone else walked.

Chaney seemed too tired to speak, and Sabas was glad because he didn't want Chaney reminding him that he had left them defenseless. Poor Chester had been hastily buried, but at least Chaney was still alive. And it seemed Godlip was fine, too. The former Grand Comrade seemed a bit sensitive about the wound on his chest; he kept his left hand covering it as they walked. Aside from that, everyone was okay. Sabas took some comfort in that.

When they arrived at the safe hole, Camara held tightly to Sabas' arm.

"Remember what you promised me," she whispered into Sabas' ear. "You will kill him, won't you?"

Sabas didn't answer. He just acknowledged that he heard her with his eyes.

They found the man awake and a light glowing at the bottom of the hole. Godlip called out. "What's your name?"

After a short pause, they heard, "Why don't you come down and find out?"

Camara squeezed Sabas's arm tighter.

"Or we could just leave you down in this hole. Let you starve. We were about to head out on a two days' journey. We won't be back here for quite a while."

There was a pause as the man seemed to consider his situation. "Laudus."

Godlip nodded at Michelina and the others, indicating that he recognized the name.

"You know Sarah and Greeson Harriser?"

Another pause.

"Who are you?" the man asked.

"Name's Godlip."

There was a long pause of silence. "Godlip Harriser?" the man asked.

"Yes."

"Seriously? Are you kidding me?"

"No. It's me, aunt... uh... uncle Laudus. It's me, Godlip."

Soon, Laudus was outside with the others. He and Godlip spent some time getting caught up. Sabas felt uneasy giving these two former enemies their freedom, and Camara made sure that she stood very close to Sabas, who held a knife in his hand in case he needed it. But when Laudus asked Godlip about his family, the fear of Laudus lessened, at least for Sabas.

"So how is your brother?" he asked.

"My brother?" Godlip shrugged. "I never got to meet him. Dad sent me to Volmar before he was born. Do you know anything about him?"

"About all I know is that your mom took him to Mainz, and they took him in." Sabas began to sweat, and his heart began to pound. "I saw your mom one more time before she died."

"What was my brother's name?" Godlip asked.

"I forget. Sounds like Sabbath or something. Sabas maybe?"

All eyes fell on Sabas, who dropped the knife he'd been holding, nearly cutting his foot.

Chapter 27
Odilia Jilted

The town of Bandonderry was built inside a long, wide tunnel that had once been part of a four-lane highway. In its heyday, it must have handled thousands of cars every day, but now it served as shelter for about six hundred people who called themselves Bandarians.

The day after leaving Mainz, late in the evening, the Dicarers began arriving in this secluded tunnel town, and the Bandarians welcomed them warmly with food and medical attention for those who had nearly succumbed to the heat. They showed the Dicarers to the gymnasium where a couple hundred cots and mats had been carefully laid out.

Jutta found his mat, and Odilia went to thank Pastor Hylebos, the town's pastor, for helping them. Hylebos, who served not only as the pastor but as the mayor as well, said, "Nonsense. It is our pleasure to have you here. We're so sorry to hear of your troubles." Hylebos invited Odilia to sit at a table in the dining area.

Odilia said, "Again, thank you so much. It's good to be here with friends. Did Yaro and Fargus stop here?"

Hylebos sat down across from her. "Yes. They left yesterday, I think, to visit the Council and to file a complaint against Volmar. They took a letter from me along with them. We're demanding that action be taken against the Avogo. Odilia, we are well aware of the treachery of Volmar against Mainz, but recent hardships have left us weakened."

"I'm sorry," Odilia said. "What happened?"

"Well," Hylebos said, leaning back in his chair. "About a year ago, one of our teenage girls was kidnapped." He paused and gazed at Odilia sadly. "She was about your age."

Odilia nodded. "Yeah. I heard about her. Father told me."

"Well," Hylebos continued, "the father of the missing girl believed that Volspat was to blame. One night, he left Bandondary, armed to the teeth and carrying a bomb. He got as far as the heaps when, I guess the sensors went off, and he was discovered by Sogmols. He was killed, but not before shooting one of the Sogmols and tossing his bomb towards the group. I don't know how many Sogmols were injured, but I guess Volspat decided we were attacking Volmar; ever since then, Sogmols have been randomly appearing at our gates, breaking into the City, threatening us and stealing things from us, like traversers and guns."

Odilia described the events that happened to Mainz since rescuing Jutta, and Hylebos shook his head in anger. He seemed ready to say something monumental when a young Bandarian guard notified Pastor Hylebos that a peculiar-looking group claiming to be from Mainz were outside the city gates. Hylebos and Odilia went to the gates and saw Sabas, Godlip and Chaney there with two strangers.

Odilia ran to Sabas and held his face in her hands. But he didn't look her in the eye for long. Instead, he hugged her and then stepped back and said, "Odilia, you won't believe what happened." He put his arm around Godlip, who appeared to be recovering nicely from the gunshot wound. "Notice anything similar about us?"

Odilia shook her head no.

"Come on. Nothing?"

"I'm sorry," Odilia responded. "I don't know what you want me to say."

"Turns out, Godlip is my brother!" he said. "And this. This is Laudus, my uncle, who I never even knew existed."

Odilia covered her mouth and then reached out to shake Laudus' hand, but she did not do the same for Godlip.

"And this," Sabas continued, his voice slightly shaking, "...is Camara." Camara stood next to Sabas and put her arm on his back.

Odilia nodded. "How do you do?"

Camara didn't answer back. She just nodded and then whispered something into Sabas' ear.

Michelina stepped up towards Odilia and said, "Hey, what am I, chopped liver?" Odilia hugged Michelina and shook Chaney's hand.

"Nice stretcher," she said to Chaney.

"They carried me like I was the ark of the covenant..." Chaney said.

Hylebos asked to speak with Odilia in private, and when he learned that Godlip used to be Gangry and that Gangry used to be the leader of the Sogmols, he insisted that Godlip be kept in their jail. And when Hylebos asked about Laudus, Camara told them he had kidnapped her and mistreated her. Hylebos ordered Laudus to be kept in jail, too. Sabas protested at first, but Laudus just shrugged and said, "Don't worry, nephew. I'm used to it."

Godlip concurred, "It's the right thing, Sabas. I wouldn't expect them to trust me either. Laudus and I will be fine."

After Godlip and Laudus were locked up, Hylebos took his leave, and Odilia showed the others to the gym, where many Dicarers and Bandarians were talking together in groups. When Odilia announced to everyone that Sabas, Michelina, Chaney, and Godlip were not only alive, but they had two new guests, the gym erupted in cheers. The people swarmed around the newcomers and gave them hugs and pats on the back. They welcomed Camara with open arms, and Sabas relayed the news that he and Gangry were brothers and that Laudus was their uncle.

Someone said, "This calls for a celebration, don't you think?" Some of the Bandarians who had instruments began playing lively music. One Dicarer pulled out a bottle of liquor he had brought and passed the bottle to Sabas, who was grateful for a drink.

Camara followed Sabas like a lost puppy. She leaned against him and rested her head on his shoulder. Odilia stood alone, turning red in the face.

Wilton came running up to her, being chased by a little Bandarian girl with ponytails. He used Odilia as a safe base, leaning his back to her and reaching behind himself to grab her leg, all while giggling at the little girl. Soon, Wilton ran off, and the little girl chased after him. Odilia decided to follow him, and the little boy ended up leading her to Jutta, who was sitting alone, apparently lost in thought.

Odilia sat down beside Jutta, and Wilton used both of them to hide from the little girl, who gave up her chase when her mother called to her.

"What are you thinking about?" Odilia asked after Wilton ran off to find the girl.

He glanced at her without answering, as if he hadn't been aware that she was there. "Oh, um. The virus."

"The virus?" She had almost forgotten. "Ah. The virus of repentance. We really should stop calling it that."

There was a long pause as Odilia watched the others, particularly Camara and Sabas, who were now as thick as thieves.

"So...what about the virus?" she said, inching closer to Jutta.

"I have it figured out."

"You do?" Odilia turned and gave him her full attention, ignoring her boyfriend's flirtations with the new girl.

He nodded. "We have it already. I don't need to write it. You have it," he said, pointing to her pocket where he last saw her put the DNI.

"You mean—Father's last memory?"

He nodded.

"What is it? What did you see?" Odilia asked as she pulled it out of her pocket.

He laughed, not in a condescending way but in a way that indicated he could never explain it. "You wouldn't believe it even if I could describe it."

"Try me," she said.

"I said, even if I could describe it. There's something on that disk. If you hadn't unplugged it, I..." he paused. "I don't know what would have happened. It was like I was being split apart. Part of me was being drawn to this incredible brightness. The other was held down, not by someone else, I don't think, but by myself. I, that side of me, it couldn't let go."

"Let go of what?" Odilia asked.

Jutta didn't seem to hear her question. "If I could get the Avogo to experience this," he shook his head. "I think the same thing would happen to them. If no one unplugged it, and they saw the whole thing, they would...be dead. At the very least, they would freak out and either go crazy or repent."

"The beatific vision!" Odilia said. "It must be. Father saw Jesus right when he died!" She glanced back at Sabas and the new girl, then down at Jutta's hands.

"I think you may be right. The Avogo probably couldn't handle the experience of Jesus since they lived such evil lives." Odilia tried gazing deeply into his eyes, but Jutta was fixated on the people talking and singing.

"What beauty!" he said.

Odilia nudged him playfully, and he grabbed her hand and cupped it lovingly between his hands. She did not pull away. "Odilia," he said. "This has made me a different man. Before, I heard you talking about religion, about God, and none of it made any sense. But this. This is different. It goes beyond words, beyond reason, beyond anything that my mind can explain."

Odilia smiled widely and glanced to see if Sabas had noticed them holding hands, but he was too busy talking to others, including Camara.

"Odilia," Jutta said. "I learned something about myself. I understand now what Father Rawley was saying the day he died. I understand why he would be willing to die for this." He paused. "It's all I want. I don't even know how to explain it, but it's all I want. I want to give my life to this, whatever it is."

Odilia pulled her hand away, taking Jutta to mean that he didn't need or want her. She stared at him a moment, trying to read his face to see if it were true. Tears welled up in her eyes, and she tried to look at something else, but all she saw was Camara clinging to Sabas's arm. Sabas noticed that Odilia was glaring at him, and he pulled himself away from the new girl.

"Odilia," Jutta said. "If I can get into Volmar, I can talk to my old friend, a Sasjovian, who can help me get what's on that DNI uploaded into the weekly updates for the Avogo. When they see it, they will change their ways, or they will die."

Odilia put the DNI in his hands and stood up. "It sounds promising," she said in a hurt tone. "You can talk about it tonight with the others before you go to bed. I'm going to see how Chaney is doing." She stood up and walked away, fighting back the tears and trying to be strong.

Chapter 28

The celebration had gone for a little over an hour when Hylebos suggested that everyone should turn in early.

"We're likely to have a very big day tomorrow. We should get some rest," he said. When the crowds began to disperse, Hylebos invited Jutta, Sabas, and Michelina to discuss what they should do about Volmar.

"We should include Godlip and Laudus," Sabas said.

"Okay. And what about Odilia?" Hylebos asked.

Jutta said, "She is talking to Chaney. Want me to go get her?"

"I'll go get her," Michelina said. The others went to the holding cells where Godlip and Laudus were. Once locked inside the small room, they began a strategizing session. Michelina joined them after about ten minutes, unable to find Odilia.

Sabas shared his thoughts about the militia, and Godlip offered advice on where the attack could take place. Jutta was sharing his idea about using Father Rawley's last memory as the virus that could be embedded into the weekly updates when he heard a faint buzzing sound. Jutta stopped talking. The group grew quiet, and soon, they all started searching for the source. Jutta caught the flying insect with cupped hands without squashing it.

"That's no mosquito," he said. "It's from Volmar." He was about to squash it, but Michelina asked if she could have it for research. She wrapped it in cloth and stuck it in a plastic bag.

"I'm not sure how much they heard. Did anyone hear this mosquito before?"

No one had heard it.

"Maybe it just got here. Maybe it didn't hear anything," Michelina said. "Everyone, look around for more."

Everyone searched the cell but didn't see any more suspicious insects. Michelina rummaged around in her toolbag for something to detect electrical current. She saw Redhing in her bag and handed it to Jutta without explanation.

Jutta accepted it gladly. "Perfect," he said. "I needed this."

"There will be Sogmols around," Godlip said as Michelina scanned the room for other listening devices.

"I'll go look," Sabas said and then called for the guards to open the cell.

"Look for Odilia, too," Michelina said. She found no more spying devices in the cell, so she suggested they whisper for the rest of the time.

Jutta quickly finished revealing his plan. Jutta would need to enter in as quietly as possible in order to meet with his old Sasjovian friend, who was responsible for the weekly updates. He would explain that he had been kidnapped and that Redhing had an important report to file. Getting inside would be very difficult; Abaidus was dead, and the Dicarers had no other spies on the inside, so they would need to rely on Godlip, who would enter into the Vauller and somehow take back command of the Sogmols. Hopefully, the Sogmols would still follow him since he had only been gone a couple of days. Michelina and Sabas would be there to back him up.

Since Odilia was not in this planning session, they decided she would wait in Bandonderry for Yaro and Fargus, who should be returning from the Council soon. She would lead the militia, made up of Dicarers and Bandarians, in an attack on Volmar after Godlip and the others had infiltrated the inside. When Godlip's crew gained control of the Sogmols, they would open the doors to let in the militia.

Godlip whispered, "I'm fairly confident the Sogmols will follow me.

Hopefully, Volspat hasn't announced that Scullion was the new Grand Comrade. Normally, Volspat would have some big ceremony for such an event. But, even if he did make the announcement, I will tell them Scullion tried to overthrow me. Besides, I know a lot of them secretly hate the Avogo. Once I take over the Sogmols, the rest should be easy. Most of the citizens of Volmar will be helpless, since they aren't allowed any weapons."

"Yeah, but," Jutta explained as he held up Redhing, "the Avogo control the PASbots, which essentially control the people. Volspat could tell the PASbots to attack us. We just have to be aware of that. There could be some resistance from them."

"You're right," Godlip said. "We should keep the Vaipwo locked out of the Vauller in that case."

By midnight, they had all agreed on the plan and decided to implement it as early as possible.

Jutta needed to sleep but couldn't. He had to write the program to get Father Rawley's last memory into the Avogo updates. Michelina agreed to stay up and help him.

"I need to install Father's memory into Redhing. Then, I can write a program that will send something that acts like a typical behavior report (BR) file, like those reports that all PASbots send everyday about their humans. Those BR files are scanned, and any anomaly, like sadness, anger, despair, is examined by someone in the COGOPT's office. In the report, I could put a message that an update to the Avogo direct neural interface was ready. Then, once someone uploaded it, the Avogo would be forced to see what was inside that memory. The update will start the transfer of the memory."

Michelina examined the DNI. "You really think this memory is that powerful?" She asked.

"Yes," Jutta said. "Believe me."

Michelina shrugged and said, "Okay. Let's get to work." She broke out her computer, and Jutta grabbed Redhing, which he plugged into a charger, but it wouldn't charge.

"How did you disable the auto-charge?" he asked. Michelina stopped what she was doing and got Redhing to start charging. After a few minutes, Jutta took a deep breath and turned it on for the first time since the safe hole incident.

While the PASbot was initializing, Jutta said, "I wish I could have turned it off when I was in Volmar. When did you enable that function?"

"When you first arrived," Michelina said. "You can still wave your hand to mute it, but now, it's not a temporary mute. It'll be quiet as long as you like."

"Nice," Jutta said.

The bot's lights were fully activated now, and it stood up. Jutta's favorite female Avatar appeared. "Jutta. How could you?"

Jutta rubbed his arm, feeling some phantom pain at the sound of the avatar's voice. He got goosebumps all over and began to get a sickly feeling in his stomach.

"This is such an embarrassment to me. I was given a job to do, Jutta. To take care of you and advise you and guide you. You have made me so sad. I have failed the Avogo. What will become of me?" The avatar was standing in a short plaid miniskirt, her hands twisting the skirt and lifting it higher, tears filling her big black eyes.

Michelina scowled. "Oh, my God," she said. "Unbelievable."

Jutta waved his hand to silence the PASbot, and the light on the underbelly began blinking. "Whatever, Redhing," Jutta said. "It's time for me to give you some advice. Don't try to threaten me, gas me, or guilt-trip me. If you do, I swear I will turn you off and destroy you."

The blinking light went solid. Michelina had turned her computer into a wireless mainframe to mimic the one in Volmar. She stood up and offered her computer to Jutta, who took it and began overriding Redhing's BR files.

Jutta spent the entire night working to turn Redhing into a virus carrier. Finally, at about 6:30 a.m., the task was accomplished. Redhing was now reprogrammed and ready to go. All that was left to be done was to get Redhing into the hands of his Sasjovian friend.

Michelina had fallen asleep about four a.m., and Jutta decided not to wake her to tell her he was finished. He poked around on her computer a little and noticed a folder named Library. He opened it and found all those books Chaney had told him about back in Mainz and thousands more. He chuckled and said to himself, "I should put these into Redhing. Make him read them to me sometime."

So he started the transfer. After nearly twenty minutes, Jutta decided he had enough books. Even just the Bible was enough. He couldn't believe he would be able to read it on his own someday. He turned off Redhing, put it in his pocket, and slipped out of the room, trying not to wake Michelina.

Jutta found his way to the mess hall where breakfast was already being served. A few people were there eating their breakfasts of tofu and vegetables, along with a porridge made from millet seed.

Jutta chewed tiredly, recalling the delicious food in Volmar. He had a real craving for a big plate of bacon and eggs and orange juice. He thought about what he would be doing in Volmar at that very hour had he never left. He would have probably just finished breakfast and be about to enjoy a nice hot bath.

The more he thought about it, the more he missed the luxury and the food. He thought about his friends and little Bibiana. He was getting lost in a daydream when someone sat down across from him. He saw a man with a big, black tattoo on his forehead.

"Morning, Jutta," Laudus said.

"Morning," Jutta said, a bit confused. "How did you get out?"

Laudus pointed to the door where a guard was standing.

"Hylebos likes me, I guess."

"Oh," Jutta said, trying hard not to stare at all the tattoos. After a bit of silence, he spoke up, "Can I ask you something?"

"Is it about the tattoos?"

Jutta felt a bit embarrassed. "Sorry. Yes. Mainly the one on your forehead."

Laudus put down his fork and finished chewing his strip of dried tofu, then washed it down with some water. "Tastes like crap," he said.

Jutta smiled in agreement.

"I bet you're used to a lot better than this in Volmar, aren't you?"

He nodded again, and then Laudus began to explain the tattoos one by one. "This one is for my brother, Godlip's and Sabas's dad," Laudus said, pointing to the ones on his arms. "This one is for my lost little sister." Many of them were for losses. One of them he really couldn't remember what it meant. Another represented the days he first began to think he was a man.

"I didn't start out as a man, you know. I was born a girl. The operations and treatments were pretty hard to come by outside of Volmar."

"So why didn't you just come to Volmar?" Jutta asked.

Laudus just laughed and shook his head as he picked over his food.

"Where did you grow up?" Jutta asked.

"Believe it or not, I spent several years in a town like Mainz, when I was a child."

Jutta was intrigued. "You don't look like a Dicarer."

"No. Not anymore. But that might explain this tattoo that you asked about earlier." He said, lifting up the graying hair of his bangs that covered it. "I always felt a little different than the others there. I went through the catechesis and had my first Communion. You probably don't know anything about that, do you?"

Jutta shook his head. "Never heard of it."

"It's complicated. It was good for a while. But as I grew older and realized I was different and that their beliefs didn't seem to have any room for me or for who I was, I stopped...I guess I have to explain the Eucharist first. You see, the Dicarers are Catholics. They believe that when the priest prays over the bread and wine, that it becomes the body and blood of Jesus.

"Ah. That makes sense. That's why I heard them say, 'Body of Christ.'"

"Right. So when you eat the body and blood as a Catholic, you have to do so with a clean conscience. You have to be free of any mortal sin. And unfortunately, as I grew older, just about everything I liked was a mortal sin. So, once I realized this, I stopped taking the Eucharist. I never felt worthy, so I got to where I would just cross my arms and take a blessing from the priest instead of eating the Eucharist."

"I see," Jutta said. "So, the tattoo there on your forehead is a person crossing his arms to receive a blessing."

"Right," Laudus said. "There's another scripture that says 'even the dogs can eat the crumbs that fall from the table.' I'm the dog sitting at the feet waiting for the crumbs."

Jutta nodded but, having just eaten and having stayed up another night with no sleep, he was fighting to keep his eyes open.

"You seem tired. Did you sleep?"

"No. I've been awake all night."

"You should get some rest," Laudus said.

Jutta stood up and said, "Thanks for telling me your story, Laudus. See you later." Jutta took his tray to the kitchen and went back to the gym for a bit of sleep.

Chapter 29

Kidnapped

Jutta slept about two hours in the gym until everyone started gathering there. Jutta was awakened by Wilton, who kept giggling in his ear. Jutta offered a very tired, "Morning, little guy."

He sat up slowly on his elbows and listened to the people talking all around him. Everyone else was awake, and soon, the gym was overflowing. Jutta stood up and folded his blankets, then searched for a place to sit. Eventually, the gym was overflowing, and people were leaning on the walls. Jutta stood near Wilton.

Pastor Hylebos turned on a microphone and addressed the crowd. "Good morning, everyone. I'd like to officially welcome our friends from Mainz this morning. I know I speak for all Bandarians when I say that we are delighted to have you here with us. We only wish it was under better circumstances. I also know that I speak for all Bandarians that we are with you in this fight. Our town council met until late last night, and I'm happy to say that we've approved the use of our militia. We will join with the Dicarers in the fight against the Avogo. Our militia are well-trained. We will fight alongside you. Sabas?" Hylebos motioned for Sabas to stand next to him. "This is Sabas Harriser. He and I will be leading our forces into battle."

Jutta felt in his pocket to make sure Redhing was there. He glanced around the room and noticed that when Hylebos announced Sabas, Odilia slipped away through the back doors.

Sabas took the microphone and tapped it. "Thank you, pastor," he said. "And thank you to all the citizens of Bandonderry for your hospitality and your willingness to join us. As you know, the Sogmols attacked us a couple of days ago. They killed Father

197

Rawley and carried off ten of our own, four men and six women. Two of them are only fourteen years old."

A murmur moved across the crowd of Bandarians who must have been recalling the teen girl who had been kidnapped from them as well.

"But we already have a plan." Sabas revealed a little about the plan to fight back against Volmar, but he said nothing about Godlip's and Jutta's secret plans. When Sabas was finished, Hylebos asked for those who were joining the militia to remain standing but for everyone else to sit down. One young boy, who appeared to be about twelve, remained standing until his mother forced him down into the seat next to her.

Hylebos continued. "I invite everyone to place a hand on one of those who are standing, or raise your hands toward them and let's bless them."

When all the hands in the crowd were lifted up in blessing, Hylebos prayed, "Lord, we stand before you here today about to march on a city that is guilty of enormous sins. It is a strong city, and it has grown haughty in its disregard of you. It's a city that persecutes your people who are gathered here. It is a city that seems impregnable to our minds, but we know that with you, all things are possible. We remember Hebrews 11:30, which says, 'By faith the walls of Jericho fell after the army had marched around them for seven days.' We have faith, Lord Jesus, that the same thing will happen to Volmar. We entrust these men and women to your hands and believe in you, that you will go before us and bring us victory in this just and noble cause..."

After the prayer, the militia was told to gather their weapons and make ready. They were told to write their last will and testaments and to say goodbye to their loved ones in case they did not return. Sabas also reminded people not to go outside the city gates and to keep watch. A Sogmol drone had been found last night, and he suspected Sogmols were around.

Jutta went to look for Odilia as soon as the speeches were over. After asking around, he discovered that she was outside the city gates, alone in a row of date trees that the Bandarians had planted seventy-some years earlier. When she saw him coming, she pretended to be reaching for a date that appeared to be nearly ripe.

"Sabas is going to lead the militia," he told her.

"I know," she said, examining the date and deciding it was not yet ripe.

"I thought he might help Godlip and me get in. But he's needed elsewhere."

She tossed the date aside and sat down under one of the trees and leaned against it.

Jutta was tired and felt impatient to get back to Volmar, but he also remembered that she had just lost Father Rawley and Chester. Some of her friends were being held captive in Volmar, and her city had just been bombed.

"You're the only one who knows her way around the heaps," he continued. "If you can get us close to the Aspodt, Godlip will try to get us in."

"I guess I'm staying here to wait for Yaro and then head the militia," she said gloomily.

"Originally, that was the plan, but I guess Sabas will handle the militia."

Jutta studied the desert landscape. It felt so different than it had that day he rid himself of Redhing when he found himself lost in this vast wasteland.

"You shouldn't be so sad," Jutta said in a moment of inspiration. "You are loved, Odilia. And you have been born in a place where you are wanted and needed. Your life has purpose. One thing I learned from Father Rawley, even though I only knew him a few hours, is that there is something out there that loves us. We need to tell them in Volmar. We need to let them know."

Odilia's expression became more life-filled. It was as if she were a seed that had been lying dormant on a desert floor that had just received rain for the first time in ten years. She blossomed, and Jutta felt that her radiant beauty had never shone brighter.

She stood up and wiped away tears. "Thank you, Jutta," she said. "I needed to hear that. Even if we are never together, you must follow your heart. You are loved, too," she said. She reached out, and they hugged.

While they embraced, three Sogmols surrounded them, guns drawn and fingers to their lips telling them to be quiet. Odilia screamed, but the Sogmols grabbed the two, gagged them, and bound their arms and legs. They riffled through Jutta's pockets and found the DNI, tossed it into the dirt and stomped on it. They pulled Odilia's rosary out of her pocket and threw it on the ground. They took everything away from them except their clothes and Jutta's PASbot. They knew never to touch a citizen's PASbot.

Jutta and Odilia were put in separate traversers, specially designed to hold prisoners. As they sped away, Jutta could hear Odilia crying through her muzzle.

Jutta watched through a slit in his cage as Odilia's traverser went in a different direction than the one he was headed in. When her traverser was out of sight, he watched the tunnel city of Bandonderry slowly disappear behind him. It seemed to him as if the walls of Bandonderry had fallen down and then risen back up around him to form his new prison. He sat back in the darkness of the cage and felt all hope draining from his limbs.

Chapter 30

Approaching Volmar

While Sabas was meeting members of the militia in the gym, Michelina grabbed her bags, found Camara, and brought her to the cell where Godlip and Laudus were being held. She updated them on what the militia was doing and said the four of them should begin making last-minute preparations to help Jutta get inside of Volmar. She checked to make sure all the gadgets she had brought with her were working. Noticing that Redhing and the DNI were gone, she asked, "Anyone seen Jutta?"

"Not since breakfast," Laudus said.

"He was at the meeting in the gym," Camara said.

"What about Odilia?"

The three of them shrugged. None had seen her.

A guard came with keys to unlock the cell and let Laudus and Godlip free. "Hylebos said you should get ready to do your thing," the guard said.

"Thank you," Michelina said. "Let's go find Jutta and Odilia. We need to get moving." They all split up to search for them. Michelina went back to the gym. "Come on, lovebirds," she said softly to herself. "This is no time for a secret rendezvous."

Michelina saw Laudus heading to the gates in front of the city, and she followed. As they walked out into the heat, they heard a child crying. Laudus followed the noise to a tree, where he found a little boy on his knees crying.

"What's the matter, little guy?" Laudus asked.

When the boy saw Laudus, covered in tattoos, he ran straight into Michelina's arms.

"It's okay, little one," Michelina said as she bent down to pick him up. She stood there waiting for Laudus, who bent over to pick something up. He came back to the two, and Wilton was crying to Michelina that Jutta and Odilia had been taken.

They went back inside Bandonderry and told Godlip that Jutta and Odilia had been kidnapped. Wilton, who was always fond of sitting at the gates of the city, had seen the whole thing. Laudus showed them what he had picked up, the crushed DNI and the broken rosary. Michelina put Wilton down and sat on a nearby sofa to deal with her shock.

"I should have known," Godlip said. "After that mosquito last night, we knew they were around. I should have warned them better." He knelt down by Wilton, who was now in Michelina's arms, and asked, "Did you see where they went?"

But the boy just tucked his face into Michelina's arms.

"He saw them carted off on traversers towards Volmar," Michelina said as she patted Wilton on the back and squeezed him tight.

"They are probably on their way back to Volmar. We need to tell Sabas," Godlip said.

When Sabas heard that Odilia and Jutta had been captured, he pressured Hylebos to dispatch the militia earlier than they had planned. Hylebos agreed they would march that night to Mainz and then march on Volmar the next day.

Godlip gathered Michelina, Laudus, and Camara and said, "If we leave now, we might catch up with Jutta and Odilia. Even if we don't catch them, we can go ahead with our plan for me to get inside and retake the Sogmols." So Godlip's group of four set out on two traversers.

After passing Mainz, Laudus, who was riding with Michelina because Camara had refused to ride with him, tapped her on the shoulder. "Michelina," he shouted. "Can we stop? I have an idea."

Michelina pulled over, and Goldip stopped next to them. "What's the problem?" he asked.

Michelina pointed her thumb at Laudus as if to say, "Not me; it's this guy."

"It appears that we won't catch up with Jutta. I just thought it might be better if we had a backup plan in case you, no offense, nephew, in case you don't succeed."

"What do you suggest?" Godlip asked.

"I was thinking; you know I was originally on my way to Volmar to sell Camara to the Avogo. They were expecting me. We could certainly get in that way. I could just walk up to the front gate with her and..."

"Oh, no," Camara said. "You're not going to let him take me back again."

Godlip shook his head. "I'll get in. Don't worry."

They all got back on their traversers and continued riding, but after a while, Godlip began to think that Laudus was right. If they all entered the city at the same time, there would be no backup if the plan failed. About five miles away from Volmar, he stopped.

When Michelina stopped next to him, he said, "Laudus is right. Laudus and Camara should wait behind us and stay together in case something goes wrong. Maybe they can help from the inside somehow. Nobody knows they're on our side. They could at least be spies for us."

Camara shook her head vehemently.

Godlip said to her, "Look, I know you don't trust Laudus, but think of the others who are depending on us. I know you don't have a stake in this matter. You're not from Mainz or Volmar, but if you can help us, we will be forever grateful."

Camara thought a minute. "I'll do it for Sabas. But keep your hands off of me, Laudus."

Michelina got off her traverser and rode the rest of the way to Volmar with Godlip. Laudus followed them with Camara sitting behind him, holding on to the traverser bars rather than Laudus's back.

After almost two hours, they pulled over behind some heaps outside the motion-monitored perimeter of Volmar. They dismounted the traversers and squatted down to survey the terrain. It was familiar territory to Godlip.

They discussed their final plans, and once they were ready, Michelina set off a small electromagnetic pulse device that she got from Bandonderry. The EMP disabled the motion sensors, and soon, Godlip and Michelina were crawling through the chute that led to the Aspodt. The room where Jutta had been rescued was empty, and the two moved quickly through it.

Outside the room, it sounded like a party was going on. They had made it in undetected. Godlip led Michelina quietly through a long corridor to the Vauller. He slowly opened the door to find that no one was there. The Vauller was completely empty. He ran to the holding cells where the Dicarers were the last time he saw them, but the cells were empty, too.

"This is strange," he whispered to Michelina. "Where could everyone be?" After a moment, he heard a movement deep inside the cells. When he shined a flashlight, he saw that there was only one prisoner there, and she was gagged.

"Odilia!" Michelina said, a bit too loudly. Godlip put his hand over her mouth to silence her. Then, he tried the codes he knew when he was Grand Comrade, but none of them worked. After trying the last possible code, he heard the voice he feared the most.

"Welcome home, Gangry." It was Volspat. "Have you brought me another Dicarer? That was kind of you. I'm getting quite the collection."

Chapter 31

Slave

Jutta had been riding in the Sogmol's cage for quite some time, trying to peek through the air slits to search for Odilia, but her traverser was nowhere in sight. It was dark inside the small compartment, and wanting to see better, he decided to turn on Redhing.

As he waited for the bot to power on, a pale glow from Redhing gave him a better view of the solid metal enclosure that appeared to be made without any seams. There were no weak spots to exploit, and no matter how hard he kicked the door, it didn't budge.

When Redhing finally spoke, Jutta nearly threw the bot against the wall. A flood of memories came crashing in on him, but he refrained and just held Redhing at a safe distance to make sure the bot couldn't latch onto him.

"Master Jutta. You have treated me very poorly these last few days. How could you, after all we've been through?"

"Light," Jutta said. The cage lit up, and Jutta said, "We've been through nothing together, Redhing, nothing."

"That is very hurtful, Jutta. Your badacts are piling up on you. You know that we are not supposed to say hurtful things."

"Oh. But I suppose it's okay for you to try to KILL me?"

"What are you implying?"

"I'm not implying anything. I'm saying you tried to gas me. Remember that? You tried to kill me."

"Absurd! I didn't try to kill you. I'm your PASbot. I was trying to save you from yourself. You had just torn me off like no good Sasjovian has ever done in history, and then you were about to leave me down in the hole. The gas was just to make you sleep until your mind could understand clearly what the rightact was.”

“It’s all lies. Everything you ever told me was a lie. The whole city was just a lie, and you can report all of this to the COGOPT. I don’t even care.”

“Of course, I will have to do that. I am adding it to the BR...That’s strange.”

“What?” Jutta asked.

“I was going to add it to the BR file, but it seems corrupt. I can’t write to it.”

Jutta began to doubt that turning Redhing on had been a good idea. “I’m sure it’s just because you’ve been off for so long. You’ve never been shut down before. Who knows what it can do to BR files? Anyway, the good news is that we’re on our way back to Volmar. They’ll fix you up in no time, I’m sure.”

“That’s wonderful news, Jutta! I’m so happy for us. You and I can certainly do with a little reprogramming right about now.”

The humming of the traverser began to slow down, and just minutes later, the traverser came to a complete stop. Jutta could hear a Sogmol’s voice but couldn’t quite make out what he was saying. He shouted out Odilia’s name several times, but there was no answer. Jutta kicked at the door to no avail. After a few moments, the traverser started up, and they were on their way once again.

“Why are you so concerned about that conniving little girl?” Redhing said.

“Shut up, Redhing. Sleep,” Jutta said, and the PASbot went to sleep.

In a couple more hours, Jutta sensed that they were arriving in Volmar. When he heard the gates opening, Jutta woke up Redhing and muted it, then took a deep breath and allowed the PASbot to crawl back onto him.

The door of his prison swung open, and two Sogmols reached in and pulled him out of the cage. Jutta quickly realized that he was not in Volmar. He didn't recognize the place, but he saw twenty or thirty people walking around in a courtyard surrounded by a tall fence with barbed wire at the top. The whole complex had many tarps that served as shade, and giant fans were blowing to keep the people cool.

The Sogmols forced Jutta to walk to the gate, where a giant man who reminded Jutta of Laudus was standing. They spoke in a language Jutta could not understand, and it sounded like they were arguing. Eventually, the man pulled out a digital wallet from his pocket and punched a few numbers into it. The Sogmols checked their own wallets and then left Jutta with the man. Jutta was then forced into the cage where a large group of dejected people stared blankly at him.

"I've been sold to CHAI," Jutta said to Redhing hopelessly. "I'm a slave now. I'll never get to Volmar. I'll never see Odilia again. Oh, God! Help me."

He felt the bot crawl up his shirt and stop near his armpit. "God? I'm your PASbot," Redhing said. "I am here for your protection, for your service, for your pleasure..."

Chapter 32
The Council

Yaro and Fargus had been waiting patiently for two days to plead their case to the Council of United Townships, an organization that had been formed nearly 100 years earlier to solve disputes among the settlements. When their turn finally came, the president welcomed them into the general assembly.

"Thank you for hearing our case," Yaro said. "For quite some time now, Volmar has been engaged in the practice of killing its own citizens who are too old or decrepit or who have some infirmity that the Avogo don't like. Recently, they attacked our city and killed our priest..."

"Hold on," the president said, "I am going to stop you there. We have received numerous complaints from Volmar that the city of Mainz has been engaged in covert operations aimed at destabilizing their government."

Yaro tried to speak, but the president said, "I'm not finished. They say that you had a spy living on the inside of the city? Is this true?"

"But..." Yaro said.

"And is it also true that you kidnapped several of their citizens?" the president asked.

"No. We didn't kidnap them. We rescued them," Fargus said.

"Semantics," the president said. "It also says here that you have tampered with their sensors and have made numerous attempts to brainwash their people with your own opinions on religion."

"There's a reason for all of that," Yaro said, growing agitated.

"I'm quite sure there is," the president said. "I'm quite sure. But what I'm hearing now is that you admit to these crimes that are in violation of the CTR code 1831.2 section B."

"But, Mr. President, if I may speak," Yaro said, "we were just trying to stop them from murdering people."

"Murder, euthanasia, refreshing, whatever you call it, our codes ensure the sovereignty of each town," the president said. "And you are not to interfere with or push your agenda on anyone else. It is our judgment that you must pay a fine for continued and repeated infringement on the rights of Volmar in the amount of 3,000 Ravi due by the end of this fiscal year."

"This is unjust!" Yaro yelled as guards entered the room and began forcefully removing them. "Did Volspat get to you?" he shouted as a guard grabbed him by his shoulder. Fargus tried to push the guard away but was met with a stick to the face. The two were kicked out of the assembly and began making their way back to Bandonderry.

At about four p.m. that day, they arrived in Bandonderry and shared the bad news with Sabas and Hylebos, who were now ready to lead the militia, made up of 120 men and 40 women, towards Volmar. They planned a very grueling march to Mainz where they would rest a few hours and then march on to Volmar the next day. Yaro and Fargus, still fuming about their treatment at the hands of the Council, readily agreed to join the fight.

Hylebos and Sabas each rode their own traverser while nearly everyone else marched on foot except for several scouts who rode ahead and also looked out for the enemy around them. When they finally reached Mainz around midnight, Sabas heard the transmitter in Michelina's office ringing.

He answered the call and heard a desperate voice on the other end.

"The Sogmols have overrun us. They are demanding that all of you return to Bandonderry and surrender the weapons."

A Sogmol's voice came over the transmitter. "Make sure you ALL come back. We watched you leave. We counted. There's 160 of you.

If you don't return with 160 people, we will destroy the town and do whatever we please with the people in it."

Sabas hung up the receiver and ran to tell Hylebos. The pastor didn't hesitate to give the order to turn back. They had not even had time to rest before they began their long, sad journey back to Bandonderry.

Chapter 33

A Ghost and a Cup of Coffee

Laudus and Camara waited in place for well over an hour, saying nothing to each other before they came to the conclusion that plan B should be set in motion.

"I guess they didn't make it," Laudus finally said.

Camara stood up as if she were going to run, but the unbearable heat made the idea of slavery in a cool place attractive.

"I've done this before, you know," Laudus said, avoiding eye contact with her. "I've sold several girls to the Avogo. Last time I went back to Volmar, I saw one of the girls. She was doing fine. One of the Avogo, Clauberg, took a special liking to her. You could probably have a good life in there. Better than what you had in CHAI."

"How could you know what it's like to be in CHAI?" she retorted.

Laudus shrugged. "Do *you* know what it was like in CHAI?" he asked.

She thought about it for a moment. "Well, at least I wasn't miserable like I am now."

"You were just part of the machine. You were only a pair of its eyes and saw nothing for yourself. That's why you're called Camera. Why did you tell Sabas your name was Camara?"

She didn't answer.

"Anyway, I did you a favor."

"Whatever. All I know is this sucks."

"You like Sabas, don't you?"

She was silent.

"Do this for him."

She nodded and Laudus said, "Good. You ready then?"

She shrugged her shoulders like a teenager who acquiesces to a parent's command. As he bound her hands loosely, she said, "You know, you're not as bad as I thought."

"I guess most people aren't," Laudus said. "If I get a bit rough, just remember, it's for show. I really do hope our plans work, but if not, I hope you are happy in Volmar. You don't have to kill anyone if you don't want to. You're free, at least from me."

The two approached the gates of the city, and as they drew near, a sterile voice said, "Welcome to Volmar. Please show your face and state the purpose of your visit."

"Business," Laudus said.

"I'm sorry. I didn't catch that. Please choose from the following. If you are interested in joining us as a citizen, please say 'Join.' If you are here to visit a citizen, please say 'visit.' If you are here for trade, please say 'business.'"

Laudus looked at Camara and rolled his eyes. "Didn't I just say that? BUSINESS."

"I'm sorry, Laudus," the computer said. "Let me get someone to help you."

"Computers. See what I saved you from?" he whispered.

She smiled, but then Laudus remembered that she was his prisoner, and they were probably being watched. He stopped joking.

"What is the purpose of your visit?" someone asked. This time it was clearly a human.

"Oh, thank God," Laudus said. "Yeah. I'm a ghost delivering another cup of coffee."

"One moment, please."

After a few seconds, the gates opened, and Laudus pushed Camara into a waiting room where people with any interest in Volmar were vetted. The gates were closed behind them, and an attendant greeted them from behind a thick bullet-proof window.

She messaged the Avogo and told Laudus and Camara to have a seat.

After a long wait, the ancient-looking man named Clauberg came and began to examine Camara. "Took you long enough," he said to Laudus.

"Yeah. But she's top-notch coffee, just the way you like 'em."

"Age?" Clauberg said.

"About 18," Laudus said.

"22," Clauberg said.

"I mean, she told me she was 18, man," Laudus said.

"No. Ravi. 22 Ravi."

"Sheesh, are you kidding me?" Laudus said. "She's worth thirty-two at the least."

"Okay. Take her somewhere else if you think you can get that."

"Ah, come on, Clauberg, work with me here. If I'm going to keep you caffeinated, I've gotta be compensated. You know you need me. And this one, believe me. Nice rich flavor. Bold roast for sure."

Clauberg said, "Twenty-six, take it or leave it."

Laudus thought about it a moment. He lifted a lock of Camara's hair and sniffed it, acting as though he were savoring for the last time something that he would be missing.

"Throw in a three night's stay here, and we got a deal," Laudus said.

Clauberg agreed and called to a Vaipwo who was waiting outside the room. The Vaipwo brought in the digital currency exchanger to supply the Ravi that was promised. Laudus pulled out his wallet and watched the currency appear in his account.

"Pleasure doing business with you, Clauberg!" Laudus said.

Clauberg just rolled his eyes and said, "You can stay three days. But be sure you disappear again after you've had your fun." Then, he put his hand on Camara's arm and said, "Come, my dear. Let's have a closer look at you," and then he led her away.

Another Vaipwo accompanied Laudus to the part of Volmar that was built for guests and showed him to his room. He took a shower, ate a huge meal and considered sitting down in the pleasure craft in his room, but he kept thinking about Camara. He felt guilty thinking about what Clauberg might do to her.

He felt an urgent need to find out what happened to Gangry and Michelina. So he got dressed and began searching for signs of them. He could hear what sounded like a fantastic party coming from the inner city, but he couldn't join as a guest. Without an escort, he was only allowed in the outer reaches of the city.

"And finally," someone on the loudspeaker was saying. "The moment you've all been waiting for. The culmination of our beloved's refreshing, the beautiful and precious Eve Jutta Duc!" A loud burst of applause was followed by long ooohs and ahs.

When Laudus realized it was the returning ceremony for Jutta, the bitterness of the whole affair filled his mouth. He wished he hadn't eaten the food there. He somehow felt contaminated and restless, so he circled the perimeter several times.

At one point, a door opened, and he saw that Gangry and Michelina were being led to the Vauller in shackles. Laudus walked faster to catch up with them, shouting at the Sogmol guard, "Excuse me, sir. Excuse me."

The guard slowed down. "Do you know where the Vauller is? I was looking for a friend." He said the first thing that came to mind.

"You need to have a pass to go there," the guard said. "Let me see your pass."

Laudus slapped his forehead. "Oh. Shit. I forgot. It's in my room. Just took a shower. I'll go get it. Is the Vauller right there, though?" The guard said it was, and Laudus went back to his room. Michelina and Godlip did not do anything to betray the fact that they knew each other.

He returned to his room and racked his brain to figure out how to get a pass to the Vauller. But eventually, he concluded that getting a pass would be impossible, so he waited until late at night when he thought there would be fewer guards. He made his way to the Vauller and checked the door, which, to his surprise, was unlocked. He slowly stepped in and saw the cells where Godlip and Michelina were being held. The guard seemed to be playing some sort of game at his station about thirty feet from the prisoners.

Laudus entered quietly. Michelina saw him approach, and she motioned that he should hurry. She pulled off her shoe and took something out of it. When he made it to their cell, she handed him a small electronic locator, and he put it in his pocket, whispering in his ear, "I put a tracking device on Jutta's PASbot. He's not in Volmar. If you find Jutta, help him get to Volmar. If he's dead, find the bot and bring it to Volmar. It should install the virus when it connects to the mainframe."

That was all she had time to say. The guard pulled out his gun and told Laudus to step away from the cell. Laudus held his hands up. "Sorry, I was just trying to find an old friend of mine named Skyte? Do you know him?"

"You're not supposed to be here," the guard said.

"I know, but I just wanted to see my old friend. Lovely prisoners you've got here. Where are they from?"

The guard snickered and said, "Never mind the prisoners. Why don't you tell me why you're really here."

"Look, I just came to town to sell someone to Clauberg. He said I could stay a few days, and I thought I'd see if Skyte was here."

The guard yelled, "Skyte is a Sogmol. We don't have friends outside the city. So how about you tell me how you know his name and what you're doing here."

Laudus was usually good at spur-of-the-moment lies, but this time, he couldn't think of anything.

"I'm sure Clauberg would like to know what his guest is up to," the guard said as he lifted up a receiver to report him.

"Look," Laudus said, "he just paid me for the girl. I've got money. If you let me go, I'll give you five Ravi."

The guard sized him up and hung up the receiver. "If that's the case, I'm sure your freedom is worth double that. Ten," he said in a lowered voice.

Laudus acted disappointed at the price, but he pulled out his digital currency wallet and punched a few numbers into it. The guard waved his own wallet across Laudus's and verified that the transfer was complete.

"Now, get the hell out of here," he said, pushing Laudus out of the Vauller.

He went back to his room, grabbed some food and supplies and then made his way to the traversers that they had left hidden outside the city. He struggled to find them in the dark, but once he did, he pulled out the locator that Michelina had given him and set off in search of Jutta.

Chapter 34

Escaping Bandonderry

In Bandonderry, Sabas and the militia returned and surrendered to the Sogmol army, which had begun terrorizing the people. They searched through all the homes and confiscated all the guns. They vandalized and destroyed things, especially Bibles and other religious contraband. And just for fun, they ran through the city screaming and threatening the people. After a couple of hours, they began to settle down and instituted a lockdown.

Sabas wondered why the Sogmols didn't arrest or kill him as the leader of the militia, but then he thought maybe it was because Scullion and Gangry were both gone, and they probably didn't have a new Grand Comrade. For whatever reason, Sabas was still as free as any other citizen. When the lockdown order came, and he saw Sogmols sweeping through the hallways looking for stragglers who were not in their rooms, he ducked into the closest room, which happened to be where Chaney, the injured Dicarer, was recovering.

Chaney was sleeping when Sabas entered, so he found a place to sit and tried not to fly off into a rage as he itemized the number of mistakes he had made. He blamed himself for everything, starting with the death of Fr. Rawley, to Chester's death, to Odilia's kidnapping, right down to the captivity of the entire town. After all, he was the one who had pushed Hylebos to march earlier than they had planned.

A few minutes of this self-blame session had passed when two men were forced into the room with Sogmols shouting after them, "Stay in there or die."

It was Yaro and Fargus. As they entered, he nodded at them and said glumly, "Godlip and the others are probably prisoners by now.

They probably got to the city, and Volspat surprised them. It was like he knew every detail of our plans."

"Was there a spy among you?" Fargus asked.

"I don't know," Sabas answered.

"Tell us more about Laudus."

Sabas appeared surprised. "Why? Do you think he could have betrayed us?"

He couldn't stand the thought that it would have been his own relative to betray them. But then he said, "Could have been him. Who knows? There were Sogmol spies and mosquito drones. They probably had drones everywhere. We were careless. I should have known." Sabas stood up and punched the back of the chair he had been sitting in, then paced back and forth, running his hands through his hair.

Chaney woke up coughing, and Yaro and Fargus ran to his side. He smiled when he saw the two men around his bed.

"The saints have returned!" he said weakly, reaching out his hand to Yaro, who took his hand and held it.

"I take it from your sad faces that you don't have good news."

Yaro shook his head. "How are you feeling?" Yaro asked.

"I've been better."

After telling Chaney everything that had happened, Yaro had more information that he hadn't yet told Sabas. "While we were out, we heard some other bad news. There are rumors that Volspat sold our friends to CHAI. I'm afraid it may be too late to help them."

"Why does CHAI need more people?" Chaney asked.

"Bodies. It just needs bodies. Who knows what a super-intelligent network of computers and brains thinks? But it does need bodies. Just like we need a body to move around and take care of ourselves, to feed our minds."

"Something bad is happening," Sabas said. "If Volspat is selling people to CHAI, something is happening for sure. Have you ever known Volspat to sell anyone? He always preferred killing them to selling them."

"Well," Fargus said. "What we need to consider is what to do now. How can we get out of here or start fighting back?"

Ultimately, they all agreed it would be best to sneak out and start with Volmar. Sabas wanted to leave immediately. Hylebos had shown him a secret tunnel that he could use to get out of the city. "Let's go, now. Let's go," Sabas said.

"We must rest first," Yaro said. "We have been traveling for so long and haven't had anything to eat. I don't remember the last time I've slept."

Sabas rummaged through the cabinets in the room where he found some stale bread that he offered to the two deacons.

Something about Sabas offering them bread set Chaney on a long sermon that apparently no one was interested in. Yaro and Fargus lay down on the floor to rest, and Sabas sat in a chair, restlessly bouncing his knee up and down as Chaney kept talking.

After about fifteen minutes of Chaney's discourse on the meaning of life, Fargus got up and felt Chaney's forehead. "You're hot," he said. Then he poured Chaney a cup of water and helped him drink it. After a moment, he said, "Enough philosophizing. Let's pray. Let's ask the saints, Mary, and the angels to pray for us. We need all the prayer we can get. Then we will sleep awhile."

Yaro sat up slowly, pulled out his rosary and, caressing it lovingly, he said, "Father used to say this was his weapon. He was carrying around a fifty-round clip."

Fargus sat on a chair and took out his own rosary and announced the first sorrowful mystery.

Sabas tried to calm his mind and pray, but he just couldn't do it. He stood up in the middle of the second decade when he should have been contemplating Jesus being scourged at the pillar and announced that he had to go.

"Have you forgotten the Sogmols are still here?" Yaro asked. "Who knows how long they'll stay to ensure we are under control."

"That just means they aren't at Volmar. Now's the time to attack Volmar. I will sneak out through the tunnel Hylebos told me about. If I get caught, then I'll resort to praying. But as long as there's a chance for me to fight, my action will be my prayer."

"You may be right. Listen, if you make it out, go to Acedia," Yaro said as he pulled himself up off the floor. "We were planning to go there tomorrow. Ask for a man named Putrm. Tell him about Father Rawley. Maybe he can help. We will try to meet you there later. But for now, we should rest and stay here to help the others."

Sabas told them where the secret door was and then slipped quietly out of the room.

Chapter 35

Perduring

Jutta was led into a large group of people who sat around moping quite hopelessly in the growing darkness. He surmised that they, too, had just been sold and were prisoners like him. As the sun set, the only light came from campfires glowing in metal bins around the camp. Jutta found a place to sit down and take a rest. A few desperate voices could be heard talking quietly. He didn't like the sound of sadness, so he sought a distraction from Redhing.

When he remembered that he had installed the Bible on to Redhing, Jutta said, "Read me something in the Bible."

Redhing answered, "I'm sorry, Jutta. That one is not...Oh. Yes. Here it is. That's strange. I suppose it is approved."

Jutta smiled, knowing that he had been able to override the permissions' settings in Redhing. Maybe Redhing would send the virus, after all...that is, if he ever got back to Volmar. "Genesis Chapter 1," Redhing began reading. "In the beginning, God created the heavens and the earth..."

The camp slowly grew silent. Though he had turned Redhing's voice low, others heard it. Some people began to gather around Jutta. An older lady sat down next to him and asked, "Can you turn it up?" They all seemed interested in hearing the PASbot read Scripture. The lady looked familiar to him. Others came up closer and gathered around. Some of them were familiar to him as well. He paused Redhing. "Do I know you?" he asked the lady.

She gazed at him sadly. "Yes, Jutta. You know me."

"You're all from Mainz, aren't you?" he said, suddenly realizing who these captives were.

The lady said softly, "I'm sorry, dear. We thought you could help us. But you're here. You're a prisoner, too." A murmur that Jutta was with them went through the camp full of Dicarers who had just been sold from Volmar.

"Never mind that," someone said. "Let's listen to some more. Play some more, Jutta." So, he turned up the volume and let Redhing read the Scriptures to the crowd. Redhing didn't read passages in order. He skipped around and read chapters from different books. The last one that was read before the camp guards came to enforce silence was from the book of Wisdom:

In Wisdom is a spirit intelligent, holy, unique, manifold, subtle, agile, clear, unstained, certain, not baneful, loving the good, keen, unhampered, beneficent, kindly, firm, secure, tranquil, all-powerful, all-seeing, and pervading all spirits, though they be intelligent, pure and very subtle. For Wisdom is mobile beyond all motion, and she penetrates and pervades all things by reason of her purity. For she is an aura of the might of God and a pure effusion of the glory of the Almighty; therefore nought that is sullied enters into her. For she is the refulgence of eternal light, the spotless mirror of the power of God, the image of his goodness. And she, who is one, can do all things, and renews everything while herself perduring;

And passing into holy souls from age to age, she produces friends of God and prophets. For there is nought God loves, be it not one who dwells with Wisdom. For she is fairer than the sun and surpasses every constellation of the stars. Compared to light, she takes precedence; for that, indeed, night supplants, but wickedness prevails not over Wisdom.

The guards barked at the people to go to sleep. The others quickly dispersed. Jutta silenced Redhing and lay down on the ground, thinking about all the Scripture he'd just heard. He thought what a beautiful world it would be where wisdom could prevail and the refulgence—he had never heard that word—of eternal light would shine. As he fell asleep, it was as if the light were consuming him again. This time it was different. While it was the same light, rather than striking terror, it brought with it an overwhelming sense of peace, like everything he had ever loved and enjoyed most in the world times two.

Early in the morning before the sun rose, he was awakened by someone's foot on his back, rocking him to and fro. "Wake up. Get up. Let's go."

Jutta tried shielding himself from the person who was accosting him. A couple of arms reached down and stood him on his feet. The blood began to rush to his head, and he started to wake up.

"Let's go. Someone's here for you."

"What? Who?" he asked.

"Just hurry up. Walk faster."

Jutta was led to the gates of the makeshift compound that served as the prison for the Dicarers and other new slaves. Standing there at the gate was a familiar, tattooed face.

"This the one?" the guard asked in a tone of urgency.

"Yeah. That's him," Laudus said. ·

"30 Ravi, let's see it," the guard said. Laudus pulled out his digital currency wallet. They waved their wallets next to each other, and the transaction was completed.

The guard with the wallet nodded to the other, confirming they had the money. "Quick. Give him the prisoner. You guys need to hightail it out of here. If you're caught again, you just wasted your Ravi. You won't be getting it back."

Laudus beckoned to Jutta, "Let's get out of here, Jutta. Come on."

The two mounted the traverser and left the other Dicarers in captivity. They only got a few miles away before the traverser ran out of energy, and they had to stop. They found a hidden place to rest, and Laudus explained to Jutta all that had happened.

Chapter 36

The Tavern-Goers

Sabas found his way to the entrance of the hidden tunnel, but two Sogmol guards were talking almost directly in front of the tunnel door. Sabas hid behind a column and cautiously peered out to make sure he was at the right place. The number on the door that the guards were standing next to read 88, and the wall had a decorative wainscot section just as Hylebos had described. All he would have to do was push down and up on part of the wainscot to open the door. The tunnel was behind the wall, and it ran to a drainage tube. It would be a nasty escape when he got to the drainage, but it was better than staying there.

After about twenty minutes, the guards began to argue about who was the better shot. One challenged the other to a shooting contest, and they went to the nearby back entrance and began shooting into the desert.

As soon as they left, Sabas opened the hidden door, slipped into the narrow tunnel, and then closed the door behind him. He emerged about a quarter of a mile from Bandonderry just as the sun was beginning to come up. He had only one hope in mind: make it to the outpost called Acedia, like Yaro said. Acedia was frequently used by ghosts and mendicants and was only about five miles south of Bandonderry. He had been there a couple of times in his life when he went hunting, and he knew it to be nothing more than a rest stop with a tavern.

He didn't know why Yaro suggested he go there, but he had a hunch something good would come of it. And if nothing else, he thought someone there might know where he could get some explosives that he could bring into Volmar with him. Maybe he would try the same thing that the distraught father of the missing girl from Bandonderry did; just walk up to Volmar with a bomb and see what kind of damage he could do before he died.

After a long hot walk, he came to the dusty tavern with only a small wooden sign hanging on the door, the word *'Acedia'* carved crudely on it. An old man with a long gray beard was lying at the doorway, apparently drunk. As Sabas carefully began to step over him, the old man opened his eyes and sat up.

"What brings you here?" he asked in an unevenly curious voice.

Sabas was reluctant to speak. He scanned the place carefully.

"Something bad," the old man said, standing up and brushing himself off. He entered the tavern and turned on a dim light behind the bar.

Sabas followed him into the bar slowly to give his eyes time to adjust to the poorly lit interior.

"Want to hear a poem?" the man asked as he busied himself behind the bar. Sabas sat down cautiously on a barstool and didn't answer. As his eyes adjusted, he started to discern what he thought were booths and tables. But he didn't see any other people.

"Today, like every day, we are ruined and lonely," the old man said. "Don't retreat, fleeing your emptiness through the doorway of thinking. Try making some music instead. There are hundreds of ways to kneel in prayer—hundreds of ways to open toward the heart of the Friend's beauty."

Some archaic music began to play softly in the background. Sabas could make out the chorus, which repeated "band on the run."

The old man stood behind the bar, smiling at him as if he were waiting for Sabas to say something.

After a moment, Sabas said, "This is going to sound weird, but, I mean, just a couple of hours ago, I was trying to pray, but I couldn't. I just couldn't pray that way. How did you know to say that?"

"To say what?" the old man asked as if he had forgotten about the poem he had just recited.

"That part about there being a hundred ways to pray. I just told someone that my actions would be my prayer."

"Ah. You're a man of action," the man said. "That's good. But 'don't look down on those of inaction. They may be acting in their own way.' But, as Sa'di said, 'A monk and a lover can't live in the same room.'"

The old man finished making a drink and put a metal cup filled with a brown liquor in front of Sabas.

"Will you drink? Are you really a man of action?"

Sabas looked around again as if to see if he were being set up. His eyes were seeing more clearly now, and he slowly realized that others were there in the bar as well, sitting in the booths and at the tables. He stared first at the drink and then at the man whose expression bewildered him. Something didn't feel right. The others appeared to be drunk. *Ghosts*, he thought. *I have a job to do.*

"I just came here to see if you knew where I could get some explosives," Sabas said, pushing the drink back to the other side of the bar.

"Stop acting so holy and putting down the tavern goers! Another person's sins will never be tallied by you. Whether I'm good or bad, mind your own business! In the end, everyone reaps what they have sown. Each person, whether sober or drunk, seeks the Beloved; every place is love's home, whether synagogue or mosque. My head surrenders, lying on the bricks of the tavern's door...Stop trying to rob me of heaven's grace."

The man pushed the drink back towards Sabas, who said, "What are you even talking about? I'm not trying to rob you of anything,"

The old man smiled at him and said, "It's a Sufi poem."

"Oh," Sabas said. "Look, I'm not here to rob you or whatever. I'm from Mainz, and I am supposed to ask for a man named Putrm. Have you heard of him?"

"You're from Mainz?" a deep voice asked from the darkness.

Sabas turned around slowly, hoping to see who was talking.

"We heard Mainz was attacked by Volmar," the voice continued. "Something should be done about that place."

Not sure if the stranger had meant Volmar or Mainz, Sabas asked, "What place?"

"Volmar, of course."

The person who had been speaking stood up and started walking towards Sabas into the dim light as if he were an apparition gradually getting brighter and bigger. He was a towering figure nearly seven feet tall. He appeared to weigh about 300 lbs. He held out his hand and introduced himself. "I'm Putrm. You are?"

"Sabas."

Another voice in the darkness called out, "The Avogo are getting out of hand, if you ask me. Them and that stupid council of theirs!"

Sabas grabbed the drink in front of him. The smile on the old man's face bought his trust, and Sabas drank it down. Putting the empty cup down on the bar, he said, "The Sogmols attacked us and killed our priest, and kidnapped ten of our citizens. A couple of days ago, two more Sogmols came in and killed one of our men, but we killed both of them. We found out the Avogo were going to bomb us, so the whole town went to Bandonderry. We got together a militia and were on our way to rescue our people, when out of nowhere, the Sogmols showed up in Bandonderry. Now the whole city is occupied, and our militia has surrendered. I just snuck out this morning. Yaro told me to come to Acedia. He said maybe you could help. The Avogo have taken everyone I love."

Putrm asked, "What was the name of the priest who died?"

"Father Rawley."

The big guy's shoulders slumped. "He was a good man."

A squirrely looking girl came out from the dark recesses and said, "I heard that they sold a lot of Dicarers to CHAI yesterday."

"Where did you hear that?" Sabas asked.

"Oh. We hear things," she said.

"I heard that, too," Sabas said.

"Should we help him?" the girl asked the big guy.

Putrm winked at the girl and said, "Naturally."

"Kickass!" someone shouted, and the whole bar erupted in excitement.

People began coming out of the darkness like cockroaches out of old woodwork. There must have been twenty or thirty men and women, all dressed in whatever scrap of clothes they could find.

The old man brought Sabas a plate of dried bean curd and some dandelion tea. By noon, the motley group had loaded up on vehicles they called three-wheeled plowders and headed towards Bandonderry to liberate the Bandarians from Sogmol control.

Chapter 37

The Eye of the Tiger

As the sun came up, Laudus and Jutta had run out of energy in their traverser. But they were able to see the city of Volmar glimmering like a diamond in the distance. It was a beautiful city, indeed. Jutta found himself daydreaming about being back inside, living a life of comfort. He told Laudus about the food there and the fun that he had from time to time. "Even though I didn't really fit in there, I guess it was pretty nice just to have all your needs taken care of. That was nice. But then there were the refreshings and all the secrets that the Avogo kept." Then he paused a moment and asked, "Was Odilia okay when you saw her?"

Laudus said, "She seemed okay in the cell next to Gangry and Michelina. Who knows what they will do with her, though?"

Jutta nodded. "Volspat has wanted her for a long time." As they surveyed at the city in the distance, an idea came to Jutta.

He turned toward Laudus. "What is today?"

Laudus shook his head and struggled to remember. "Let's see, we were in Bandonderry two nights ago? That was Wednesday...it has to be Friday."

Jutta's heart began to beat faster. "And what time do you think it is now?"

Laudus studied the shadows being cast off the mountains in the distance. "I'd say around 7:30?"

Realizing he could just ask Redhing, he woke the bot up and asked, "What time is it, Redhing?"

"It is 8:05 a.m., Master."

Jutta turned on the settings to allow the bot to search for a signal. "Can you connect with the mainframe in Volmar?"

"Searching," it said. "I'm sorry, Master Jutta. There is no signal here. Only some other strange signal that I can't quite make out."

"Very good, Redhing. That will be all."

"But..." Redhing's voice stopped mid-sentence.

Jutta smiled at Laudus. "I love being able to shut this thing up. Can't do THAT in Volmar." He stood up and said urgently, "Let's go. There's time, Laudus. We can do this, but we have to hurry."

"Do what?" Laudus asked. But Jutta said, "Follow me," and started running in a straight line directly towards Volmar, leaving the traversers behind him.

"But, Jutta?" Laudus shouted. "Where are you going?"

"To Volmar!"

"But we can't just waltz back in there. They'll kill us."

Jutta slowed down a little to let Laudus catch up. "We don't need to get in. We just need to get close enough for Redhing to connect. Remember the virus of repentance? It's here, on Redhing! If this really is Friday, we'll be just in time. The updates take place every Friday morning at 9:00."

"Really?" Laudus said. "I figured they'd want to update at night when they're sleeping."

"No. Computers can, but with direct neural interfaces, the people have to be awake. They have to experience what is happening. And when they experience this, when they see what Father Rawley saw, the light, the light," Jutta could hardly contain his happiness. "Let's go. There's not much time!"

Just after he said that, he stopped abruptly, and Laudus ran into him, nearly knocking him over. "Sorry," Jutta said. "Forgot to turn on Redhing's transceiver. Okay. Got it. Let's go."

The two ran toward the city, as the sun was beginning to bake the earth. They didn't even think about bringing water from the traverser or any other supplies to survive in the desert. They just ran, like madmen on a mission and with very little time to complete it. Jutta held Redhing out in front of him—half-watching where he was going and half-watching the bot, whose voice he had muted.

"Redhing, show me the clock and the transceiver. Let me know when you can connect." The bot did as he was told and didn't talk back. "I should have thought of programming Redhing like this sooner!" he said to Laudus, panting. Laudus was trying to keep up, but since he'd had no sleep that night, he was exhausted. "I could have done that when I was in Volmar, before the refreshing. Maybe I could have figured things out, and I could have joined the resistance. I could have been a Dicarer on the inside." Jutta was excited and babbling, but Laudus fell behind.

After what seemed to be an eternity, Jutta stopped. The clock showed 8:30. Jutta looked ahead at the city, which still seemed to be no closer than when they started. "Can't you connect yet?" Jutta asked Redhing. But there was no answer from the muted bot. Jutta could tell from the display that it was still disconnected.

Laudus finally caught up and had to sit down because he was having trouble breathing.

"You go on, Jutta. I'll catch up later."

Jutta resumed his march straight toward Volmar. "We've got to be in range," he said, worried that he wouldn't make it close enough before 9:00. "If I don't make it now, it'll be another week."

Though he was sweating, and his legs were hurting, Jutta picked up his pace and pushed on. He ran as fast as he could. He had never run so fast or hard in his life before. His side began to hurt, and his mouth felt like it was only collecting dust. His side hurt so badly that he finally had to stop. "Maybe just a minute to rest," he said to himself. Redhing displayed 8:45, but the transceiver still did not connect.

"Come on, side. Stop hurting." He pushed through the pain and ran a few more minutes until the terrain began to look familiar. "We must be close enough, Redhing." He unmuted Redhing, hoping to hear something encouraging.

"Master Jutta, you are quite overdoing it. Your heart rate is through the roof! You must take a rest now."

"No, Redhing. I can't rest now. We have to get closer to Volmar. You have to connect!"

"But Jutta, I'm afraid for your life. It is getting so hot now. I am your PASbot. I…"

"Never mind. Just connect!" Jutta shouted hoarsely; his throat parched. "And play some music."

"What do you want to hear?"

"Anything really old," he said, breathing heavily.

"Here's, 'Keep On Loving You' by REO Speedwagon." Redhing read the song title and artists before playing. "Too slow, skip!" Jutta said. "Now playing 'Bolero' by Maurice Ravel."

"Skip!" he said. "Don't you have anything upbeat? Something to run by?"

"Playing 'Eye of the Tiger' by Survivor."

The song gave him energy, and he ran as hard as he could as long as it was playing, but when the song ended, Jutta glanced at the clock. 8:50. Still not connected. Jutta had to slow down to a walk.

"Why can't you connect? Volmar is right there!" he said, pointing to the city, which towered above him no more than a half mile away. "We have to be in range by now. What's wrong with you? Hurry up!"

"No signal yet, Master Jutta. I do not understand the urgency of what you are doing, but I look forward to reporting everything that has happened these past few days since the refreshing ceremony to the Avogo. They will know what to do."

"Are you screwing me over, Redhing?" Jutta asked.

"Whatever do you mean, Master Jutta?"

"Nothing." Jutta tapped on the clock as if it were broken. "Six minutes left. We are so close. You've got to be able to connect now. Are you just not trying?"

"Believe me, I am trying, but I just can't get a signal. Maybe they have turned it off," Redhing said.

"They never do that. Why would they do that?"

"Maintenance? Sometimes they reboot the system before the updates," Redhing suggested.

Jutta could go no further. He sat down on a hot rock and watched the seconds slip away on the clock. It turned to 8:55.

"I guess there's no hope. Not this week anyway," he said, not really talking to Redhing. "We'll have to wait out here another week. Until next Friday. How will we survive that long out here?" Jutta began to cry as the clock ticked to 8:56.

"The heat must be making you delirious, Master Jutta," Redhing said. "We will just go into Volmar now, and everything will be sorted out."

Jutta didn't respond. He just sat there and continued to cry.

"One thing, I'm sure, Jutta. None of this is part of the refreshing."

Jutta sniffled, but an idea came into his mind. "Refreshing. Rebooting. That's it. I'm so stupid. I need to reboot you!"

"What? But you can't..."

Redhing's voice stopped. Jutta had already turned him off. "Why didn't I think of this? Reboot, reboot. It always works." It took about 30 seconds for the bot to shut down and another thirty seconds to turn back on. When the screen finally lit up, the clock read 8:59. "Come on. Come on. Connect!"

A green light lit up on the transceiver. "It's connected!" Jutta shouted. As soon as the connection was made, the clock turned 9:00. Redhing seemed to be sending everything that Jutta had programmed, but Jutta was still uncertain if the connection had been made in time.

"You really aren't supposed to turn me off, Master Jutta. I assure you that was in my reports I just sent," Redhing said after sending and receiving updates.

The time was 9:03, and Jutta had no way of knowing if he had done any good.

Chapter 38

Who are These Wearing White Robes?

Odilia had spent a fitful night in a cell next to Godlip and Michelina, unable to sleep and unable to communicate with them because of the guard who kept licking his lips and making vulgar sounds every time she glanced his way. For most of the night, she sat up on her cot with her back in a corner and her knees pulled to her chest.

Around five or six in the morning, she finally nodded off and slept until eight a.m. when she was awakened by the changing of the guards.

She studied the new guard a moment and then closed her eyes again but could not go back to sleep.

Not long passed before this new Sogmol took a small metal pipe and banged it on the bars of Odilia's cell. "Wakey wakey," he said, smiling at her and revealing a missing tooth.

Odilia had already planned what she would do if someone came into her cell and attacked her. When the Sogmols threw her and Jutta into the traversers, they had not found the small field knife that was still in her right boot. She inched back into the corner of her cell.

"Somebodys wants to see you," the Sogmol said. He stormed into her cell, grabbed her by the hair, and dragged her out.

"Stop it, Flator!" Godlip yelled from the next cell over. "Let her go."

"Or what?" the ugly Sogmol said, baring his missing front tooth, which had been knocked out by Gangry not long ago. "You're nothing now, Gangry. Just yous sits tight. Me and the boys is gonna have some fun with you too soon."

Flator pushed Odilia to her knees and wrapped a rope around her neck. She put her fingers between the rope and her neck, trying not to choke. She could not reach her knife. He led her around the room a moment and then grabbed her from behind.

Odilia surprised him with a kick in his shin, and when his balance was off, she bent over quickly, throwing him over her shoulder. He landed on his back with his feet near Godlip's cell. Godlip pinned his foot down while Odilia tried to get the rope around the Sogmol's neck. But Flator was too strong. He pulled her onto himself and would have rolled over on top of her if Godlip and Michelina weren't holding his feet.

Odilia tore herself away, while Flator tried to wrest his feet free, kicking at Gangry and Michelina. Odilia was about to reach for her knife when she noticed the metal pipe on the ground next to her. As she raised it to hit him over the head, someone entered the room behind her and grabbed the pipe, pulling her backwards into his arms.

"Enough," the old man shouted. It was Clauberg. He pulled the pipe out of her hands, and it clanged on the ground. Godlip let go of the Sogmol immediately; years of conditioning to be subservient to the Avogo kicked in.

Odilia struggled to free herself from Clauberg, but the nearly 200-year-old man held onto her with inhuman strength. The Sogmol stood up and brushed himself off. "Sorry, sir, we was just trying to bring her to yous when this has-been grand comrade grabs us."

Clauberg saw that Godlip had moved back to his bed, and Michelina was sitting next to him, holding his hand. "No more of this nonsense," Clauberg said. "Gangry, I'll be back for you and your girlfriend soon. Right now, all I want is a little peace and quiet so I can get to know little Miss Odi here."

Odilia squirmed and shouted, "No! Help!" as Clauberg dragged her through the Vauller door and handed her to another Sogmol, who had been waiting outside.

"Take her to my room," he said. Odilia kicked and screamed all the way but still ended up in Clauberg's room. Clauberg dismissed the Sogmol and locked the door so that Odilia couldn't escape.

"I knew you were a feisty one," he said. "That's what Volspat always liked about watching you."

Odilia felt sick. "What do you mean, watching me?"

"Oh. Nothing, really. We put a camera in your room a couple of years ago. It's kind of our way of getting to know whether we like someone or not." He stood directly in front of her and caressed her face. "And we like you."

Odilia stepped back and spat on him. "What camera in my room?"

"We always did enjoy Sabas's visits. So cute and innocent."

Clauberg opened a closet, revealing various implements that looked like they were designed to torture. While his back was turned, she reached into her boot and grabbed her field knife. Clauberg chose a length of nylon rope and ran it through his hands as he turned towards her. Odilia put her left hand out as if to tell him not to come any closer. But her right hand was behind her back, gripping the hidden knife.

Clauberg inched closer and closer, teasing her with the rope. "Just think, I've been watching you grow all these years. Like a farmer watching his crops get ripe."

He took off his shirt, revealing scars on nearly every square inch of his chest and stomach. The old man's body resembled a patchwork quilt that had been sewn together from many parts. On his chest, Odilia thought she saw something moving under his skin. "It's time for a little...harvesting, don't you think?" he said in a maniacal voice.

Odilia's left hand was still out, telling him to stay back while her right hand was hidden behind her thigh, spinning the knife back and forth. She kept inching away from him until she backed into a wall and could go no further. "How evil you have grown with age!"

she said. "Your sins will come to term."

Clauberg lunged for her with the rope between both hands as if he were using a net to catch a wild animal. When the rope hit her neck, Odilia countered with her right hand, plunging the knife into his scarred belly and pushing it deep inside of him until she felt the warm blood squirt onto her hands.

The old man dropped to the floor, screaming. Odilia sank the knife into him again, this time into his throat, and the yelling stopped. He only made gurgling sounds for a short while longer before he fell over and stopped moving. The third person of the Avogo trinity lay dead at Odilia's feet.

She dropped the knife and put her blood-covered hands to her mouth to keep from screaming, but the blood got in her mouth, and she spat it out. She pulled the sheets off the bed, wiped her lips, hands and tongue, and then covered the body with the sheet. She frantically scanned the room, trembling. Above the bed was a digital alarm clock that read 9:01. Odilia turned to run back to the Vauller to release Godlip and Michelina, but when she opened the door, Volspat was there, apparently having heard Clauberg scream. He pushed her violently to the floor. Pointing to the sheet covered in blood, he shouted, "What is that? Clauberg?" Volspat shouted again, "Clauberg?! Herta!"

He was calling for the nurse who had been with them from the beginning. He pulled Odilia by the hair and threw her onto the bed. Then he jumped on her and started punching her in the face. She held her arms up to deflect the blows, but they kept coming. He paused a moment to move her hands out of the way, and when he had her hands pinned, he lifted his right arm and threw a punch that landed squarely on her jaw. The next blow landed on her ear because she was trying to turn away from it. Her ear started ringing. He raised his hand again, but his clenched fist stayed high in the air, ready to come down hard.

The blow never came.

Volspat remained on top of her a moment, and she could feel him start to tremble. Through squinting eyes, she saw that the old man had turned completely white. He crawled off of her onto the floor and got on his knees, mumbling and pleading with someone. His whole body shook violently, and he made terrifying noises and screams like she had never heard before in her life. They were more demonic than human. Herta stumbled into the room as well and fell down next to Volspat. She began screaming in terror and ripping her hair out.

Odilia heard Volspat cry out in bitter despair, "Who are these wearing white robes, and where did they come from?" As soon as he had said this, his body fell over, and his flesh began to rot. Herta experienced the same fate.

Odilia buried her nose in her elbow and tried not to watch as maggots and all kinds of bugs crawled out from under their skins and attacked the carcasses of the unholy trinity, consuming them quickly as if she were watching a time-lapse video.

Soon, all that was left were brittle bones, and the place was eerily silent. She felt her face; everything hurt tremendously. Her jaw was dislocated, her ears rang constantly, and she thought her nose might be broken. But she gathered herself together and went back to find Godlip and Michelina.

In the corridor, she passed an enormous ancient grandfather clock made of gold that marked the transition between Disibodenberg and Volmar. It was 9:15.

Odilia found her way back to the Vauller. She could hear Flator taunting Godlip and Michelina, and as she slowly cracked open the door, she saw that he had a taser and was laughing as Godlip flailed around on the ground. Her head was throbbing, but she pushed back the pain and slid inside quietly. She picked up the piece of pipe from the floor and smashed it against the back of the

Sogmol's head. Flator dropped to the ground and grabbed his head. Odilia fumbled through his pockets and found a key card that opened the cell. Then, she closed her eyes and leaned against the wall, unable to bear the pain in her head any longer.

Godlip stopped moving but did not wake up.

* * *

When Michelina saw that Flator was getting up, she ran out of the cell, grabbed the pipe, and finished him off with a brutal blow to the head. "Nighty nighty," she said as she dropped the pipe, and it clanged on the floor. She ran back to Godlip's side and listened for a heartbeat. She rested her head on his chest to make sure he was still breathing. That's when she got a good look at Odilia's badly beaten face. She gently put a pillow under Godlip's head and then helped Odilia into the cot but would not let her lie down.

"Odilia!" she shouted. "Stay with me, Odilia! Don't fall asleep." She found some water near the guard station and ripped off Flator's shirt to use as a rag for wiping Odilia's wounds. Odilia grabbed Michelina's shirt and saw through swollen eyes that the person touching her was trying to help.

"Oh, make it stop," she said, shielding her face with her hands.

Godlip slowly came around, and once he was aware of their situation, he pulled himself up and locked the door coming into the Vauller, then dragged Flator's lifeless body into Odilia's old cell and locked it.

While Michelina did her best to keep Odilia awake, Godlip scanned the room for painkillers. He found a stash of whiskey in the guard's station and offered the bottle to Odilia to help numb the pain.

"The Avogo are dead," Odilia said, refusing the whiskey.

Godlip took a swig of the whiskey himself and nearly choked. "What?" he coughed.

"They're dead. I saw it. I killed one of them. But the others, it was like they suddenly started rotting from the inside out, and they just disintegrated."

There was a long pause as everyone took in the news. Michelina said, "He must have done it, then! It must have worked. Laudus must have found Jutta and brought him back to Volmar. The virus of repentance! It worked. Jutta's here! Jutta did it!"

Odilia's disheveled hair fell over her right eye, which was now completely swollen shut. She was silent for a moment. "You may be right! That's the only explanation. That's what he said would happen." She started to get excited. "He did it. He actually did it!" Odilia said laughing, but when she laughed, her head hurt, so she took the bottle from Godlip and tried whiskey for the first time in her life.

Michelina stood up and danced around Godlip while she quietly hummed a silly victory song.

Odilia sat there in bed with her head propped against the wall and smiled. "Ah! Don't make me laugh," she said. "It hurts."

Godlip said, "If the Avogo are dead, it's safe to go out and get something for your wounds. I'll be right back." He returned moments later with bandages, medicine, food, and water for Odilia and Michelina.

As Michelina nursed Odilia, the three of them talked about their next move. "Wonder where all the Sogmols are," Godlip said.

"Probably fighting our militia," Michelina said. "I bet they were sent when they saw Sabas and the others coming. Maybe we should go help them. Nobody knows the Avogo are dead yet, except us. Volmar will keep running itself for a while."

"You're right," Godlip said. "With the Avogo dead, we can easily take the city again. I should go help Sabas."

"What's this 'I' stuff?" Michelina said. "I'm going, too."

Odilia tried to stand up, but Michelina put her hand on her shoulder. "Where do you think *you're* going? You've done quite enough for one day. You stay and rest. We'll leave you with the radio, food, water, keys, a pipe, a taser..." Michelina chuckled as she gathered things for Odilia to keep her safe. "If you feel better, you can get up and look for Camara. Keep the radio tuned in to this frequency. We'll call you and let you know what's happening."

Odilia gave Michelina a one-eyed dirty look, but she was in no condition to argue. "Okay," she said.

"Try not to sleep. You probably have a concussion," Michelina said.

Chapter 39

Reuniting

Jutta and Laudus were struggling to find the traverser that they had left behind earlier when they heard someone calling out.

"Jutta! It worked! You did it!" It was Michelina.

"What worked?" he said to the wind, believing he had imagined the voice.

"The virus of repentance! It worked! The Avogo are dead!" Godlip and Michelina approached, and Jutta realized what was going on.

"It worked?" Jutta asked with a very dry voice. "The Avogo are dead?"

"Yes," Michelina said, handing him a flask of water and throwing her arms around him.

Godlip must have seen that the two were about to pass out from the heat. He set up a canopy to block the sun and gave them more water while Michelina filled them in on what had happened.

Jutta couldn't believe it. "It worked!? I thought we were too late!" he said incredulously. Jutta stood up and scratched his head. His eyes fell on something off in the distance. "Look," he said. Godlip and Michelina saw what appeared to be a considerable group of people marching towards them. Godlip and Michelina steeled themselves for a battle, but it wasn't long until they saw it was Sabas leading a mix of Dicarers, Bandarians, and a group of odd-looking strangers on plowders and a few traversers.

Michelina stood in the open to wave them down.

Sabas said, "Look at you! You're alive. We've just come from Bandonderry, where we crushed the Sogmols with the help of our new friends from Acedia."

It almost sounded as if Sabas were boasting. So Michelina

responded, "Yeah? Well, we just came from Volmar, where we crushed the Avogo!"

A cheer went in waves through the eclectic army at the news that the Avogo were dead. Everyone headed towards Volmar, and when they arrived, Jutta ran straight to the Vauller, where he found Odilia and did everything he could to care for her. When Sabas saw that Jutta was with Odilia, he went through the town, searching for Camara, and found her imprisoned in Volspat's room.

Chapter 40

The Returning Ceremony

Several days after secretly taking over Volmar, the mixed group of Dicarers, Bandarians, and others from Acedia were ready to announce the liberation of Volmar to the Vaipwo and Sasjovians.

Jutta was sitting alone on a couch in Disibodenberg when Odilia entered.

"Jutta," Odilia said, holding out her hand. "It's time."

Jutta stood up and took Odilia's hand. Then they walked down to the city together. When they arrived, they stood in front of a large crowd on the same stage where Jutta had waved goodbye to Volmar not so long ago. Fargus came on stage carrying a baby girl. He handed her to Odilia, and Jutta stood by her side as Yaro said a blessing over the baby. Yaro then poured water over her tiny head, and everyone applauded.

Once the baby was baptized, Jutta took her in his arms carefully. She was dressed in an outfit that let everyone see her clubbed foot. Jutta gazed deep into her eyes and felt that he caught a glimpse of what he'd seen in Father Rawley's last memory. Odilia held onto his arm and stood close to him. He lifted his eyes and took a deep breath, then he and Odilia stood on the spot on the stage where they would speak to the town of Volmar.

Knowing he had a moment before the ceremony began, he handed the baby to Odilia and pulled Redhing out of his pocket and unmuted him.

"It worked, Redhing. It worked."

"What worked, Master Jutta?"

"The refreshing, of course."

"But I thought…"

"Shh. The pains are gone. That sense of hopelessness I used to have, you know? It's gone."

"That's wonderful," the bot said. "The Avogo are amazing. They did it! Who is this baby next to you?"

"Her name is Eve Jutta Duc."

"But that's not..."

Jutta muted Redhing and put him back in his pocket.

He looked around at his new friends. Camara and Sabas were holding hands. Godlip and Michelina were standing together, and Odilia was standing right next to him on the stage where he had had his Refreshing ceremony.

On the other side of the curtains was a large crowd of Vaipwo and cameramen who had been assembled for a mysteriously important announcement. Jutta kissed Odilia's cheek and made the sign of the cross. He took the baby back in his arms and nodded that he was ready.

The curtains opened, and all the TVs throughout Volmar, all the pleasure crafts, and all the PASbots tuned in.

A collective gasp went up among the Vaipwo as they began to recognize Jutta and the baby with the clubbed foot that he was holding.

About the Author

Randall Martin received his Master's in English from the University of Central Oklahoma in 1996. In 1999, he began a two-year stint as Senior Editor at Taiwan News in Taipei. While there, he worked with a journalist who turned out to be a member of Opus Dei. The journalist introduced him to an Opus Dei priest in Taipei, and a seed was planted that took around thirteen years to germinate. In 2012, after listening to Sacred Heart Radio for several months, Randall enrolled in RCIA at St. Charles Borromeo in Tacoma, WA. He came into the Church during the Easter vigil of 2013. He loves Jesus and the Catholic Church. He says that going to Mass is like sinking into a warm Jacuzzi for his soul. He lives in Tacoma with his wife and has two grown sons. *Refreshing Jutta* is his second book.

Published by
Full Quiver Publishing
PO Box 244
Pakenham ON K0A2X0
www.fullquiverpublishing.com